The Fairetellings Series

Kristen Reed

The Fairetellings Series: Books 1 through 3

Other Tiles by Kristen Reed

The Fairetellings Series

The Jilted Bride: A Footnote to Cinderella's Happiness
Eirwen's Dream: Inside Snow White's Sleeping Mind
Ingrid's Engagement: How A Beauty Tamed A Beast
Salvation by the Sea: The Tale of the Innkeeper's Maid

The Beginnings Series

Out of the Garden
Five Nights With Pharaoh

The Clara Robinson Series

The Way of Escape

Table of Contents

The Jilted Bride

A Footnote to Cinderella's Happiness

Chapter 1

Demetria's pulse thundered more wildly than her favorite mare's hooves during a fierce hunt as she stared at her reflection in the full-length gilded mirror. The cream-colored satin gown she'd just donned was trimmed with a deep flounce and handmade lace that no commoner could ever afford. Her veil, which was nearly as long as she was tall, was held in place by a wreath of fragrant orange flower blossoms that the seamstress had adorned the expensive, heavy gown with.

As the youngest daughter of Lord Aurelian, the Duke of Isidor, Demetria had been preparing for her wedding day since the moment she was born thanks to the tutors, instructors, and governesses he'd hired to help her become the perfect wife. Their instruction would have been all for naught if she hadn't inherited her mother's beauty since many men were willing to overlook a lack of accomplishments or refinement in favor of a pretty face. With perfectly porcelain skin, doe-like eyes the color of coffee, full lips that were almost always curved into a smile, and waist-length dark mahogany hair that blazed auburn in the sunlight, she had impressed her fiancé and, more importantly, his father.

Demetria had heard that King Tresillian was more excited about the match than his son and heir Prince Caspar, but the charming prince had praised her beauty and kissed her hand with a stunning smile after their fathers agreed to the betrothal. At the time, Demetria had silently appreciated his slightly wavy dark blond locks, sapphire eyes, and dimpled chin, but that attraction and mild infatuation hadn't yet turned into the all-consuming love she craved in her heart of hearts.

Elizabeth, Demetria's mother, had assured her that true love would come with time. After all, she and Aurelian had grown to love and respect each other deeply during their happy marriage despite not meeting until their wedding day. However, when Prince Caspar spent the entire ball several nights later dancing with a mysterious girl and took off after her when she abruptly tried to leave at midnight, she knew that his heart belonged to someone else.

She'd spent the whole night maintaining her composure and dancing with members of the royal household and other courtiers who no doubt wanted to distract her from Caspar's poor behavior, but her calm exterior gave way to uncontrollable sobbing once she was alone. Demetria cried herself to sleep in her mother's arms, fearing that her marriage was over before it even began while her father had words with the king. The next morning, she received a heartfelt apology from the guilt-ridden prince, and he reaffirmed his commitment to marry her with a beautiful ruby necklace. Of course, Demetria had to forgive Caspar and accept his gift, but from that moment on, she had a niggling fear that she would never be the future queen of Aspasia.

Even as she rode to the cathedral with her parents, Demetria nervously played with the lace trim on her gown with unsteady hands and kept her eyes on the passing countryside to avoid their unrelenting scrutiny. Aurelian had been on edge since the ill-fated ball, and poor Elizabeth had been torn between concern for her uncharacteristically anxious daughter and her ireful husband. Thankfully, the ride from the palace to the cathedral was a short one, and Demetria had some time to calm herself with prayer and to make sure her ensemble was in place as the ceremony began.

When the doors were opened, Demetria walked down the aisle and smiled as she saw how handsome Caspar looked. His blond hair shone in the candlelight as it brushed the collar of his red jacket, and the blue sash he wore perfectly matched his eyes. Caspar flashed a disarming smile, but keeping his eyes on her seemed to be a struggle as he periodically glanced at his parents and the three women who quietly wept in the back pew. Demetria's hands perspired, and she clutched her bouquet even harder, determined not to embarrass herself by dropping the pristine white roses at the sight of Lady Morwenna and her daughters openly mourning on her wedding day.

Just as Demetria reached the altar, the creak of the old wooden doors reopening reached her ears, and the crowd began to murmur. Caspar's eyes widened, and a rident grin more genuine than any smile he'd ever directed at Demetria stretched across his handsome face. Even though she already had an idea of what or rather who stood behind her, Demetria slowly turned around and took in the girl standing at the back of the room. At first glance, the young bride thought that some audacious peasant had tried to sneak into the ceremony, but her stomach churned as she recognized the girl's sparkling emerald eyes and halo of blonde hair. Despite the ashes that soiled the girl's milky white skin and tattered brown dress, Demetria recognized her as the mysterious girl who had stolen Caspar's attention and heart at the ball.

The cinder-covered girl never even met Demetria's devastated gaze because Caspar ran to her and pulled her into his arms with a kiss that inspired even more gasps. The bride stood absolutely still, hoping that no one would notice her mortification as the prince's coachman strode forth with the glittering glass slipper the destitute usurper had foolishly—or maybe calculatedly—left behind at the ball. Caspar knelt before her, his eyes never leaving her radiant face as he wordlessly slipped the sparkling shoe on her dainty foot. His impossibly large grin widened even further as he picked her up and carried her from the room, her beautiful shoe twinkling in the sunlight with every step.

One by one, everyone in the room swiveled back around to face the altar and gave Demetria their undivided, unwanted attention. Her small chest heaved, her quick breathing turned into gasps for air, and the room became blessedly blurry as tears filled her eyes and obstructed her view of the voyeuristic crowd. Demetria didn't even realize that her parents had risen until her mother took her quaking hand and guided her from the room. The last thing the devastated bride saw as she passed back down the aisle and out of the cathedral with gossiping Aspasians watching her every step was her father boldly walking over to the slack-jawed king with a baleful gaze that would have set the monarch on fire if there'd been any magic behind it.

Once Elizabeth successfully whisked Demetria out of the church, they immediately piled into the awaiting carriage, and the jilted bride shook with uncontrollable sobs in her mother's arms until they received word that they were to return to the palace without Aurelian. As the two women fled the cathedral in the beautifully decorated carriage, Demetria rested her head in her mother's lap, soaking the blue silk gown with bitter, salty tears as she drifted into a fitful sleep.

◆　◆　◆

Hours later, Demetria and her mother watched as Aurelian arrived at the Aspasian royal palace with the king and queen. The dour duke came straight to his daughter's room, and his rage gave way to pity only to resurge again when he saw his little girl's disheveled hair and the tearstains on her blotchy face. It had taken a lifetime to prepare Demetria for a man of Caspar's caliber, but it took less than a minute for the mysterious peasant girl and thoughtless prince to ruin his plans for Demetria's future and to shatter her already bruised heart into pieces. He couldn't decide who he was angrier with … the prince for his inconsiderate disregard for his daughter's feelings or the king for his refusal to force the prince to keep his word. Either way, the duke's round face was crimson with rage, but he didn't want to add to his dejected daughter's pain by directing his anger at her.

"How are—"

"Who was she," Demetria interrupted. "Who was that girl and why was Caspar kneeling at her feet and fawning over her like she's some sort of queen?"

"They call her Cinderella. Whether that is her birth name or a term of endearment, I'm not sure, but she has been a servant in her stepmother Lady Morwenna's household since her father died twelve years ago."

Demetria scowled at the mention of Lady Morwenna. The uppity, overly ambitious noblewoman had been trying to thrust her insipid yet gorgeous twin daughters on Caspar for months while their betrothal went unannounced. In a strange turn of events, the two girls she'd placed her bets on had been defeated by a lowly servant. While the thought of losing Caspar and her chance to be queen to the peasant pest still made her stomach lurch, knowing that the disrespectful Morwenna was also suffering consoled her a tiny bit.

"How was she able to go to the ball if she was a servant? Did she steal that tacky dress and those ridiculous glass shoes from her stepsisters or from someone else?"

"She didn't steal anything. Apparently the other servants saved up their money for God only knows how long to have her dead mother's wedding dress fixed up. The shoes also belonged to her mother."

"How does she know Caspar? Has she been seducing him this whole time or did they meet at the ball?"

"The girl is too pure to seduce anyone," Aurelian sighed. "They met in the woods when Caspar went hunting several months ago and fell off his horse. He twisted his ankle, so she took care of him until the rest of the party caught up with him. She'd been posing for a portrait for some apprentice painter wearing one of her stepsister's old gowns, so he thought she was a noblewoman. It just happened that every time he came to visit her after that day, Morwenna, Drusilla, and Lystra were on the prowl looking for him at court, so she was able to keep up the ruse that she wasn't a servant."

Hearing that the provincial tart had dressed above rank and manipulated Caspar for months stoked the inferno inside of Demetria, but she remained calm.

"Well, he must have found out what she really was because he didn't seem too surprised to see her in that dowdy dress today."

"Cinderella told him the truth at the ball, but he spurned her. That's why she left so abruptly. Caspar's reaction upset her so much that she fled the palace as fast as possible, and she lost her shoe in the process," Aurelian explained. "Her stepmother sold her to some count when she found out about their relationship, but the old man freed her today so she could stop the wedding."

"How considerate," Demetria sneered. "I'm assuming you've met her since you seem to know everything about her."

"Yes, she wanted to explain herself and extend her apologies to our family and to you specifically for what she did," he answered carefully. "She would also like to have a word with you in private about what happened, but she also sent a written apology in case you weren't up to seeing her just yet."

Aurelian pulled a letter emblazoned with the royal seal from his pocket and handed it to Demetria. The young woman glared at the epistle, her face growing hot at the thought of the reading the servant girl's words. In a moment of rage, she snatched the letter from her father's hands and ripped it into pieces, paper fluttering to the floor and joining the trampled rose petals that were strewn from the door to the where Demetria had hurled her tattered bouquet upon their arrival.

"I never want to see or hear from that ash-covered wretch again," Demetria shot back. "If she was truly sorry she would tell Caspar to be a man of his word and marry me."

"It sounds like they're in love, Demi," Elizabeth softly spoke up. "Do you really want to marry a man whose heart belongs to someone else? With her only a short distance away, he would likely take her as his mistress, and she would be a thorn in your side your entire life."

"What I want is to be celebrating my new marriage with a grand feast and dancing," Demetria wept, "not standing in here in this ridiculous dress while they get to start their life together. When everyone finds out that Caspar left me at the altar, I'll be a laughing stock. No one will want to marry me."

Elizabeth wiped away her daughter's bitter tears while Aurelian clenched his fists, struggling to maintain his composure as he witnessed his daughter's anguish. If Caspar wasn't a prince and Aurelian wasn't a duke, the protective father would have gladly thumped the thoughtless young man for his behavior.

"You are a beautiful, accomplished, delightful girl," Elizabeth reminded her. "Prince Caspar was a fool to abandon you for Cinderella, but that doesn't mean every man is as shortsighted and dishonorable as he is. The right man will see what a prize you are and steal you away from us before you know it. Then your father and I will be the ones weeping."

"As soon as we return to Isidor, I will make finding you a husband a priority," Aurelian swore. "The Duke of Wolstan was very taken when he saw your portrait and was quite disappointed that you never had a chance to meet in person."

The jilted bride bit her lip and tears stung her eyes again at the thought of being paraded before another nobleman and facing more disappointment. Even before her disastrous betrothal to Caspar, she had been rejected by Prince Dryden, who had been holding out for his childhood sweetheart. The count she'd had her heart set on after him, Ulric, had been carrying on an affair with a parlor maid in his kingdom … a maid who they learned was pregnant with his *second* illegitimate child.

"Perhaps this conversation can wait until we're back home," Elizabeth suggested, sensing her daughter's apprehension.

Aurelian nodded and spoke again.

"Do you want to stay the night or would you rather leave now, Demi?"

"I don't want to be here for another second."

"Then I'll have the carriage prepared for the two of you. I'll stay behind to settle things with King Tresillian and make sure all of your belongings make it back to Isidor."

With that decision, Aurelian left the two women to prepare for their hasty departure from Aspasia, a kingdom none of them ever wished to see again.

Chapter 2

When Demetria and Elizabeth arrived at their castle in Isidor, the sun was barely peeking over the cloud-shrouded mountains to the east. Despite her emotional fatigue, Demetria hadn't slept a wink that night. Instead, the disheartened girl slouched against the wall of the carriage and watched as the full moon crawled across the inky sky while she reviewed every interaction she'd had with Caspar in an effort to pinpoint when she had lost his favor.

Unfortunately, the prince had been so charming up until the ball that she'd begun to wonder if his charisma was just an act that he used to blind and beguile women. After all, with his dashing good looks, captivating smile, and rapier wit, he had captured more hearts than he knew what to do with. She had once looked down at the fawning noblewomen and peasants with pride as she saw how they panted after the man her parents had secured for her, but now she realized that she was just one of many who had been fooled by his charm without winning his affections in return.

Yet a peasant girl had stolen his heart.

Demetria shook the image of the two newlyweds kissing from her mind and watched as a shepherd on the nearby pasture looked after his sheep. As much as she cherished the luxuries that came with being a girl with a titled father, she found herself envying the simpler lives of the common folk. Being in the company of powerful men and women meant constantly putting on an act. The more your life was falling apart, the more pristine it needed to seem to outsiders.

Facing financial ruin? Throw a lavish party that people will be raving about for weeks. Plagued by a cheating husband? Sing his praises more loudly than anyone else does. Grieving a broken heart? Move on to the next suitor and flirt boldly with the flourish of your fan. Demetria had been relatively sheltered until she came of age, but she'd encountered enough scandal and humiliation to last a lifetime. Despite learning how to pick herself up, put a smile on her face, and play the part of a carefree girl, her heart was heavier than any eighteen-year-olds ought to be that morning.

Maybe that's why he loves her, she pondered. *She's simple and naïve to the scandals and intrigues of court life.*

Demetria's mother roused when they neared the castle, and her heart ached as she saw the forlorn look in her daughter's fatigued eyes. Elizabeth's journey from a wealthy merchant's daughter to the Duchess of Isidor had happened without incident, but poor Demetria had endured three devastating disappointments with nothing to show for them but eyes that were red and puffy from countless tears and a heart that she prayed wasn't irreparably shattered.

As much as it pained her to admit it, Elizabeth also realized that Demetria's suffering was in part her own doing. Had she and Aurelian been more discerning in the men they chose for her, their daughter's heart would have been better protected from pernicious princes and careless counts. Unfortunately, all of the men had spoken well of because few would *dare* sully the noblemen's reputations.

The young men were extremely amiable, but they were as disingenuous as they were charismatic and as vile as they were handsome. Prince Caspar had been the most charming of them all, but he had humiliated and hurt Demetria more than the others combined. It seemed that the current generation of men rebuffed their fathers' moral teachings in favor of the enticing hedonistic lifestyle that had become increasingly popular with each kingdom's growing prosperity. They made decisions based on their feelings and desires instead of wisdom and ignored their consciences, which they seemed to consider an inconvenience on their quests for self-gratification.

Perhaps we should introduce Demi to some older gentlemen. They may not be as debonair as the men closer to her age are, but their affections are more constant and they're far more honorable.

"How are you feeling?" Elizabeth asked, smoothing Demetria's wild hair out of her face.

"I just keep wondering why Caspar abandoned me for her."

The duchess sighed and clutched her daughter's hand.

"I wish I could tell you why Caspar behaved the way he did, but I can tell you that there is a man out there who won't be so careless with your heart. He will love and protect you as if you were his own flesh, and no woman whether peasant or princess will ever come between you."

Demetria pulled her hand away and crossed her arms. As delightful as the hypothetical man Elizabeth spoke of sounded, she couldn't bring herself to believe that he was real. Not even her closest friends had found such men. They'd married well from a financial perspective, but there was no love in their households. The men were cold, unfaithful, and occasionally cruel.

"Do we have to start looking for new suitors immediately or can I have some time to myself?"

"That's up to your father, but I'll discuss it with him. I'm sure he'll oblige."

Demetria nodded and wordlessly turned her attention back to the countryside, longing for the privacy of her bedroom so she could close her eyes and escape into whatever fantastical world her mind dreamed up.

◆　◆　◆

When the two women arrived at their home in Isidor, servants knitted their brows in confusion at the sight of Demetria, who should have been waking up in the arms of her husband and not shuffling into her parents' home with her dark eyes trained on the floor. Once the servants realized what had happened, they gossiped amongst themselves in the safety of the kitchen and their other work areas, speculating as to why the much anticipated royal wedding hadn't gone as planned.

The only servants who abstained from the gossip were those who were too old or too oblivious to be bothered by the family's personal affairs, but the between maid Marianne was neither old nor unaware. The young woman, who was only weeks older than Demetria, had just finished her tasks for the morning and was taking a much-needed reprieve from the drudgery of her life by reading when the cook called her over.

"I need you to deliver this to Lady Demetria's room," Celeste instructed. "She hasn't eaten since breakfast yesterday, and the duchess is worried about her. Don't come back until she eats at least half of this plate."

"What if she tells me to leave?"

"Tell her to take it up with her mother. I know the girl is hurting, but I'd rather you anger her than the duchess."

Marianne opened and closed her mouth several times like the colorful fish that swam in the pond on the estate as she struggled to find the words to dissuade Celeste. When she couldn't think of a good enough protest, Marianne exhaled slowly and nodded. The young woman swept a few stray strands of blonde hair behind her ears in a meager effort to make herself look more presentable before picking up the tray of delectable food and leaving the kitchen. Marianne walked through the castle, smiling and nodding as she passed her hardworking friends, and silently prayed that her interaction with the duke's daughter would go well.

Demetria had never been rude or unkind to the castle staff, but she more or less acted as if they didn't exist. She rarely made eye contact with them and never said thank you despite the great example her parents set. Knowing her prideful nature and a few passing details about her disappointing wedding day, Marianne didn't think the duke's desolate daughter would react terribly graciously to a servant awkwardly standing over her as she ate.

Lord, please keep me from being a discouragement to this poor girl.

Upon reaching Demetria's room, Marianne softly knocked.

"Come in," a voice groaned.

The servant reluctantly entered the room and greeted the should-be newlywed with a brief curtsy.

"I've come to deliver your breakfast, milady."

Demetria sat up, rubbing her puffy red eyes with a yawn. When she saw Marianne with her flowing blonde locks and green eyes, her face flushed and her breathing quickened as she ripped the covers off her body and vacated the bed. After barreling across the room and drawing close enough to see that the peasant girl wasn't Cinderella, Demetria realized that she wasn't dreaming. The girl standing in front of her with her eyes trained on the floor was just one of the many servants her parents employed and not Aspasia's new princess. As much as she loathed the glass slipper-wearing usurper, she was slightly disappointed that she didn't have the chance to give her a piece of her mind.

Marianne's hands trembled, but she fought to maintain her poise under the noblewoman's silent scrutiny. Demetria's baleful gaze softened slightly as she saw Marianne's discomfort, but she couldn't help being bothered by the girl's resemblance to her nemesis.

I wonder what else the two ragamuffins have in common.

"You can leave the tray and go," she dismissed, walking back to the bed to pull her recently discarded robe on over her nightgown.

Marianne bit her lip and firmly clasped her hands in front of her as she lowered her eyes to the floor.

"The duchess asked that I stay with you until you've eaten," she said softly.

Demetria turned to face Marianne again with a roll of her deep brown eyes.

"Fine."

A soft sigh of relief eased through Marianne's lips, and her hunched shoulders returned to their normal posture as her agitated charge sat down at the table and began to eat. Unfortunately, as Demetria's only company, she immediately fell under the young lady's watchful stare again.

"What is your name?"

"Marianne, milady."

"What exactly do you do here?"

"I'm a between maid, so I do a little bit of everything, but I mostly help with the cooking and cleaning."

"Do your parents also work for my family?"

"They did."

"Did?"

"They passed away ten years ago."

"Are you married?"

"No, milady."

Demetria halted her line of unexpected questioning to eat several forkfuls of her meal, but her eyes never left Marianne.

"What do you think makes us different?"

Marianne furrowed her brow and lifted her eyes slightly to make eye contact with Demetria. Her heart ached for the poor woman when she saw the dejection in her eyes, but the maid wasn't quite sure how to answer her question.

"I don't understand."

"How old are you?"

"Eighteen."

"As am I," she said. "We're the same age, same build, and you're a decently pretty girl. What makes you different from me?"

"Well, you're of noble blood, and I'm only an orphaned servant. You're wealthier and more important than I'll ever be."

Demetria tilted her head and narrowed her eyes slightly. Marianne had laid out their differences in breeding and economic status without a hint of bitterness or jealousy in her voice.

"Does that bother you?"

"No, not at all. I may not have fine dresses and jewels, but I'm happy with what God has given me."

"So you think God is responsible for our lot in life."

"Yes."

The young noblewoman raised a single dark eyebrow.

"Then you think he's responsible for the prince humiliating me on my wedding day to run off with an ash-covered servant girl?"

"If the prince and the girl you speak of sinned against you, that wasn't God's doing," Marianne clarified earnestly. "He doesn't tempt us or make us sin, and I'm sure he's saddened by what happened to you."

Demetria sighed and turned her eyes to her suddenly unappetizing meal. If God was as loving and omnipotent as she had been taught, why didn't he save her from Caspar and the others? It seemed to her that either he wasn't as good, or he wasn't as powerful as she'd believed he was. The fact that the archbishop had stood beside idly as the prince dishonored her also didn't sit well with Demetria.

"Maybe your misfortune serves a greater purpose," Marianne offered. "Who knows what—"

"You may go now," she interrupted.

Marianne glanced at Demetria's half-eaten plate and decided that the distressed lady had eaten enough to appease her mother. With another low curtsy, she ducked out of the room to move on to her next task for the day, praying for her young mistress' broken heart with every step.

Chapter 3

The Duke of Isidor wasn't one for pacing, but he was well on his way to wearing a trough in the floor of his parlor as he and his wife waited for Demetria. He had been so sure that his downtrodden daughter would welcome his good news when he left Aspasia, but he'd grown more agitated with every mile that passed between the accursed kingdom and his duchy.

Elizabeth sat in her chair, poised as usual with her hands primly clasped in her lap, but she too was full of nervous energy. In the days since Demetria's deplorably disrupted wedding, the poor girl had only left her room when she was summoned for supper. She knew that her daughter was at least eating well thanks to the reports from the soft-spoken between maid, but a full stomach meant nothing when her heart had been torn in two.

When Elizabeth first learned that her cook had sent Marianne to make sure her daughter was eating, she silently berated herself for not having been more specific in her instructions. While Marianne didn't have the spirited, lighthearted demeanor that Cinderella possessed according to Aurelian's anecdotes, she bore a remarkable resemblance to the newly crowned princess. Fortunately, Demetria hadn't complained about the meek girl, and Marianne hadn't given the impression that she was being treated harshly.

Maybe she hasn't noticed the likeness, Elizabeth contemplated. *After all, Demi only saw the girl for a moment at the wedding and at a distance during the ball.*

As if on cue, Demetria entered. Elizabeth rose to greet her daughter with a warm embrace and a smile, but she ached when she saw the despondency in the eyes that looked so much like hers and that yet again her daughter hadn't bothered dressing.

"I'm so happy to see you, Demi," she rejoiced. "Come and sit down for tea."

Demetria wordlessly took her seat and Aurelian did the same, guilt gnawing at him as he beheld his youngest child's misery. The family of three remained silent as the servants began the tea service. Demetria took a timid sip of her tea but barely glanced at the scones and biscuits before her. Hating the oppressively heavy silence, Aurelian hastily spread clotted cream on his scone as he spoke.

"I have good news for you, Demi," he began. "We're going to have a visitor next week."

"Oh?"

"Yes, Lord Ferdinand will be staying with us."

Demetria set her teacup down with a bit more force than necessary, but not so violently that either parent could justifiably berate her for it.

"Why is he coming here?"

"Well, as you know, the Duke of Wolstan had been our next choice for you, and I thought you might like to meet him."

"You might want to send some of the servants away before he arrives if you want anything to come of this visit," Demetria retorted.

"There's no need for that," Elizabeth softly interjected. "You have nothing and no one to fear in our household."

"You also have much more to offer than any servant or even a woman of your rank," Aurelian added. "As a peace offering, King Tresillian has given you a dowry worthy of a princess."

"That's very kind of him," Elizabeth approved. "Money aside, Ferdinand is an honorable, sensible man. Your father knows him very well."

Demetria stayed silent, willing the unkind, spiteful words that were threatening to burst forth to stay hidden in the recesses of her mind. While she wasn't thrilled with the prospect of having to entertain the likely deplorable man, she didn't want to insult her father by voicing her reservations about his ability to choose a husband for her. After all, he had sung Caspar's, Dryden's, and Ulric's praises as if they had been the handsomest and most principled men in the world.

Yet they had all disappointed her.

"Very well then," she said coolly.

The duke and duchess stared at Demetria for a moment, waiting for some sort of protest, but she simply nibbled on a biscuit as she silently vowed never to open her heart to her new suitor.

◆　◆　◆

That evening, Demetria decided to skip supper. While the headache she complained of was nonexistent, her parents didn't push the issue and allowed her to remain cloistered in her room. However, her stomach began to make some embarrassingly feral sounds sometime after dusk, so she snuck down to the kitchen. When she strode into the large, sweltering room and found only Marianne scrubbing the pots and pans Celeste had used, the lady lifted her chin and gracefully lowered herself onto a stool by the door.

Hearing the familiar creak of the stool, Marianne looked up, her green eyes widening like a stag caught in a hunter's sights, before she addressed the duke's daughter.

"Can I help you with something, milady?"

"I'm starving. Is there anything down here I can eat?"

"I can prepare a plate for you," she offered. "Would you like me to bring it to your room when it's ready?"

"No, I'll eat in here."

Taken aback by Demetria's unusual choice of dining venue, it took Marianne a moment to recover before she began to plate some of the leftover food from that night's meal. Once she finished, the girl set the plate in front of Demetria with some wine.

"Do you need anything else, milady?"

"Have you eaten supper already?"

"No."

"Why not?"

"I don't feel right eating until all of my tasks are done for the evening."

"Well, make yourself a plate as well and join me."

"I'd rather not disturb you. If you'd like, I could serve you and take my meal when you're done eating."

"You didn't seem to have a problem *disturbing* my meals before," Demetria shot back, immediately wincing at her needlessly harsh words. "I'm so sorry. That was incredibly rude. Will you please forgive me?"

"Of course, milady."

There wasn't a trace of bitterness in Marianne's voice, but Demetria still hated herself for lashing out at the servant. No matter how much the between maid reminded her of Caspar's new bride, Marianne didn't deserve her unchecked enmity.

"Now, would you please sit and eat with me? You wouldn't be disturbing me. I'd just like a little company. That's all."

"All right," Marianne conceded.

The timid servant fixed herself a plate and sat down with Demetria. Though she kept her green eyes on her plate, Marianne remained alert in case her unlikely companion needed anything. Surprisingly, Demetria didn't ask for her services again and only made conversation.

"You're very quiet," she observed.

"I just don't want to disrupt your meal, milady. I thought you'd want to eat in peace."

"Because you heard about what happened to me?"

Marianne looked up and met Demetria's dark gaze.

"I know what everyone has been saying," Demetria maintained. "I don't have to be in the servants' quarters or in the kitchen to know that you've all been talking about the prince jilting me for Cinderella. All I have to do is look at your annoyingly attentive stares. It's like you're all waiting for me to fall apart again."

"There has been some talk, but only because we're concerned for you," she began cautiously. "I've never been in your position, but I do know that what the prince did was inconsiderate at best and cruel at worst. I can only imagine how much pain you're in."

A tear found its way down Demetria's cheek, and it wet her plate before she could control herself. She broke eye contact and wiped away the evidence of her pain with a sniffle.

"I can leave if you'd like some privacy," Marianne offered.

"No. Please stay," she pleaded. "I'll go mad if I don't talk to someone other than my parents."

"What would you like to talk about?"

"I don't know," Demetria said, dabbing away another tear before it could spill forth. "Did you know that my parents are already trying to find a new man for me to marry?"

"I heard that we are having a guest, but I didn't realize he was a suitor."

"Even though my father speaks well of him, I don't trust that he's judged him accurately," she confessed. "I don't blame him for praising these men. I'm sure they're as charming to his face as they are to mine, but there is so much I don't know about them. They could be the wittiest, most well-read men in all the land and be tragically careless or unreliable."

"Not all men are like the prince," Marianne said without thinking.

"Have you met many noblemen?" Demetria sneered. "They're so drunk with whatever power and freedom they have that they do whatever pleases them with no regard for anyone else … especially a woman."

"I've never met anyone of noble blood but your family, but I have faith that not every nobleman is as you say. While the lure of power and pleasure can be tempting, there are men who know what their role is as husbands and take their responsibilities very seriously," she answered. "The duke is a great example of that. I may not know him as well as you do, but anyone can see that he adores and respects your mother."

Demetria took a sip of her wine as she contemplated Marianne's words. The maid was right. Her father loved her mother with unparalleled devotion. He had never strayed or even flirted with other women.

"What do you think a husband's role is?"

"To love his wife selflessly."

"And what about marriages where man and wife aren't in love before the wedding?"

"Well, a man can love a woman in word and action even when he hasn't developed a deep affection for her yet by being patient, kind, and faithful."

Demetria chewed on her food thoughtfully as she mulled over the servant's surprisingly poignant views.

"If there is a man like that who has a title and fortune that my parents would approve of, I would gladly marry him. However, whether gladly or reluctantly, I have to marry at some point," she breathed. "Are there any men who have caught your eye?"

Marianne nearly choked on the morsel of bread she'd been swallowing upon hearing Demetria's unexpectedly personal question.

"Milady, I …"

"Your secret is safe with me. I won't tell anyone."

Marianne studied Demetria for a moment, seeing that the girl was completely sincere.

"There's a really nice boy who works in the stables, but we've been just friends for longer than I can remember."

"What is he like?"

"He's the most selfless, hardworking, sweet man I've ever met," Marianne answered, looking down as a smile crossed her lips. "He also makes me laugh, but never at someone else's expense. He's just genuinely funny."

Demetria studied Marianne thoughtfully, seeing her genuine affection for the nameless stable boy. Even though he was nothing more than a peasant, she couldn't help wondering if he was just as unreliable and selfish as Caspar had been.

"Well, I hope he's the man you think he is," Demetria said as she rose from the table. "Thank you for dinner."

"You're welcome, milady."

As Demetria left the kitchen, Marianne realized that was the first time the young noblewoman had ever thanked her for anything.

Chapter 4

For the next three days, Demetria crept into the kitchen to break her fast or eat supper with her unexpected companion. She asked Marianne question after question about her life of servitude and slowly realized that the young woman neither envied nor resented her family for their wealth. The youthful servant also took her duties very seriously, rising early and turning in late each day to complete her daily work and to selflessly help others with theirs.

Despite all of her hard work, Marianne seemed rested and at peace … two things that Demetria craved. Since her would-be wedding, she'd spent her nights tossing and turning as nightmares about Caspar and his lowborn bride tormented her, and her waking hours were helplessly agitated. Nothing brought her pleasure or enjoyment, but her time interrogating the serene servant in the dimly lit kitchen helped some of her dejection lift.

As mitigating as their conversations were, Demetria was still hesitant to dive into her old hobbies and habits. She took no pleasure in donning the expensive gowns that had been tailor-made for her and having her hair arranged in the most current styles. Knowing that Caspar had tossed her in all of her bridal fineries aside for a dirty peasant in rags made her feel as if the time spent beautifying herself daily was wasted. Her mother had commented on her dark waves hanging loosely one morning but never mentioned her unadorned appearance again thanks to the glower she'd received in response.

Frustrated by another night of fitful sleep, Demetria decided to go for a walk on the property. Having not left the castle for almost a week, breathing in the fresh summer air and watching the sunrise was a nice change even though she wore nothing more than an old nightgown. When she strolled along the property, Demetria was surprised to see Marianne sitting under one of the trees reading a book. For a moment, she simply observed the servant, who seemed more content with that simple task than Demetria had felt since the ball in Aspasia.

Tears filled her dark eyes again, and she hugged herself as her envy for Marianne resurfaced, comingled with her hatred for Caspar and Cinderella. Nothing in her life felt right anymore, but she hadn't the foggiest idea of how to find the joy that had been mercilessly ripped from her. For all of the luxuries and diversions at her fingertips, everything seemed so meaningless.

"Are you all right?"

Demetria gasped and jumped slightly, wiping away the evidence of her despair as she turned to face the source of the concerned, accented voice. The noblewoman was surprised to see a man only a few years her senior standing at the stable entrance. His chestnut-colored hair was pulled away from his handsome, unshaven face in a low ponytail, so Demetria could clearly see the compassion in his heavily lashed hazel eyes. Judging by his rumpled, plain clothing and tanned skin, she immediately assumed that he was one of the servants who spent his time working outdoors. When she heard the whinny of a horse and recognized that she was by the stables, her dark eyes widened.

She was probably in the presence of Marianne's stable boy sweetheart.

"Are you all right," he repeated, stepping closer.

Demetria took a step backward.

"I'm fine. Just getting over a cold," she lied.

He glanced at the completely oblivious Marianne and back at Demetria.

"Most women don't cry when they're sick with a little cold … at least not to my knowledge," he disputed gently. "Would you like to talk about whatever's troubling you or should I fetch one of the other women on staff to comfort you?"

Demetria blinked once or twice, taken aback by his words. Whoever this man was, he clearly didn't realize who she was. While she wasn't arrayed in the finery a duke's daughter was expected to wear, surely all of their servants knew her face … and they wouldn't be as bold as he was even under such circumstances.

"No, I'll be fine," she finally answered. "Are you new to the house staff?"

"I'm visiting from Eusebia."

"So you came with the Duke of Wolstan?"

"Yes, my name is Ric," he answered, extending his hand with a dimpled grin.

Rather than rebuffing the informal greeting, Demetria played provincial and shook his hand, her heartbeat racing as his large, rough hand enveloped and squeezed hers in a hearty shake. She flashed a demure smile and averted her eyes momentarily as her cheeks warmed. For all of her balls and suitors, Demetria had never spoken with a man alone.

Being unchaperoned with the foreign servant made her feel exposed but unrestricted at the same time. Without her parents demanding propriety and other nobles watchfully taking in their interaction, she didn't have to take up the stifling mask of decorum and gladness that she had been dreading donning in the Lord Ferdinand's presence. She was free to express herself without earning her mother's gentle correction or busybody aristocrats' whispers.

"I'm Dora," she lied, pulling inspiration from the name of her father's duchy.

"It's nice to meet you, Dora," Ric said with another genuine smile. "Have you lived here long?"

"My whole life."

"How do you like living here?"

"The castle is beautiful, and the duke and his wife are very kind," she trailed off.

"But?"

"But I just feel discontented. Fate has dealt me a cruel hand recently, and the things I used to love don't hold the joy that they used to."

"Do you mind telling me what happened?"

Demetria hesitated, realizing that telling the truth would give away her identity. After all, if Ric had been traveling with Lord Ferdinand, he would have known all about her unlucky wedding day. She had to be creative if she wanted to keep playing a peasant.

"Someone stole something that meant a lot to me … something irreplaceable."

"I'm sorry to hear that. Did that young maid steal it?"

"No, of course not. She's—"

Demetria's eyes widened as she heard footsteps. When she turned and saw Marianne approaching with her book in hand, the duke's daughter broke away from Ric and welcomed her new companion with a smile.

"Good morning," she greeted. "Are you ready to start preparing breakfast, Marianne?"

"Yes, but—"

"Great. Do you mind walking back to the servants' quarters with me? I burned my apron cooking supper last night and need to borrow your spare today," Demetria hastily interrupted before turning back to Ric to shake his hand again. "It was nice meeting you, Ric. Have a nice day."

"And you as well, Dora."

Marianne furrowed her brow but kept her mouth shut as she witnessed the strange interaction between Demetria and the unfamiliar servant. Correcting the duke's downtrodden daughter for her duplicity in front of the man didn't seem wise despite their recent familiarity, so she waited until they were out of earshot to broach the topic.

"Who was that, milady?"

"He's one of Lord Ferdinand's servants … a groom I assume since he's at the stables."

"Are you previously acquainted with him?" Marianne asked carefully.

"No, not at all. In fact, he thinks that I'm a servant," she laughed. "Normally I'd be offended, but I guess I look the part."

Demetria glanced at Marianne and saw concern flicker in the girl's green eyes.

"Don't worry. I'm not so disenchanted that I'm going to sink to Ulric's level and abuse my position by having an affair with a servant," she assured her.

Despite her unwillingness to take part in castle gossip, Marianne was well aware of Demetria's cancelled engagement to the carnal count. Ulric had visited the duke's castle on numerous occasions, and she'd caught his eye on one such visit. Thankfully, her dear friend Vane had interrupted Ulric when he attempted to corner her by calling her to the kitchen for an imaginary chore. From that moment on, the stable boy had ensured that she never walked the halls alone while Ulric was visiting.

Whether the count just had a penchant for servants or women in general, Marianne wasn't sure, but she'd been enormously relieved that the domineering nobleman's loose morals were revealed before he could marry Demetria. As badly as he, Dryden, and Caspar had disappointed Demetria, Marianne knew that her fate would have been much worse had she married someone so unfaithful and overbearing.

"Of course you wouldn't," Marianne replied as they entered the castle. "Are you going to tell him who you are?"

"If he's in the house for long, he'll find out who I am sooner rather than later."

Marianne set her lips in a firm line, willing herself not to admonish Demetria. Despite their time together, Marianne had to remember that she was nothing more than a between maid … she had no place telling a duke's daughter what to do. All she could do as Demetria bade her farewell and retreated to her room was pray that God would give the heartbroken young lady discernment and keep her from dishonoring herself and her family.

♦   ♦   ♦

That afternoon, Demetria shuffled into the parlor for tea with her parents and the Duke of Wolstan. Lord Ferdinand, a smiling man in his twenties, greeted her by bowing and tipping his hat, which added to his considerable height. His mustache, which was just a shade darker than his blond locks, was groomed with just enough wax to keep it upturned at the tips while his cropped hair was perfectly coiffed with a part on the right.

The young duke was handsome with his shining blue eyes, white teeth, and radiant smile, but something about him rang false to Demetria. Even though everything he said was pleasant and interesting, she felt as if he was just putting on a show. As she nodded and gave her rehearsed smile while he told a story about a performance he'd recently seen, Demetria realized that she was likely seeing the cracks in his façade because she was growing weary of wearing her own mask.

The Duke and Duchess of Isidor watched their interaction carefully in hopes that some sort of affection would spark during the afternoon tea, but there was no fire between the two young nobles. Fortunately, Aurelian and Ferdinand planned to spend the afternoon at the horse races, so Elizabeth had the opportunity to get her daughter's opinion of Ferdinand as they played a game of chess.

"Ferdinand seems like a nice man, doesn't he," the duchess probed.

"Yes, he does."

"And fine-looking too."

"Yes, he's very handsome."

Elizabeth studied Demetria, who was trying to decide the next move to make with her knight.

"You don't seem terribly enthusiastic about Ferdinand. Do you have any objections to him?"

"Not yet," she answered. "Lord Ferdinand was very agreeable and witty, but everything seemed rehearsed. I felt like I was part of a performance, not a conversation."

"Well, I'm sure he was only trying to make a good first impression. Once you get over the initial awkwardness, I think you'll get along just fine."

Instead of replying, Demetria finally made her move, snatching up one of her mother's pawns.

"Why do I have the feeling that there's something you're not saying?" the duchess asked.

"Because you're my mother," Demetria sighed, sitting back in her chair. "How soon do you expect him to propose if he's interested in marrying me?"

"I'm not sure. Your father is better acquainted with the duke than I am. Why do you ask?"

"Well, I wouldn't feel right agreeing to marry him without knowing more about his character," she said carefully. "Is he honest? Does he truly care about me? Does he love someone else?"

Guilt inspired a pang in Elizabeth's chest and gnawed at her conscience as she listened to her daughter's concerns. Had she and Aurelian been more fastidious, Demetria could have been saved some of the pain she'd endured. Now, her beautiful daughter was guarded in ways that most young women never had to be, and her apprehension could cost her a good husband if she didn't find a way to shake it.

"Ferdinand is not Caspar," Elizabeth reminded her.

"No, but is he Dryden or Ulric? None of their faults were exposed until I'd placed my hope in them, and I've only had one trivial conversation with Ferdinand. He may prove worse than all of them combined."

"Demi—"

"I don't expect him or any man to love me so soon, but I need to know that he will be committed to loving me in action even if the affection hasn't developed yet," she continued. "I can't tell if he's a patient, kind, selfless man when I feel like every line that comes out of his mouth has been practiced in front of the mirror."

Elizabeth stared at her daughter, powerless to come up with a wise response that wouldn't enable her reservations. She was also stunned by the boldness and underlying wisdom in Demetria's comments. While the duchess valued the characteristics that the young lady mentioned, she'd never had the courage to voice those desires to her parents. The fact that she'd married a good man was purely God's doing.

"I have a headache. May I be excused?" Demetria asked.

"Of course, sweetheart."

The duchess knew that her daughter wasn't ill, but she allowed her to end their game and retire to her room. As her brown eyes settled on the chess pieces, Elizabeth prayed that she would have the wisdom to guide and encourage her disheartened daughter before she spoiled her chances with Lord Ferdinand.

◆　◆　◆

"You didn't like him?"

Demetria shook her head as she swallowed the bite of leftover turkey she'd been chewing. The duke's daughter had skipped dinner that evening and elected not to eat until she knew Marianne would be finished with her duties so she could leave her room without fear of running into her suitor or her parents. Sitting in the kitchen wearing a nightgown and having the freedom to be herself instead of dressing up and putting on a show for the Duke of Wolstan was a welcome relief, but what she truly cherished was the company of her newfound friend.

"I don't dislike Ferdinand, but nothing about him seemed genuine. It makes me wonder if he's hiding something."

"Maybe he was nervous. This was your first meeting after all."

"You sound like my mother," she said, more amused than annoyed.

"I'm sorry, milady. I wasn't trying—"

"It's all right. I'm not angry," Demetria clarified. "I suppose I'm just jaded."

The sound of footsteps caused the two women to turn their attention to the kitchen door where a familiar hazel eyed groom appeared. Marianne's eyes widened, and Demetria met her surprised gaze with a very slight shake of her head.

"How are you ladies doing this evening," Ric greeted.

"Good, thank you," Demetria replied, noticing that he had the same fast speech and rippling accent as Ferdinand, but that it lacked the duke's practiced bravado.

"And you, Marianne?"

"Very well."

"Do you mind if I join you for supper? I've barely eaten a thing since breakfast this morning."

"No, go ahead," Demetria consented.

Marianne began to rise to fix Ric a plate, but Demetria waved her off and rose to her feet. While the between maid knew her way around the kitchen better than Demetria, the noblewoman knew how exhausted she was after working all day. After spending time with her newfound friend that week, Demetria had also seen enough of the kitchen to figure out where to find everything she needed to fix her own plate earlier that evening and Ric's as well. She was also glad to disperse some of her nervous energy by arranging some of the remaining food on the Eusebian servant's plate.

"Thank you," he said with an appreciative grin when she set the meal before him.

As the daughter of a highborn nobleman, Demetria was rarely on the receiving end of gratitude, but the little satisfaction she derived from serving Ric warmed her heart, and his easy smile made her heart beat faster.

"You're welcome."

Demetria took her seat again and addressed the cheerful groom as she resumed her meal.

"So, do you like living in Eusebia?"

"Yes, it's a very fine country."

"Do you get to visit the ocean very often? I've heard the beaches are spectacular."

"My duties keep me pretty occupied, but I try to make it to the coast whenever I can," he answered. "What do you two do for fun? Some of the footmen were telling me that they like to play cricket now and then."

Marianne relaxed a little bit upon hearing that Ric's attention wasn't solely on them. Considering Demetria's recent troubles, the between maid wanted to protect her from Ric if he proved to be a wolf in sheep's clothing. The fact that he addressed them both with equal attentiveness and had taken the time to converse with the men of the house set her mind at ease.

"I've taken to reading and going on walks lately," Demetria answered.

To isolate herself and escape her troubled thoughts, she had turned to the written word. While Demetria had her own favorite novels, Marianne had lent her a book by John Bunyan. Demetria had seen a nicer edition of the book collecting dust on her father's bookshelf, but she'd never had any interest in reading it until the meek maid suggested it some days before. Though her plight didn't quite match the protagonist's, she certainly felt as if she was looking at life with new eyes and had a burden weighing her down since her wedding day.

"Reading is definitely a relaxing way to pass the time. I just finished *A Tale of Two Cities*," he divulged.

Demetria raised an eyebrow.

"Are you hoping for a revolution in Eusebia?"

"No. Not at all. I just think it's a very well-written book," Ric chuckled. "Are you an avid reader as well, Marianne, or do you have another favorite pastime?"

"I read when I can, but I enjoy drawing more than anything," she admitted.

"My sister is a very talented painter. You'd probably get along well."

"How many siblings do you have?" Marianne asked.

"Five. I'm the youngest."

"So am I," Demetria piped up. "Did your parents indulge you as a child?"

"Oh yes," he laughed. "They didn't expect as much from me, so I had more freedom than my older brothers to do as I pleased."

"What did you do with your freedom?"

"Well, not having as many duties meant that I could pursue my passions more freely so I could study and write in my spare time instead of being pressured to learn my father's trade."

"What subjects did you study?"

"I've been really fascinated by the concept of living a servant's life."

"I'm not sure I follow," Demetria said, tilting her head slightly.

"Our Lord came not to be served but to serve others, and I believe that we ought to do the same. Not just out of obligation or to earn a wage as many people do, but to love others and to help carry their burdens so they can see Christ in us."

Demetria studied Ric with renewed interest as he took a bite of his turkey. While the duke and duchess took their daughter to church services regularly and she wholeheartedly believed that Jesus had died for her sins and risen on the third day, she had never heard anyone preach about the virtues of serving others. The little volunteering she'd done by giving to the poor and organizing events for their benefit had been done more out of obligation and to socialize with other women than a genuine desire to live out her faith.

This revelation also made her look at Marianne with a new perspective. Was her companion a faithful servant and good friend because she was committed to her work or because she was devoted to her Lord? Considering how often Marianne's nose was in the Bible and the other books she read, Demetria was tempted to believe the latter and not the former.

Unfortunately, contemplating the source of Marianne's hardworking, kind nature also made her mind drift to the servant girl from Aspasia, who had caused her greatest heartbreak. Had Caspar been drawn to Cinderella because she possessed the same sweet meekness and selflessness as Marianne? While Demetria didn't see herself as particularly selfish or demanding, she'd lived a pampered and sheltered life and rarely tried to meet the needs of the less fortunate.

Servants, however, weren't so disconnected from the lower classes that they were blind to the plights of the lowborn people in the country. After all, hadn't it been a servant who'd suggested donating the excess food that was wasted every day to the local orphans? And didn't Marianne weary herself every day helping the other servants when she had her fair share of work to do?

"I'm sure that was an interesting course of study," Demetria finally said. "What did you discover?"

"Well, after pursuing the righteous life for a while, I decided to take a step back to see if my old hobbies still brought the same satisfaction, and they didn't quite fulfill me anymore. The diversions were innocent enough, and I took some joy from them, but knowing that I'd had a positive impact on someone's life was so much more rewarding."

Marianne found Ric's assertions fascinating and encouraging, but she'd decided to let Demetria take the lead in the conversation. The young between maid had been hesitant to be so bold about her faith with Demetria because of the disparity in their stations, so she welcomed Ric's unabashed dissertation. Marianne was very fond of her master and mistress because of how well they treated the castle staff, but for all the money and goods they gave to the poor, they rarely gave their time or their love. They had instilled gospel-centered beliefs in their daughter without teaching her what to do with her faith.

However, it hadn't escaped Marianne's notice that Demetria had actually washed both of their plates after supper the previous night and served Ric's meal. As much as she hated what the young lady had been forced to endure in Aspasia, she'd been praying that there was a silver lining in the mortifying, painful experience. Marianne couldn't help thinking that perhaps God had sent Lord Ferdinand's forthright groom to play a part in Demetria's journey. She didn't approve of the duke's daughter concealing her identity, but if Ric viewing her as an equal enabled him to speak truth uninhibited, maybe some good could come of it.

"I feel the same way," Marianne added hesitantly. "I love spending time drawing and reading, but helping the orphans in the village is so fulfilling."

"How often do you do that?" Demetria inquired.

"One of the footmen usually drops off the extra food each night, but I visit the children every Sunday and when I can during the week."

"So you're going tomorrow?"

"Yes, I leave as soon as afternoon tea has ended."

"Would you mind if I go with you?"

Marianne beamed at Demetria's request.

"Of course not! I'd love that."

"May I go as well?" Ric asked.

"I don't see why not," the servant replied.

"Well, if we're going to spend the afternoon with a group of rambunctious children, we should get some sleep," he asserted, rising from his seat and gathering their empty plates. "I'll take care of cleaning up so you ladies can rest."

"Thank you," Demetria said with a smile.

Ric returned her grin and went to work on their dishes as the two young women exited the room, both feeling as full of hope as they were of the delicious food they'd devoured with the visiting servant.

Chapter 5

The next day, Demetria could scarcely contain her enthusiasm as she ate her breakfast and dressed for church. Listening to the wizened pastor preach each Sunday had never been something that truly excited her, but her ears perked up a bit more intently as he spoke about the letter to the Ephesian church.

"'For by grace are ye saved through faith; and that not of yourselves: it is the gift of God: Not of works, lest any man should boast. For we are his workmanship, created in Christ Jesus unto good works, which God hath before ordained that we should walk in them,'" he quoted.

The man of God went on to talk about the gospel and salvation through grace and faith, but that last part of the passage pierced Demetria's heart just as Ric's words had the night before. She had never thought about the concept of doing good works until recently, and the idea of focusing on someone other than herself for the sake of truly living her faith after spending over a week wallowing was refreshing.

Aurelian and Elizabeth noticed their daughter's lifted spirits and cheerful demeanor after the service and during tea. While the young lady hadn't taken the same care with her appearance that most girls her age and rank did, she laughed and smiled with a lightheartedness they hadn't seen since before King Tresillian's ball, and Lord Ferdinand was enchanted by how animated and jovial she was that afternoon. Much to their dismay, Demetria asked to be excused after tea to visit the orphans in the village.

The duke gave his blessing and silently hoped that Ferdinand would offer to join her, but the young suitor simply praised her choice of diversion and wished her well. While her parents were a bit disappointed by that turn of events, Demetria was delighted to trade conversations about court life and the latest plays for an afternoon with her newfound friends.

Demetria flitted into her bedroom and quickly changed into the dress that Marianne had loaned her. She frowned at how the rough fabric felt compared to her usual silk and satin, but compassion outweighed her discomfort as she realized that Marianne wore that dress and others like it on a daily basis. As the noblewoman slipped on the borrowed shoes that came with the dress, she noticed that though Marianne's clothing was unfashionable and a bit worn, it was immaculately clean and well taken care of.

Once Demetria was dressed in the servant's clothing, she grabbed a few books from the library and crept down to the stables. Ric had asked the ladies to meet him there that afternoon, and she was glad he'd chosen a location that wasn't frequented by her parents or their esteemed guest. Had any of them seen her provincial ensemble, she would have been forced to reveal her true identity to Ric and to answer for her odd behavior.

As she strolled to the stable, Demetria noticed that only Ric was present. The young lady hesitated for a moment, not knowing if she should wait for Marianne or join the groom without another person with her. However, he looked up from the horse he'd been walking back to the stable and gave her a dimpled smile and a slight bow. Demetria's apprehension fled, and she returned the grin with a slight nod, resuming her trek to the meeting place.

"Good afternoon, Dora," he welcomed warmly. "You look beautiful today."

Demetria smiled, and her cheeks flushed at his greeting. Men tended to praise her beauty when she was in her finest clothes and jewelry, but Ric's compliment somehow seemed more genuine. Then again, the groom had only ever seen her wearing her nightgown, so even Marianne's plain, cotton dress would have been an improvement.

"Thank you. You're also looking well," she replied.

Even though Ric wasn't wearing the finery that men like Lord Ferdinand and her father donned on a daily basis, he didn't need a tailored coat and top hat to look dashing with his smiling full lips, endearing dimples, and kind, deep-set eyes. Even the light dusting of freckles across his Roman nose that she hadn't noticed until that afternoon added to his allure instead of diminishing it. However, even as she appreciated Ric's good looks, Demetria couldn't help realizing that she was more impressed by his authenticity and depth than the masculine beauty he'd been blessed with. After all, she'd met more handsome men than she could count since coming of age, but none with such a benevolent spirit.

Thankfully, Marianne joined them a moment later with a basket of food and an armful of her own books, so Demetria had a pleasant distraction from the delightful servant. Ric immediately took the basket from the maid and Demetria lifted the books from her hands, stacking them on top of the collection of childhood favorites she'd pilfered.

"You don't have to do that," Marianne assured Demetria.

"No, but I want to," she protested with a smile.

It felt strange for Marianne to be assisted by the woman she should have been serving, but she was more concerned about the flush on her mistress' cheeks and sparkle in her eyes. Ric had proven to be nothing short of a gentleman so far, but he wasn't an appropriate match for Demetria. If he thought that she was available for marriage or if she developed feelings for him, one or both of them would wind up heartbroken or disgraced. With that in mind, Marianne resolved to be more diligent in somehow guiding their interactions and prayed for the wisdom to do so as they walked to the village.

The trio spent their stroll talking about the weather and discussing the day's sermon. While Demetria hadn't been convicted about giving her time to serve others until very recently, her parents had instilled in her a reverence for the Bible, so she knew enough about scripture to participate in the conversation about salvation through grace. Ric's knowledge of the Old Testament impressed her when he brought up the difference between their faith-based salvation and the intricate instructions the Israelites had to follow under the Law. He even cited how different people and items in the Old Testament had all pointed to Christ and seemed genuinely distressed that so many people were blind to that connection. Eusebia had a large Jewish population, and his mother had grown up in that faith until her adolescent conversion, so they held a special place in his heart.

When they reached the orphanage and the symphony of giggles, squeals, and crying reached their ears, Demetria tightened her grip on the books and bit her bottom lip. The few children she had been around as an adult had been raised by parents who thought that children were meant to be seen and not heard, so the wild sounds that came through the half-open windows terrified her. Would they sit still long enough for a story or would she have the impossible task of calming them?

Before they could even set foot in the orphanage, a portly woman stumbled out of the house, wiping her sweat slicked brow with the corner of her apron. Demetria immediately recognized the exhausted woman, but she couldn't remember where or how she would have met her.

"Marianne, thank goodness you're here," she gasped. "I see you've brought friends with you."

"Good afternoon, Martha. These are my friends Dora and Ric. Ric is a groom visiting with the Duke of Wolstan, and Dora is a new servant at the castle."

Marianne hated lying to Martha, but Demetria's true identity wasn't hers to expose. The plump woman gave her two companions hasty but firm handshakes and waved them inside, fanning herself as they entered the orphanage. She led them straight into a large room that was filled with twenty children ranging from infants to a girl who was at least twelve years of age. They had been playing and interacting with one another, but the toys and books lost their appeal as soon as they saw their visitors.

Several of the children ran to Marianne, greeting her with hugs while a few others rushed over to Ric, who laughed as they jumped on his back and clung to him as if he was a tree to climb and not a grown man. A baby girl with big brown eyes and a tuft of dark hair crawled over to Demetria, and she hesitated for a moment before awkwardly lifting the infant into her arms.

The duke's daughter had never held a baby before and was terrified of dropping the chubby, drooling babe, but some of her fears fled when the little girl seized her thumb with her plump, dimpled fingers and giggled with delight. Demetria laughed as well and adjusted her grip on the child on her hip as she glanced around the room.

When they entered, she'd been too distracted by her anxiety and insecurity at the thought of entertaining the children to notice that she was intimately acquainted with most of the furniture in the room. While they weren't in the pristine condition she remembered, Demetria recognized the couches, chairs, and tables that had been in various rooms of the castle when she was a child. The piano her parents had replaced with a nicer instrument on her sixteenth birthday was even pushed into a corner, where a little girl with her hair in braids and two missing teeth curiously poked at the keys.

"All right, children! Settle down," Martha bellowed, making Demetria jump slightly and the infant in her arms gurgle gleefully.

Despite their raucous behavior, the children almost immediately sat down in front of the burgundy armchair that Marianne had pulled in front of the fireplace. The servant girl sat down in the chair, and Demetria carefully lowered herself onto the piano bench beside the plait-wearing girl. Ric, who had a little boy riding on his shoulders, stood beside the duke's daughter as Marianne spoke to the starry-eyed orphans.

"What story do you want to hear today?"

The children all began to speak at once, making the adults laugh at their eagerness. Eventually, someone suggested a story about a mouse and the idea caught fire amongst the children. So, Marianne pulled out the book and read the story. Every child listened attentively to the story, which they'd all heard a dozen times before. At the conclusion of the tale, they clapped wildly, smiles stretching their cherubic faces wide.

"What do you want to hear next?" she asked.

"I want to hear that story," a little boy exclaimed, pointing to one of the books stacked by Marianne's feet.

The between maid picked up the book and inspected it, realizing it was one that Demetria had brought.

"I've never heard of this story before. Do you want to read it?" Marianne offered, meeting Demetria's gaze.

"Sure," she stammered, getting up with the baby still in her arms and taking Marianne's seat at the front of the room.

As Demetria sat in the chair where she'd curled up in her father's lap so many times before, she was reminded of the simpler times. Memories of her happy childhood and the familiar, beloved story she read lifted her spirits. The further she got into the fantastical tale about a fairy and her friends in the forest, the wider her grin grew and the more animated she became, doing her best to imitate the voices her parents had once used to read the book. At the end of the story, the audience applauded again, but the squirming children were far too restless to sit through another tale no matter how captivating it was.

Martha dismissed them to continue playing, and the three visitors were left to fend for themselves. Marianne played dolls with several of the little girls while the boys gravitated toward the tall Eusebian groom. The same little girl who had been tinkering with the piano before story time turned back to the instrument and began to poke at the keys. Careful not to awaken the sleeping infant in her arms, Demetria sat beside the little girl again.

"My name is Dora," she introduced. "What's your name?"

"Cindy," the girl lisped in a sweet, almost chirp of a voice that brought a smile to the young woman's face.

"Do you know how to play the piano, Cindy?"

She shook her head, her dark plaits whipping from side to side.

"Would you like to learn?"

Cindy's dark eyes lit up and she beamed up at her, joyfully showing off a pair of missing teeth and making Demetria's heart swell.

"I'd love to!"

With the child's enthusiastic assent, Demetria began to teach her the basics. After writing the notes' names on the ivory keys with a wax pencil, the noblewoman played each one and recited its name before encouraging Cindy to do the same. Once she seemed to have the names of the keys, Demetria showed her that multiple notes could be played at once to create a chord.

As the afternoon progressed, the two bonded over the instrument that Demetria herself had learned her first songs on thanks to the instruction of a far less compassionate tutor. At Cindy's behest, Demetria played one of her favorite hymns, singing quietly so the girl could hear how the vocal melody complimented the instrumentals.

"Be thou my vision, O Lord of my heart; naught be all else to me, save thou art - thou my best though, by day or by night; waking or sleeping, thy presence my light."

Eventually, the sound of music and delicate singing reached Ric's ears and drew his attention away from the boys, who were currently enthralled by the towering structure they were building with a set of old wooden blocks. When he realized that Demetria was the source of the sweet sound, he stopped playing for a few beats, momentarily getting lost in the familiar, beloved tune. The perceptive little boys also turned their eyes and ears to the music and listened as Demetria unknowingly performed to a rapt audience. When the duke's daughter finished the song, she turned to Cindy again.

"If you'd like, I can drop off some sheet music—"

Applause and cheers interrupted Demetria's offer, and her cheeks reddened when she saw Ric was her most vocal admirer. She flashed him a demure smile and quietly resumed her lesson and conversation with Cindy, vowing to return for another lesson with sheet music. While Demetria didn't sing or play any other songs that afternoon, her dulcet voice and skillful playing echoed in the Eusebian groom's head for the rest of their visit and their walk back to the castle.

Chapter 6

Demetria continued to visit the orphanage each afternoon for the next week to continue her lessons with Cindy and play with the other children. Marianne was too busy with her duties to join her each day, but Ric accompanied her when his schedule allowed. Spending each day serving, teaching, and entertaining the children left Demetria exhausted by the time she began the evening stroll back to the castle, but her heart was the fullest and happiest it had ever been when she remembered their smiling faces and affectionate greetings.

While she certainly enjoyed visiting the orphanage and making the children smile, Demetria also noticed that the Duke of Wolstan never expressed any interest in joining her when Aurelian and Elizabeth suggested that he tag along. He would give her money to purchase toys, sweets, and other items for the children, but whatever commitments and leisurely pursuits he had planned outweighed any desire he had to visit the children. Lord Ferdinand wouldn't even give up a game of chess with her father to give Cindy and the others the affection they sorely needed.

Demetria missed her friends' company the afternoons when they were performing their duties at the castle, but she shared stories and updates about the children the nights that they were able to eat together in the kitchen. It warmed Marianne's heart to see how Demetria's afternoons at the orphanage brought much-needed light to her life and inspired a giving spirit in her, but the maid's stomach knotted with unease when her mistress and the Eusebian servant visited the children alone.

The young groom was the picture of proper, gentlemanly behavior and had never spoken to or touched Demetria in an inappropriate way, but Marianne saw the way he watched her as she served or cleaned up after their suppers and feared affection that could never be reciprocated was developing. Even though Demetria hadn't outright rejected Lord

Ferdinand, Marianne recognized that she wasn't expressing any interest in spending time with him unless her parents specifically requested her presence. With that in mind, the maid decided to broach the topic during their early morning walk the next Saturday.

"Lord Ferdinand has been here for over a week," she commented. "What are your thoughts on him?"

"He's very ... polite," Demetria answered indifferently. "He's also well-read."

"But do you like him?"

Demetria exhaled slowly and crossed her arms.

"No, I can't say that I do."

"Is it because you don't know him or because you don't like what you do know?"

"It's a bit of both. He's polite, educated, and very handsome, but I haven't seen any depth or kindness in him. It seems like his life is all about allowable pleasures and socializing."

"Have you made an effort to know if he cares about more than those pursuits?"

Demetria chewed on her bottom lip, contemplating Marianne's unwanted but valid question.

"I suppose I haven't, but I don't think I want to know," she confessed.

"Have you already dismissed him so completely?"

"No," she breathed. "I'm just not sure that I want to be courted by anyone right now. After everything that happened in Aspasia, I don't want to let my guard down with another man."

"If you try to protect yourself from pain, you'll also cut yourself off from the opportunity to love and be loved. You can trust that God will carry you through anything that happens with Ferdinand or the other men you meet," Marianne gently pointed out. "What do you make of Ric?"

"I've never met anyone like him before," she smiled. "He's kind, genuine, and thought-provoking. He makes me feel at ease, but he challenges me at the same time without even realizing it."

"Why do you think that is?"

"I don't know ... maybe because there isn't so much pressure on our friendship. I don't go into every interaction knowing that my parents want me to marry him and that he's sizing me up as a wife."

"But what if he is?"

"What do you mean?"

"What if Ric is developing feelings for you? Would your father let you marry him?"

Demetria stopped walking, staring at the horizon as she imagined the gracious groom asking Aurelian for her hand in marriage.

"No, he would never allow it. I hadn't even considered that he might be thinking about that."

"Well, he *does* think that you're of the same class, so he may not be looking at your relationship purely as a friendship with no intentions."

The duke's daughter nodded and some of the levity she'd awakened with that morning went out of her. She'd been so focused on her own desires that she'd completely neglected to think about Ric's feelings. For all he knew, she was a young, unmarried maid who had agreed to spend a considerable amount of time with him during their acquaintance. While it was nothing short of a miracle that he hadn't realized who she was, he would find out eventually and be devastated if he desired more than friendship.

Demetria would be a fraud and no better than the men who had hurt her... or the cinder-covered servant girl who had stolen her fiancé. That humbling thought also brought to mind the torn up letter from Cinderella that was sitting on her dresser. She had been so angry after her wedding that she hadn't even considered forgiving the new princess. Now, as she faced her own failings, Demetria realized that she needed to forgive her and Caspar. Even if the duke's daughter couldn't piece together Cinderella's message, she owed the prince and princess the same absolution that she hoped Ric would give her.

"I need to fix this," she resolved. "I have to tell him the truth before it goes on any longer and Ric gets hurt."

"I think that's very wise," Marianne agreed.

As the two women neared the castle, they saw Ric and Ferdinand at the stable. Neither man saw them as they continued their discussion, which looked very heated. Ferdinand pointed toward the castle and shouted something at Ric, who took the tirade in stride. When he finished saying his peace, Ferdinand stalked away, and Ric went after him, their argument continuing as they walked toward the woods.

"I wonder what they were fighting about," Demetria whispered.

"I don't know, but I've never seen a servant argue with his master like that," Marianne said, shivering slightly.

"Perhaps now isn't the best time to speak with him."

As much as Marianne wanted Demetria to be honest with Ric, she nodded in agreement. If Ric was still hot from his conflict with Ferdinand, she had no doubt that their conversation wouldn't go well. So the women entered the castle, Demetria vowing to tell Ric the truth as soon as they were together again.

◆　◆　◆

That day, Demetria looked at Ferdinand with new eyes. She listened intently when he spoke, asked probing questions, and even played a game of croquet with him while her parents observed and conversed nearby. There was no trace of the anger she'd witnessed earlier, but her curiosity and resolve to give the young duke a chance made her more attentive and forced her to soften her heart.

"I don't think I've ever seen a lady play croquet so well and with such delicacy," he complimented after their game. "You must play quite frequently."

"You're quite a masterful player yourself," she replied in kind.

"How do you normally spend your days? I don't have any sisters, so the lives of young ladies have always been quite a mystery to me."

"I've always enjoyed reading and playing the piano. In fact, I've been teaching a charming six-year-old girl at the orphanage how to play. Cindy has no prior training, but I think she'll be quite good one day. She has a real ear for music."

"Well, you'll have to play a song or two this evening. If you're as good with a piano as you are with a croquet mallet, it would be a pleasure to hear you perform."

Demetria smiled, but she couldn't help noticing that he'd paid no attention to her comment about Cindy. However, determined to give the duke a chance, she pressed on with the conversation.

"What activities do you enjoy back home?"

"Oh, I love hunting. Few things get my blood racing like going after a fox or a stag on a warm day," he replied. "I also enjoy a good ride when I can manage one."

"Have you had a chance to ride much since you've been in Isidor?"

"Yes, I actually went for one early this morning."

"I think I may have seen you," she blurted out without thinking. "Was your groom giving you some trouble?"

Ferdinand's smile faltered, but his cheerful disposition returned as quickly as it had left.

"No, it was just a gentleman's disagreement," he quickly explained. "Do you enjoy dancing?"

This time, it was Demetria's turn to hesitate.

The last time Demetria had danced was at the Aspasian ball. She'd spent the night being passed from duke to earl to count while Caspar spun Cinderella around the dance floor. Demetria had been careful to watch their every dance with tearful eyes, and her spirit had broken a little when they eventually disappeared into the garden together. While she had loved the rhythmic spinning and stepping that came with dancing, that ball and the events that followed had stolen some of her zeal for the pastime. However, Demetria knew that men expected an unmarried woman of her age to dance well and with enthusiasm, so her reservations would have to remain private.

"What young lady doesn't?"

"Well, my good friend Lord Devereux is hosting a ball on Wednesday night. I've secured an invitation for your family, and I'd be honored to dance the first waltz with you."

"Then the dance is yours," she agreed as Aurelian and Elizabeth joined them.

"You two certainly look like you're having fun," Aurelian observed with a grin.

"Your daughter is excellent company, and I'm sure I'll learn that she's an even better dancer later this week," Ferdinand said with his usual flattery. "Now, if you'll kindly excuse me, I have some business to tend to in town. I shall return for supper."

"I'll walk you back to the house," Demetria's father offered.

The Duke of Wolstan surprised Demetria by kissing her hand as he bowed. She could feel herself blushing, but she still managed to maintain her composure, keeping a small smile on her face as he bid farewell to her mother and strode away with Aurelian.

"How was your time together?" Elizabeth probed, lending her daughter a little shade with her parasol.

"Good," she said, sounding chirpier than intended as she fought to hide her lack of enthusiasm about the duke. "He asked if I would dance with him at the ball on Wednesday."

"Did you say yes?"

"Of course."

"Did you agree because you're growing fond of him or because it was the proper thing to do?"

Demetria sighed and shook her head.

"I'm trying to give him a chance, Mother."

"I know, sweetheart," Elizabeth said, sweeping a stray hair from her daughter's face. "Let's go inside and have some tea."

The mother and daughter went back inside the castle arm in arm. Even though Demetria took comfort in her mother's presence and felt no pressure from her to immediately reciprocate Ferdinand's affections, she recognized the delicate position she was in. Demetria held at least one man's heart in her hands, and she wanted to be far gentler with their feelings than Caspar and the others had been with hers.

◆　　◆　　◆

Despite having eaten with her parents and Ferdinand that evening, Demetria still joined Marianne in the kitchen as she ate supper. Ric usually showed up about thirty minutes into their meal, but Demetria's spirits fell when an hour passed and she realized that the groom wouldn't be joining them.

"Did you see Ric today?" she asked.

"No, not since this morning."

"Have you heard anything about his argument with the duke? I mentioned that I'd seen them together this morning, but Ferdinand just said that it was a gentleman's disagreement," Demetria continued, imitating the duke's masculine voice.

"I haven't heard a word, but Vane told me that he'd been instructed to help with the horses when he and your father left for the village."

Pushing aside her disappointment about Ric, the young noblewoman smiled as she saw how Marianne's face lit up as she spoke about the stable boy she admired.

"How did the rest of your conversation go?"

"Very well. He actually asked if he could walk me to church on Sunday."

"That's wonderful!"

Demetria had been so sure that the sandy-haired stable boy was in love with Marianne when she saw them together one day, but she'd been careful not to voice her observations to the maid. After all, she knew better than most women how fickle men could be, and she didn't want to plant seeds that Vane would never water. Instead, she had made a point to visit the stables earlier that week and surprise the humble young man by subtly praising Marianne's many virtues before going on a ride. She just prayed that she hadn't overstepped and that Vane would pursue the meek maid the way she deserved.

"Are you excited for the ball?" Marianne yawned.

"Not particularly."

"But won't it be nice to see some of your friends?"

"None of my *friends* have called on me since I returned to Isidor," Demetria pointed out. "I'd rather not spend my evening making empty conversation with people, but I'll focus on getting to know Ferdinand better. I haven't seen him interact with anyone but my parents and me, so it will be eye-opening to see how he gets along with others."

"I'm sure it will be a lovely evening."

"I'm sure it will be," Demetria echoed, picking up Marianne's empty plate. "You look exhausted. Why don't you go to bed and let me take care of this."

Marianne wanted to argue that she was more than awake enough to clean up after her supper, but she knew that would be a lie. Instead, she gave her unexpected friend a sleepy smile.

"Thank you."

Then, Marianne retired for the night, leaving Demetria alone to contemplate and pray about her relationship with the Duke of Wolstan as she cleaned up after her best and only friend in the castle.

Chapter 7

By the time Wednesday came around, Demetria still hadn't seen Ric. Marianne had spied him in the stables once or twice, but he had been in a foul mood and had made himself very scarce. The children at the orphanage mentioned that he'd joined them for supper on Sunday and Tuesday, but it seemed as if the Eusebian groom was determined not to spend time with Marianne and Demetria.

Ric's avoidance should have been a relief to Demetria since she could put off telling him the truth. Unfortunately, his absence only lessened the joy she'd recently recaptured. Realizing that she'd grown fond enough of Ric to miss him also strengthened her resolve. After all, no matter how kind, funny, and selfless he was, Ric fell laughably short of her parents' standards. She had a duty to marry well, and she would be disobedient and dishonoring to them if she did anything less.

So, she asked Marianne to help her dress for the ball in the immaculately tailored rose pink silk gown she'd originally purchased for her honeymoon. Ivory raised-point needle lace trimmed the low bertha neckline and graced the rest of the dress while matching fabric ran down the bodice to accentuate her small waist. The brocade underskirt had a woven pattern of the same hues with bits of burgundy while small tassels hung from the bodice on either side of the ornate skirt.

The low ranking maid wasn't versed in the art of styling hair as a lady's maid would have been, but Demetria was patient and valued Marianne's serene presence more than an extravagant hairstyle. Knowing her friend's shortcomings, Demetria requested a simple twist with her hair parted down the middle and looped over her ears. When the unpretentious style was finished, she smiled at Marianne in the mirror.

"Thank you. You did a wonderful job," she glowed.

Marianne smiled as she began to tidy up the vanity.

"You're welcome."

"I wish you could go to the ball with me. I haven't been out since the wedding, and I'm a little scared to face the stares and whispers."

"Just remember that their opinions about what happened with Caspar and Cinderella aren't important. You are a kind, thoughtful, graceful, beautiful woman, and your value doesn't diminish because of one man's mistake," Marianne encouraged. "If they have nothing better to do than speculate about your life, then that says more about their hearts than yours."

Demetria beamed and nearly squeezed the breath from Marianne's lungs with an unexpectedly fierce embrace.

"If nothing else good ever comes of my failed engagement, I can at least thank God for bringing you into my life."

"I'm grateful for your friendship as well," the maid replied as the hug ended.

"I'm going to ask my parents if you can be my new lady's maid," Demetria announced. "I've been sharing Charlotte with my mother since I came of age, and I think she'd agree to it."

"I don't have the training—"

"You don't need it. Charlotte and I can teach you everything you need to know," she interrupted. "You'll also be paid a higher wage, and you can use that money however you see fit."

"Can I think about it and let you know tomorrow?"

"Of course. There's no rush or pressure. We'll still be friends no matter what you decide."

The chime of the grandfather clock echoed throughout the castle, heralding the hour of Demetria's departure.

"Well, I should be going. My parents are probably waiting for me downstairs."

"I hope you have a good time, but whatever happens, remember what I said. Be loving and respectful to everyone you meet, and you'll be able to leave the ball knowing that your behavior was above reproach no matter what those busybodies say or think."

"Thank you. I'll try my best."

Giving Marianne's hand a squeeze, Demetria left the room to join her parents for an evening of opulence.

◆　◆　◆

Hours later, Demetria sat with her mother, fanning herself while she watched the joyful masses swirl around the Earl of Parthena's ballroom. Lord Ferdinand hadn't arrived at the ball yet, but she had already danced with two men. One was an officer in the military, who had already downed one too many servings of punch and the other was the ungraceful albeit sweet teenaged son of a viscount.

The dancing so far had left something to be desired, but the curious stares and congratulatory conversations about her new dowry with probing women exhausted the duke's daughter more than a thousand drunken quadrilles or clumsy polonaises ever could. For that reason, Demetria was relieved to have a moment of rest with her mother. Just as she finished a glass of the less potent variety of punch, an eager young man who had no doubt heard about Demetria's new dowry began to make his way across the room.

"Will you honor me with your hand for a waltz, my lady?"

"Actually, I believe this dance is mine," a familiar voice interjected before she could give an obligatory yes.

When Demetria saw Ferdinand to her left, she actually found herself thankful to see the duke.

"I'm afraid he's right," Demetria affirmed. "I already promised the Duke of Wolstan that I'd save the first waltz for him."

The disappointed young man bowed to the duke then strode away in search of another dance partner while Demetria took Ferdinand's arm and the two young nobles walked to the dance floor.

"Will you please forgive me for arriving so late? I had some business to take care of."

"Of course," she said.

"You look incredibly stunning this evening."

"Thank you. You look handsome as well."

Demetria and Ferdinand began the dance with the other couples and glided around the room to the triple meter song. The Eusebian nobleman was very light on his feet and managed to go the entire dance without ever stepping on her poor pained toes. For the first time that evening, Demetria found herself smiling and laughing from actual delight instead of obligation, and seeing the young duke enjoying himself and being more genuine than she'd ever seen him gave her pause. As the dance came to a close, she wondered if the posturing she'd perceived during the course of his visit had just been a result of his own nervousness. After all, she'd been barely more than civil to him and for all he knew, she was possibly in love with the Aspasian prince.

Her heart softened and spirits lifted, Demetria wasn't bothered when Ferdinand sat with her after the waltz. As if on cue, Aurelian decided to introduce Elizabeth to an acquaintance of his across the room, leaving the two as alone as they could properly be at the ball. Recognizing the opportunity that had been presented to him, Ferdinand decided to continue their conversation.

"So, the reason I was late tonight was because I was actually finalizing the details of a gift for you."

Demetria tensed slightly but maintained an even, cheerful disposition.

"Oh?"

"Yes, I took it upon myself to hire the services of a piano instructor and a few nurses to take your place at the orphanage. It seemed like the children had been quite a burden to you recently, so I thought you'd appreciate having someone to look in on and instruct them full time. With them on staff at the dreary little place, you won't have to waste your afternoons looking after the people's discarded children."

Demetria's smile froze as she stared at Ferdinand, dumbfounded by his unanticipated, unwanted gesture, but he spoke before she recovered the ability to speak.

"I have grown very fond of you during our time together, and I—"

"In what way," she interrupted. "What about me are you so fond of?"

"You're the most stunning, accomplished woman I've ever had the honor of meeting, and I find your company very enjoyable."

"I appreciate the compliment, my lord, but I don't think you truly know me if you believed that I thought of those sweet children as a burden or obligation," Demetria retorted. "They have been abandoned because of their parents' carelessness or extremely bad fortune, and they need love and stability."

"Which the new staff members can provide for him," the duke insisted. "Now, you don't have to trouble yourself with them."

Demetria took a moment to collect herself, gazing pensively at her shut fan for a moment and taking a deep breath before meeting Ferdinand's blue gaze.

"While I'm sure that Martha and the others appreciate the extra help, and I'm grateful for your generosity, spending time with children like Cindy and the others is a privilege, not a burden."

"A woman of your caliber should not have to lower herself by caring for sticky-handed, forgotten children."

"And what of our duty to care for the poor?"

"I'm caring for them by providing the staff they need."

"You might be opening your wallet, my lord, but you are closing your *heart* to them. Their smiles and sticky-handed hugs have brought me more joy than an afternoon of shallow conversation and croquet or dancing at a ball ever have."

"I didn't mean to offend you, my lady," the duke clarified apologetically.

"I know, but the fact that you think I would be relieved not to spend my days giving orphans the affection they need or helping the poor in some capacity tells me that you don't know me at all. While I was admittedly standoffish when you first arrived in Isidor, I've tried to engage you about the things that I find important and to discover what your passions are. However, you only seem to be interested in pursuing the all too alluring pleasures and diversions of this world and avoiding those you find beneath you."

"I can see that I've been gravely mistaken about you, Lady Demetria," he droned monotonously as he rose to his feet. "I bid you good evening."

The duke gave a hurried bow before stalking across the room. As Demetria watched him go, she silently berated herself for speaking so harshly to Ferdinand. Yes, he had completely misunderstood her, but her words had been too severe for her liking. When she spied her parents making their way over several moments later, Demetria rose to her feet and clasped her hands before her as she braced herself for the admonishing she deserved.

"Demetria, I believe you have greatly offended the Duke of Wolstan," Aurelian began.

"I know, Father. I will apologize to him as soon as possible," she promised. "Did he tell you what happened?"

"Only that your tongue is sharper than any lady's ought to be and that he was retiring for the evening," Elizabeth explained.

"I don't care what you did or didn't say to him. Just make things right before you drive him away and sully your reputation," Aurelian instructed. "Don't give these vultures another scandal to gossip about."

"Yes, Father," Demetria agreed.

The duke spirited his wife away in search of a drink to calm his nerves, leaving Demetria alone to contemplate her conversation with Ferdinand. As she walked onto the balcony and spied a young servant performing his duties below, her thoughts turned to Ric. Demetria knew that their relationship could never progress past friendship, but she prayed that she would be fortunate enough to marry a man with a heart like his.

Chapter 8

Ferdinand had retired long before the family of three returned from the ball, so Demetria sought him out before she even broke her fast the next morning. The sullen duke was preparing to go horseback riding, so she found him at the stables, where Vane was stepping in for the increasingly absent Ric.

"May I trouble you for a moment, my lord?" Demetria whispered in entreaty.

"You may," he retorted as he pulled on his gloves. "Have you come to cut me with your scathing criticism again?"

"No, I'm here to apologize."

Ferdinand looked up and blew air from his nose, softening slightly as he met her earnest gaze.

"Go on."

"I was inexcusably rude to you last night. No matter how I felt about what you said or did, I had no place being so cruel and insolent. Will you please forgive me?"

The duke grinned and took her hand, kissing it gently.

"Of course, my lady. I could never remain angry after receiving such a sincere apology."

"Thank you," she sighed with a smile.

Receiving the duke's forgiveness made Demetria feel as if a weight had been lifted from her shoulders. However, upon realizing that he still held her hand and hadn't moved to continue his riding preparations, her breathing quickened and a nervous sweat moistened her bow.

"Thinking that I had somehow offended you and ruined your opinion of me kept me awake all night, but your presence this morning has refreshed me more than a night of slumber ever could."

"I should be—"

Ferdinand lowered himself onto one knee, smiling up at her as Vane and the other servants looked on.

"Demetria Morigan Everard, will you do me the honor of becoming my wife?"

"I— I— I," she stammered.

"I know this isn't how you expected this to happen, but I do have a ring in the castle and your father gave me his blessing upon my arrival. I was only waiting for you to return my affections."

Several tense moments passed between them as Demetria gaped at Ferdinand in horror. Finally, the sound of a horse's whinny snapped her out of her shock. Demetria withdrew her hand from his and took a step backward, wiping the sweat from her brow and willing her pulse to slow.

"Please stand," she begged.

Ferdinand rose to his full height, the hope draining from his face with every taciturn moment that passed between them.

"I truly appreciate your proposal and your forgiveness, but I cannot marry you," she quaked. "While I am positive that you will make some woman the happiest bride in the world, I am not she. Had you visited several months ago, I would have gladly said yes, but I am not the woman I once was."

The Duke of Wolstan seized Demetria's clammy hands again, her entire body tensing as her heart thundered in her chest.

"I know that Prince Caspar's rejection had a great impact on you, but I will gladly wait for your heart to heal if it means that I can have you as my wife."

"I'm not rejecting you because of Prince Caspar. I'm rejecting you because we would make each other miserable. Please accept my decision," she pleaded tearfully.

Ferdinand's sapphire eyes darkened, and he dropped her hands.

"Thank you for your honesty, my lady. If you'll excuse me, I have a ride to be getting on with."

The duke turned to resume preparing for his ride and Demetria began her walk back to the castle, unsure as to whether she should feel relieved that he had just removed a burden from her shoulders or fearful that she ruined the only chance she would ever have at marriage.

◆　◆　◆

As expected, Lord Ferdinand didn't join his hosts for tea that afternoon. Instead, he sent word that he would be leaving for Eusebia before supper, thanking Aurelian and Elizabeth for their hospitality. Demetria kept her dark eyes on her tea as her weary father relayed the message.

"I thought you were going to apologize to Ferdinand today," he said, observing her sullen disposition.

"I did, but he proposed after accepting my apology," she revealed. "I rejected him, and he wasn't very happy with me."

Aurelian set the note down, dropping two lumps of sugar in his tea.

"Were you rude to him again?"

"No, but he misunderstood my reasons for refusing him, so I tried to be as clear and respectful as I could."

"What were your reasons?" Elizabeth implored softly.

"We would never be happy together," Demetria answered, tears rolling down her cheeks and wetting the table. "He's concerned with appearances and entertainment, but I want a man whose time isn't spent on vain pursuits. I can't marry him. I just can't. Please don't make me change my mind."

Elizabeth looked to Aurelian, silently pleading with him to have mercy on their distraught daughter. The duke heaved a sigh and shook his head, placing his hand over hers.

"Demi, I would never force you to marry someone who displeases you so. Your mother and I have both noticed a change in you recently, and I can see your point about his lifestyle not being a match for yours," he said.

"Thank you," Demetria sobbed as relief flooded over her.

Elizabeth abandoned her seat to embrace her weeping child, kissing Demetria's forehead and smoothing her dark hair.

"Oh, my sweet girl. Please don't cry," she urged softly. "We aren't angry with you."

"No, not at all. Perhaps if I had been as observant with him and the others as you have been, I could have spared you some of the heartbreak and trouble you've had to endure," Aurelian admitted. "Will you forgive me?"

"And I as well," Elizabeth chimed in. "I'm as much to blame as your father."

"I forgive you," she sniffled. "I know that you only want what's best for me."

"Well, I'm going to do a better job of finding the best," Aurelian swore. "I won't have your heartbroken again because of my bad judgment."

"Thank you."

Demetria wiped her eyes, and Elizabeth dabbed away a few tears as well as they resumed their afternoon tea, the entire family feeling more serene than they had in weeks.

♦ ♦ ♦

That evening, Demetria and Marianne sat in the noblewoman's bedroom playing checkers. The unburdened noblewoman had secured her parents' blessing in taking her friend as her lady's maid, and Marianne had accepted the position, so she'd saved several meringues from that evening's supper for them to share during their celebration.

"The house steward said that I could start training now and change positions full time once a new between maid is hired," Marianne revealed.

"That's perfect. I'm so glad you decided to take the job."

"As am I. I'd like to use some of the extra money to buy some new books for the children. I heard of a few new stories that I think they'd enjoy."

"Perhaps we can go into town together one day to go shopping for them. A couple of the older children are hitting their growth spurts, and they'll need new clothes."

"That's a great idea, Demetria."

Demetria smiled at Marianne finally calling her by name, but talking about the children made her mind turn to Ric.

"Did you see Ric before Ferdinand left?" she asked.

"No, I heard that the duke sent him back to Eusebia early," Marianne revealed. "Do you think he found out that you'd been spending time together?"

"I doubt it. He never mentioned it to me or my parents," she sighed, "but it's just as well. I'll likely never see him or Ferdinand again anyway."

Marianne gave her friend's hand a comforting squeeze.

"I know you had your reasons for concealing your true identity, but Ric was very fond of you, and he surely would have been hurt if the charade went on any longer. This way, you parted on good terms as friends and will always have warm memories of one another."

"You're right, and I trust that God will bring me a man who is just as kind when the time is right. I just have to remember what I've learned from my mistakes with Ric and Ferdinand so I can keep from making them again with the right man."

"Quite right," Marianne agreed.

"What of you and Vane?"

"I really enjoyed our picnic today. He actually invited me to the theater next week."

"And you said yes?"

"Of course," she giggled. "I can only imagine how long he had to save up to buy tickets."

"Well, you can borrow one of my gowns. I'll even do your hair for the outing," Demetria offered enthusiastically.

"I'd like that."

The two friends talked late into the night before Marianne retired to her room and Demetria slipped under the covers, thanking God for opening her eyes to the maid and blessing her with the truest friend she had ever known.

Chapter 9

Over the next week, life at the Duke of Isidor's castle returned to its new normal. Demetria finally revealed her true identity to Martha and the children at the orphanage, so she and Marianne spent their free afternoons with the children and their new caretakers. She soon learned that Ferdinand had only paid their wages for the remainder of the month, but Lord Aurelian was more than happy to pick up where the young duke left off and to keep them employed for as long as the orphanage needed them.

Unfortunately, with every visit, she was reminded of the young groom who had disappeared from Isidor with no notice. Thankfully, the children's smiles and sweet company more than made up for her sorrow, and her heart was filled to the brim with gladness every day. One day as she returned from the village with Marianne, she was promptly intercepted at the door by her flustered mother.

"Demi, my dear, we have an unexpected guest," she whispered, her voice shaking as she smoothed her daughter's dark hair.

"Who is it?"

"The Prince of Eusebia. He's visiting regarding his cousin Ferdinand's stay," Elizabeth revealed. "He is speaking with your father now, but tea will be served shortly. Please freshen up and join us as soon as possible."

The color drained from Demetria's face upon hearing the news, and she immediately understood her mother's unease. Apparently she had offended the Duke of Wolstan so gravely that one of the king's sons had elected to come to admonish her family in the flesh.

"I'll be down presently," she stammered.

Elizabeth gave her daughter a practiced but tight-lipped smile and glided back toward the parlor while Marianne rubbed her friend's back.

"Everything will be all right," she insisted. "You have nothing to fear from this foreign prince whatever his quarrel with your family may be."

Demetria nodded and took a deep breath while she and her new lady's maid rushed to her room as fast as their weary legs could take them. In a flurry of activity that was a credit to both her recent training and natural skill, Marianne arranged Demetria's dark locks into one of the more simple yet sophisticated styles that she wore when the family had guests. She also helped her mistress into a dress that was more appropriate for her station since she always opted for a plainer ensemble when she served the children at the orphanage.

In a wink, the flushed young lady was descending the stairs to join her parents and the likely indignant prince in the parlor. Demetria stopped just outside of the doors to steady herself with a deep breath and prayed for gentler words than she'd used on Ferdinand. Once she felt as composed as could be expected, she rounded the corner and entered the room.

Aurelian met his daughter's eyes and rose from his seat, prompting his guest, whose back was to the door, to do the same.

"Prince Edric, I'd like to introduce you to my daughter, Demetria," the duke presented.

The prince turned around, and Demetria took a step back with a gasp, her hand flying to her heart as she recognized the royal. While she had grown accustomed to seeing him in worn slacks and a simple shirt with dirt under his nails and his chestnut-colored hair in a bit of a disarray, Demetria had no trouble recognizing Ric in his fine clothing and with his hair carefully styled.

"Demetria," he echoed thoughtfully, his eyes never leaving the stunned young lady. "May I have a moment alone with your daughter, Lord Aurelian?"

Aurelian hesitated.

"I can assure you that my intentions are completely honorable," he swore.

"Of course, your highness," the duke obliged, taking his equally bewildered wife's hand and exiting the room.

For a long, silent moment, the two simply stared at one another in complete silence; each taking in the other's uncharacteristically refined appearance and collecting their wild thoughts.

"Your name is Demetria," Edric confirmed.

Demetria nodded, still unable to find her voice in his presence.

"Where did Dora come from?"

"I—I made it up," she faltered. "I didn't want you to know who I was."

"Nor did I. I suppose that makes us both guilty," he said with an easy smile that made some of Demetria's apprehension fade.

"And Ric is short for Edric," she surmised.

"Yes, that's what my family calls me when I'm not in trouble."

Another several heartbeats of quiet had passed between them before Demetria spoke again.

"Why were you pretending to be a servant?"

"I wanted to get away from Eusebia for a spell and travel without the usual fanfare and social obligations. I enjoy animals and spending time outdoors, so I volunteered to help with the horses and give his groom a much needed holiday with his family," he explained. "Why did you conceal your identity?"

"When we met, it was refreshing to speak to someone who had no idea who I was and what had just happened to me in Aspasia," she said after swallowing the lump in her throat. "You spoke to me like I was a regular girl … not as the duke's daughter who was scandalously left at the altar for another woman."

"So Caspar was the something—or rather someone—that was stolen from you."

"Yes, he was," she confirmed, breaking eye contact to look down at her clammy hands, which she'd clasped firmly in front of her.

"Did you love him?"

"No, but that didn't make what happened hurt any less."

"Of course not," he replied. "Would you like to know why I returned to Isidor?"

Demetria nodded, still avoiding Edric's intense, inquisitive gaze.

"After the last time we saw one another, I told my cousin about you. He had no idea that the sweet servant I spoke of was the elegant young lady he was pursuing, but he could sense my affection for you," the prince said. "Ferdinand asked point blank if I intended to propose, and I said that I was considering it."

Demetria's head shot up, but she remained quiet, unsure of what Edric would say next.

"My cousin launched into a tirade about propriety and disgracing my parents, and he threatened to send word to them about my plans in hopes that they would talk some sense into me. I backed down and made a point to avoid you, so I started going to the orphanage when I assumed you would be busy with your duties and taking supper earlier in the evening," Edric explained, "but I couldn't shake the feeling that I shouldn't give up so easily. I left for Eusebia and rode through the night to plead with my parents to allow me to marry a commoner, and they agreed after some serious convincing. That's why I came back. I was going to reveal myself and propose."

The young woman lowered her eyes as she realized that Edric had spoken in the past tense, her knuckles turning white as she clutched her closed fan. Apparently her duplicity had cost her the chance to be with the man she had grown to care for. While he had been guilty of the same crime, she couldn't blame him for not wanting a wife who could be so dishonest. No man wanted to marry a woman with loose morals ... especially not a prince whose wife needed to be above reproach in every way.

However, when Edric placed his finger under Demetria's chin and gently forced her to look into his smiling hazel eyes, she realized that she had assumed wrong.

"Now, I realize that I would be foolish to propose now because there is so much more I need to learn about you. I thought you were just a kind-hearted servant, but now I see that you're a woman who has indulged in the finer things in life yet sees the value in humbling herself to help the less fortunate and who assesses others based on their hearts and not their ranks," he continued. "You're far more fascinating and remarkable than I initially thought, and it would be an honor to get to know you better. Is that all right?”

"Of course,” she grinned. "I’d love that.”

"Are you at all angry with me for lying?”

"No, I’m relieved,” Demetria laughed. "I started to accept that I wouldn’t see you again and hoped that I could meet someone like you who my parents would approve of, but this is so much better.”

"Shall I fetch your parents?”

The beaming young woman nodded, and Edric took her hand, delicately kissing her forehead and making her heart flutter as he went to the door. Seconds later, Aurelian and Elizabeth walked back into the room, both delightfully confused to see how flushed and joyful their daughter was after what they assumed was her first meeting with the foreign prince.

"Sir, madam, will you please forgive me for my unannounced visit and for being so abrupt in asking to speak with your daughter?”

"Of course, your highness,” the duke replied.

"And you, my lady?”

"Yes, I forgive you,” Elizabeth said.

"Thank you,” Edric replied with a slight bow. "Now, on to a much more personal matter. My lord, may I have permission to formally court your daughter?”

"For marriage?” Aurelian asked.

"Yes, sir. For marriage.”

The duke and his wife looked at Demetria, who gave them a nod of assent. Though he was still befuddled by their daughter’s brief, powerful interaction with the Eusebian prince, Aurelian sensed that the young royal had nothing but the best intentions and that his affections for Demetria were completely genuine.

"You have my permission to court Demetria and my blessing to proceed as you see fit,” he sanctioned.

"Perfect,” Edric grinned, dimples appearing in his cheeks. "Now, shall we have tea? I’ve heard wonderful things about your cook’s scones.”

The foursome took their seats and eased into a lively conversation about the young couple's unusual past and their hopes for the future as they spent the first of many wonderful afternoons together.

The End

Eirwen's Dream
Inside Snow White's Sleeping Mind

Chapter 1

Few things bored Princess Eirwen to tears more than preparing for events. Having to do so while she was still mourning the death of her father, King Rhys, made listening to instructions about her coronation that Friday seem about as exciting as watching her newly painted portrait dry. However, a smile graced the princess' rosy, Cupid's bow lips when she shifted her azure gaze from the Prime Minister to her fiancé.

Prince Roderick was sitting in one of the pews near the back of the abbey keeping the chubby cheeked Ifan entertained by quietly playing toy soldiers with him. Though the auburn-haired prince was twenty years older than her half-brother, the two were as thick as thieves. Four-year-old Ifan had waddled after his future brother-in-law in awe ever since the foreign prince first arrived in Talfryn a year before to court Eirwen. Roderick's bravery on the battlefield during a recent war with Aspasia had impressed the child and his mother, Nerys, but his kindness and romantic poetry had stolen Eirwen's heart and earned the king's approval.

The prince had hand delivered a beautifully written sonnet about her obsidian locks and twinkling blue eyes upon his departure, and he included a new poem with every letter he sent during the intervals between his visits. Though Roderick's first verse had praised her beauty, it became increasingly obvious during their correspondence and interactions that he valued her mind, spirit, and faith more than her striking looks. However, his comfort, compassion, and heartfelt declaration of love after her father's passing were what had truly won her over.

"Eirwen," Nerys hissed.

The princess turned her attention to her stepmother and gave the beleaguered widow a sheepish grin. While the two women had never been close, their relationship had grown increasingly strained since Rhys' death.

Treating a woman only a decade older than she was as a mother had always been awkward for Eirwen, but submitting to a twenty-year-old young lady would be equally strange for Nerys after the coronation. Those differences aside, the two beauties were bound by the mutual tragedy of losing someone they loved dearly and having their lives turned upside down by his untimely death.

At least I have Roderick, Eirwen thought as she went through the motions of her crowning. *Him coming into my life was truly a blessing from God.*

The remainder of the rehearsal passed quickly, and the four royals swiftly boarded their coach for the short ride back to the palace. Roderick took Eirwen's hand in his once they were seated and kissed her knuckles, making her cheeks flush and her heart flutter.

"You were wonderful today," he praised, "and you'll be spectacular when the time comes tomorrow."

"Thank y—"

"She'll only do well if you don't distract her again," Nerys scolded, turning her coffee-colored glare to Eirwen. "You need to be more focused tomorrow if you don't want to make a fool of yourself in front of Parliament and the other noblemen."

"Of course, Stepmother," Eirwen replied in an even tone. "I truly appreciate all of your help in planning this. I know it hasn't been easy for you."

The widow's chin quivered slightly as she blew air out of her aristocratic nose and broke eye contact to look at the passing countryside. Only five years before, Nerys had been crowned the queen of Talfryn. She'd had high hopes for her future despite forgoing the handsome young men who panted after her in favor of a significantly older husband. King Rhys had been a kind, fair, affectionate man, and his blonde bride had been convinced that he would one day change the line of succession to make their son the heir to the throne because of the love they shared. Unfortunately, the monarch died before she could persuade him to do so, which meant that she was little more than a guest who lived in the palace at Eirwen's pleasure.

The idea of bowing and scraping to the nauseatingly sweet, high-spirited girl exasperated Nerys, but there was little she could do about it. The young woman, who spent more time with her nose stuck in a Bible than a priest, would rise in power and she would fall into obscurity. Her best shot at a good life would have been to marry well a second time, but there was no man in Talfryn whose power rivaled Rhys' and her beauty was fading more rapidly than she expected.

Since Ifan's birth, wrinkles seemed to sprout like weeds at the corners of Nerys' eyes and the lines that appeared on her forehead and on either side of her mouth no longer vanished when she stopped laughing or smiling … not that she'd done much of either recently. Eirwen, on the other hand, had the glow of new love working in her favor and her ethereal beauty seemed to grow in time with her budding relationship. In less than twenty-four hours, the naïve twit would be not just the most beloved, benevolent, beautiful woman in the kingdom, but also the most powerful. And Nerys would be nothing.

It was positively infuriating.

Despite Nerys' attempt to disengage from conversing with the two young lovers, she still held Eirwen's rapt attention. The future queen of Talfryn could tell that her stepmother was hurting, but Eirwen was hesitant to disturb her. After all, everything she did or said seemed to frustrate Nerys, and she didn't want to add to the grieving woman's pain with her unwanted persistence.

Sensing his fiancée's distress, Roderick gave Eirwen's hand a quick squeeze, which she responded to by resting her head on his shoulder. The valiant prince fought the urge to pull his fiancée into his arms and console her since it was neither the time nor the place. Despite having known each other for a year, he had never done anything more than give her a peck on the lips after she accepted his proposal. Since their engagement, the two would hold hands or Roderick would place his arm around her when they were away from prying, critical eyes, but those precious, innocent moments were few. Greater displays of affection would have caused whispers of indecency and sullied her reputation.

With that in mind, the two parted ways when they arrived at the palace with only a bow and a kiss on her hand. Roderick promptly joined the Prime Minister, Lord Drystan, for a tour of a nearby village and Eirwen spent her afternoon doing what relaxing she could to conserve her energy for the next day's coronation. After letting Ifan best her in three games of marbles and reading four chapters from *Pride and Prejudice,* which Roderick had bought for her on his latest outing, Eirwen sought out her stepmother.

Eirwen found the woebegone widow in the parlor drinking tea alone. The princess took her seat at the table and greeted Nerys with a smile.

"How has your afternoon been?" she chirped.

"Dull as always. I feel like I've been drowning in boredom since your father died."

"I'm sorry. Is there anything I can do to help?"

Nerys waved off her stepdaughter's response as she sipped on her steaming beverage.

"Well, would you like to—"

"Have you and Prince Roderick been intimate at all?" Nerys asked abruptly.

Eirwen's complexion went from snow white to beet red, and her blue gaze dropped to her hands. The young mother smirked behind her teacup and watched in amusement as her embarrassed companion struggled to form a response. Intentionally causing Eirwen even a little discomfort worked wonders for Nerys' mood, but she couldn't help noticing that her stepdaughter even looked stunning in her state of shock.

"O-Of course not," she stammered. "We've only ever kissed once, and it was barely for more than a moment."

"Has he ever been intimate with another woman?"

"No," Eirwen gasped. "Why would you even ask that?"

"You were both terribly close on the carriage ride back from the abbey, and I didn't know what to think of it," Nerys lied smoothly. "Soldiers are notorious for taking more than riches and gold when they go to war. I wouldn't be surprised if Roderick spent the night with a woman or two during one of his campaigns."

Eirwen placed a scone on her plate and spread clotted cream on the pastry with quaking hands while she fought the images Nerys' words inspired of Roderick with another woman. She knew that there was some truth to her stepmother's claims, but she just couldn't imagine her sweet beloved behaving as so many others had. He was different. Not just because he was hers but also because he was a gallant, caring man. As she reminded herself of Roderick's true character and the countless times he'd proven to be a man of faith and principle, Eirwen's racing heart slowed and she was able to meet Nerys' dark eyes again.

"I don't know what gave you the impression that Prince Roderick was anything other than a man of honor, but you're quite mistaken about his character," Eirwen replied. "While holding hands and sitting as we did in the carriage may not have been acceptable in your eyes, it in no way is a symptom of debauchery on his part. He has told me that he's lever lain with anyone, and I trust his word completely."

"Well, let me give you a little advice. No man makes a habit of showing his bad side when he's courting a woman he wants to marry. Your father was a *tragically* flawed man, but I didn't realize the depths of his weaknesses as a king and as a man until after we were husband and wife. You'd do well to go into your marriage with your eyes wide open, so you can avoid making the same mistakes that I did."

"My father was *not* weak," Eirwen shot back, her voice trembling as her blue eyes darkened with fury. "He had his faults just like anyone else, but I won't have you speaking ill of him when he is still fresh in his grave."

"My, my, my … you're certainly quick to exercise your new authority," Nerys taunted. "I didn't realize you had such a fierce bark, Snow White."

Eirwen winced at the way her stepmother practically snarled her childhood nickname. Having been born on the day of the first snowfall of the winter with a fair complexion that was striking rather than sickly, the late Queen Gwenyth and King Rhys had affectionately nicknamed her Snow White. Even as she grew older, they joked that she could disappear into the snow if not for her dark locks and rosebud pink lips. That endearing moniker always brought a smile to her face, especially when Roderick learned of the name and took to using it on occasion, but having it sneered as a curse by Nerys' venomous tongue cut her to the bone. Fighting back unshed tears, Eirwen placed her napkin back on the table and took a deep breath as she rose to her feet.

"I'm going to lie down until Roderick and Drystan return for supper. I hope you enjoy your tea, Stepmother," she whispered.

"Sleep well, Snow White," Nerys grinned victoriously.

The princess balled her hands into fists as she glided out of the parlor, hoping the pain of her fingernails digging into her palms would keep the tears at bay long enough for her to escape to the privacy of her room. Once Eirwen was gone, Nerys relished in her solitude. Whenever the naïve princess had been away since Rhys' passing, Nerys had been able to rest peacefully and exert more influence in the palace, but power always reverted to the late king's pasty heir upon her return.

If the young princess were permanently absent—or rather dead—all of Nerys' problems would disappear. She would remain in power as queen regent until Ifan came of age to take on the role of king and her position would be secure. All she would have to do is make sure the little twit died of seemingly natural causes. Considering her husband's recent passing, Nerys had no doubt that she could put on a convincing show to mourn Eirwen before the kingdom. She would earn the people's pity and allegiance, which would turn into love and respect in time as she proved worthy of her crown.

But could she actually go through with it?

Even as Nerys contemplated the dark plan that swirled in her mind, she realized that it wasn't a matter of ability but one of will. The widow had the steely determination necessary to do the deed and could easily procure the means of her salvation, but one question still remained. Was she *willing* to take an innocent young woman's life to ensure that she and Ifan had the life they deserved?

Nerys vacated her chair with a sigh and inspected her reflection in the gilded mirror on the wall. As she counted the offensive silver hairs that had invaded her blonde mane and lamented the ever-present dark circles under her weary brown eyes, Nerys remembered her youth.

Ten years ago, as a young, vivacious woman, she had been the object of countless men's affections and every woman's awe or envy. No one had come close to her in beauty, wit, or even accomplishment. Men of all ranks had written songs about her mysterious dark eyes and poems about her flaxen locks. Rhys himself even said on multiple occasions that she had the most enchanting voice in the kingdom. No one had compared to her.

Then her saccharine stepdaughter came of age.

"Mirror, mirror, upon the wall," she sighed, "why bring me so high then let me fall?"

Of course, the looking glass didn't respond to her silly rhyme, but Nerys caught a glimpse of Eirwen's new portrait hanging on the wall behind her as she eyed the mirror. While she glared at the depiction of the regal, radiant royal, the widow's blood boiled with bitterness. When the king of Talfryn had claimed her as his wife, she'd found rest in knowing that her future was secure thanks to her powerful husband and eventually a beautiful son.

Then, Rhys' heart shuddered to a stop one day, and everything was ripped from her hands because he left everything to his more beloved first wife's daughter.

Just as her animosity reached its zenith, a seductive voice softer than an ermine surcoat whispered in her ear, and all of the tension fled her body.

Do it.

◆　◆　◆

When Eirwen entered the dining room for supper after a brief but fitful hour of sleep, she could barely muster up a smile to greet Roderick, Drystan, and Nerys. However, despite her troubled mind, the princess acknowledged her guest. As a close friend of her father's, Drystan's input had been invaluable as she both mourned the king's passing and prepared to replace him as the ruler of her kingdom.

"Thank you for joining us this evening," she greeted. "It's always a pleasure to have a meal with the best Prime Minister Talfryn has ever had."

"You're too kind, your highness," he smiled, taking his seat as she did the same. "It's been an honor to watch you become the most beautiful lady in the kingdom, and it will be an even greater privilege to watch you grow into our finest queen."

Eirwen cast a glance in Nerys' direction and was relieved to see that she hadn't taken any offense to Drystan's compliment. In recent months, her stepmother had grown testy every time someone paid her a compliment. However, something was different that evening. The fair-haired widow seemed more content than she had since the king's heart attack, and Eirwen prayed that her serenity would be long lasting.

"Thank you," the princess finally replied.

"She really is quite a blessing for our kingdom," Nerys added, placing her hand on Eirwen's. "In fact, I think we should celebrate your coronation with a toast."

The widow turned to the footman behind her.

"Please fetch the new Eusebian apple cider and apples for us, would you?"

"Y-Yes, my lady," he stuttered with a bow before exiting the room.

Nerys faced Eirwen again and lowered her voice.

"I'd also like to apologize for how we left things earlier. I was very insensitive and rude, and today wasn't the first time. Will you please forgive me?"

"Yes, Stepmother," the princess replied. "Of course, I forgive you."

The two women exchanged grins and Roderick smiled as well. Though he hadn't known what the two quarreled about in his absence, the prince was well aware of the tension that existed in the royal household. Any steps that could be made toward restoring Eirwen and Nerys' relationship were a blessing, and he silently prayed that the reconciliation would continue as his fiancée transitioned into her new role.

Everyone eased into a casual conversation about how they had spent their afternoons and laughter ensued as Nerys told a story about her son's sudden conviction that he could learn how to fly if she would only have a cloak of feathers made for him. When the merriment died down, the footman returned with four glasses of the crisp Eusebian cider and four apples, three of the green variety and one of the red apples the princess was known for favoring. Once the drinks and fruit were served, they all raised their glasses so the cheerful widow could toast to her stepdaughter.

"May your marriage and your reign leave a lasting impact on everyone who beholds them," she sang out. "To Eirwen."

"To Eirwen," the men chorused as the princess smiled demurely and clinked her glass against theirs.

"My brother Ferdinand told me that eating an apple with the cider enhances the flavor, so make sure you at least take a few bites," Nerys instructed. "I think you'll really enjoy it."

"Then I shall do just that," Eirwen replied, taking a sip and then a bite of the surprisingly juicy apple, which earned a smile from her stepmother.

As the meal progressed, the fruity first course didn't sit well in Eirwen's stomach. She lost her appetite for the herbaceous roasted turkey and couldn't even bring herself to try the fresh rolls her cook had baked. The princess dabbed away the perspiration that formed on her forehead with a pale, trembling hand, and the gesture caught Roderick's attention. Her concerned fiancé immediately abandoned the conversation Drystan and

Nerys were carrying on about the previous year's masquerade ball to inquire about her health.

"Eirwen, are you all right?"

"No," she wheezed. "I don't know what's wrong with me."

Nerys touched Eirwen's moist forehead with the back of her hand and frowned.

"You do have a slight fever. It's probably just the stress from all of these preparations catching up with you," Nerys cooed. "Let's get you to bed so you can get some rest before tomorrow."

"I'll fetch the doctor," Roderick volunteered.

Nerys nodded in approval and helped Eirwen to her feet. The pallid princess leaned on her stepmother for support as they shuffled through the palace to her room. Once inside, Nerys and Eirwen's lady's maid helped her out of the midnight blue dress she'd been wearing and into a nightgown. The thin fabric stuck to Eirwen's body, which was suddenly drenched in sweat, and violent tremors shook her as the women tucked her in and placed a cold, wet cloth on her forehead.

"Just close your eyes and sleep," Nerys encouraged, smoothing Eirwen's dark hair out of her face. "Sweet dreams, Snow White."

The dowager queen's melodious voice was the last thing Eirwen heard as her vision blurred and she drifted into a sleep as still as death.

Chapter 2

The moist, earthen surface Eirwen felt against her cheek when she awakened was a far cry from the soft pillow she'd fallen asleep on. When the princess opened her azure eyes and saw a forest and a seemingly endless canopy of greenery above, she furrowed her brow and sat up. Though Eirwen had ventured into the forests of Talfryn periodically for travel purposes, she wasn't familiar enough with the woods to know where she was simply by glancing at the green landscape.

Getting to her feet, which were lamentably bare, the princess dusted away the grass that clung to her nightgown and her pulse drummed loudly in her ears as she tried to decide what direction she should begin walking in … if she should even leave the spot where she'd awakened.

What if Roderick was looking for her and she wandered farther away from him? What if she stumbled upon a group of bandits? What if she encountered a wolf or some other equally terrifying beast?

In an attempt to calm her racing mind, the princess closed her eyes and told herself that she would find her way home. She just needed to remain calm. Feeling the pull of the west, Eirwen opened her eyes and began to walk with her back to the rising sun.

Some of the anxiety that greeted her that morning faded when a bushy-tailed squirrel ran down a mighty oak tree and stopped in her path to gnaw on a large acorn. A smile graced her rosy lips when the woodland creature scampered away, but her blue eyes widened and her hands flew over her mouth to quiet a gasp when a metal trap ensnared the small animal and ended its life.

"Aha," a man rejoiced.

Eirwen whipped around to face the source of the voice and blinked in confusion at the sight of an unexpectedly familiar face. Glyn was a tiny but joyful man of no more than four and a half feet tall who Nerys employed at Rhys' dismay to entertain her at court. The jester had pulled his graying black hair into an uncharacteristically sloppy ponytail, so she could see how his hazel eyes danced with excitement at the prospect of eating the little creature. Only when Eirwen lifted a hand to wipe away the tear that had sprung loose from her eyes did Glyn notice her presence.

"Oh dear," he began. "That wasn't your squirrel, was it?"

"No. It wasn't, Glyn."

Then it was his turn to be confused.

"Glyn?"

Eirwen looked away, suddenly questioning her own knowledge of the jester's name. How could she forget the name of the man who had made her laugh countless times in the past three months when she sometimes felt as if she would ever laugh again?

"I'm so sorry. I thought your name was Glyn."

"No. What kind of name is Glyn for a dwarf?" he scoffed.

Eirwen winced at his word choice. When the court jester failed to amuse her stepmother, Nerys took to calling him a dull dwarf. Why the small man before her willingly called himself by half of the widow's most scathing insult, she couldn't comprehend, but she didn't want to argue about epithets with him.

"Then what is your name?"

"The name's Lawen. What's yours, human?"

"You don't know who I am?"

"Should I?"

"I'm from the kingdom of Talfryn. My father, King Rhys, just passed away and I'm supposed to be crowned queen today."

"I've never heard of Talfryn in my life, so you must be very far from home," he sympathized. "Why don't I take you back to my cottage so my wife and I can help you find your way after a hot meal? Dwarf women are known for their flavorful stews."

"That's very kind. Thank you."

As much as Eirwen didn't want to trouble the man and his wife, she had a feeling that they would be able to shed some light on how and why she had awakened in a strange land so far from home.

◆　◆　◆

After Lawen freed the squirrel from his trap, the two made the short walk to his cottage. Despite the man's small size, his humble abode was plenty large enough for Eirwen to feel at home. Lawen's wife was as tiny as he was, but her heart was one of the largest the princess had ever encountered.

The instant she set foot in the couple's home, the woman began to fuss over her, noting her bare feet, bedraggled onyx hair, and pale complexion. Even though Eirwen successfully convinced her that the fairness of her skin was completely normal, she let the rotund, rosy-cheeked woman wash her feet and comb her hair as a pot of stew simmered on the stove. Lawen, on the other hand, decided to relax after his morning hunt by sucking on his pipe and reading a book nearby.

"So how did you come to be in our little nook of Edwig?"

"That's what's so strange. I have no idea," Eirwen answered. "I went to bed after dinner last night feeling sicker than I have in a long time, but I woke up in the forest this morning."

"Do you ever sleepwalk?" her hostess asked.

"No. Never. Even if I did, I doubt I'd make it past the castle guards."

"Then that *is* strange," she agreed. "And what was your name again? I was so focused on your frazzled state that I forgot to ask it when you arrived."

"Eirwen," the princess said with a smile, also capturing Lawen's attention again. "And yours?"

"Mair. What—"

"Eirwen?" Lawen interrupted, his eyes going wide. "It can't be …"

"Is something the matter?" Mair asked.

"Don't you remember the prophecy?" Lawen asked. "'White as snow and black as coal. Snow White shall free from the Siren's hold.'"

Mair raised an eyebrow and tilted her head.

"The name Eirwen means snow white," he explained with a sigh.

"Snow White is also a nickname my parents gave me," Eirwen admitted reluctantly. "What exactly does this prophecy mean?"

"Our land has been under the control of a deadly Siren for over a century," Lawen explained. "She lures men that she finds useful or handsome to her castle with her song and kills beautiful young women to maintain her beauty and power."

"That's terrible. Has anything been done to stop her?"

"Yes, but no one has been successful. However, there is one woman who can defeat the siren," he continued, holding up a single finger while he got to his feet. "All she has to do is use the Armor of G'lau and the Sword of Sanbryd to stand against the Siren and defeat the present darkness in the land."

"And you think this girl is her?" Mair asked incredulously. "Look at her! She's royalty not a warrior."

"Your wife is right," Eirwen confirmed apologetically. "The only sword I've ever held is the Sword of State for my kingdom, and it's hardly meant for waging war."

The tiny man suddenly walked across the cottage and seized Eirwen's hands in his.

"This isn't a fight of brawn against brawn. If it was, Edwig would've been free decades ago. It's a battle of light magic against dark magic, and a soft-handed princess with a pure heart and perseverance stands a better chance at succeeding than a soldier who's searching for gold and glory."

"None of this makes sense," Eirwen grieved, running a hand through her hair. "Where I come from, there is no magic … at least not the kind you speak of."

"What do you mean?"

"There are forces of good and evil fighting a war, but people don't have *powers,*" she explained. "Jesus, the Son of God, and some of His followers performed miracles. He even rose from the grave after being crucified, but it wasn't magic. It was God."

"Maybe what we call magic is just God at work fighting the forces of evil in Edwig," Lawen suggested. "If you ever met the Siren, you'd be a fool to deny that she has some sort of power, but she can be defeated."

"And you think I'm the one to do it," Eirwen breathed.

"Yes," Lawen insisted.

Eirwen looked to Mair for her input, but the motherly woman simply shrugged and went to stir her stew, leaving the princess to contend with her determined husband.

"What if I took you to someone who knows more about the prophecy? The village elder will be able to explain it better than I have."

"All right," Eirwen conceded. "I'll meet him, but I don't believe in spells and such, so I can't promise that I'll go along with anything right now."

The petite man grinned from ear to ear and kissed Eirwen's hand.

"You won't regret this," he swore.

Eirwen simply gave a forced smile and nodded. While the princess was hesitant to place her trust in anyone who believed in magic, she knew from reading the book of Exodus that the Pharaoh's sorcerers had wielded some semblance power that enabled them to turn their staffs into serpents. However, that had been countless centuries ago. The charlatans who claimed to be magicians in her kingdom were nothing more than scammers and illusionists. Surely there was no one left in the world who attempted to dabble in the occult as Jannes and Jambres had. Eirwen rubbed her arms as a chill caused goose bumps to rise on her flesh and prayed that the jester's doppelganger wasn't leading her down a path of darkness and destruction.

♦   ♦   ♦

After enjoying Mair's scrumptious stew, Eirwen changed into a set of clean clothes that another traveler had left behind. Even though the slim-fitting pants were immodest by the princess' conservative standards, she was thankful that the antiquated linen tunic was long enough to graze her knees and ease some of her discomfort. Like the rest of the clothing, the drab brown boots she donned were slightly too large for her, but a pair of woolen socks helped them fit a little better.

To finish off the old-fashioned outfit, Eirwen wore a black hooded cloak that blended in with her dark locks, which Mair had styled into a long braid for her. The forest was notorious for being filled with robbers and bandits, and the hairstyle in addition to the cloak would help hide the fact that she was a woman from anyone who may spy on them from a distance. With that in mind, Eirwen kept her hood on and her head down as she walked through the forest with Lawen, whose good mood had made him quite chatty.

"You know, I can't remember the last time I saw a human young lady in these woods," he mused. "I should have known something was different about you."

"Why are you calling me a human as if you aren't one as well? Being smaller than me doesn't make you less of a human or less of a man."

"I appreciate the sentiment, but manly as I may be, I'm a dwarf," Lawen disputed. "We're something between fairies and humans, but a lot more intelligent than gnomes. Those fat little things with their dunce-like hats and red cheeks aren't good for much more than sitting in gardens and picking flowers."

"I don't understand …"

"Look at my ears."

Eirwen's blue eyes widened when Lawen lifted his scraggly hair to reveal a pair of pointed ears that were adorned with several large hoops and had wiry hair sprouting from the canals.

"Your ears don't look like that, do they?"

The princess touched her ears in wonder and shook her head.

"No, they don't."

"In addition to the pointy ears, we're quick and packed solid with muscle. Any dwarf could contend with a human man in battle and hold his own with no problem. We're also each born with a specific talent or affinity for a trade."

"What's yours?"

"Writing."

"What kind of writing?"

"A little bit of everything. I just finished a volume about the history of Edwigian dwarves, and a satirical play that I wrote about gnomes is a favorite over in the city," he boasted, puffing out his chest. "I actually brought my supplies with me so I could write about your journey to defeat the Siren."

Eirwen bit her bottom lip and looked away, not wanting to confirm or deny that she would take on the questionable quest.

"Well, hopefully I'll have the opportunity to read some of your work before I go back to Talfryn."

The pair continued conversing about less pressing matters as they walked to the village. Eirwen learned that Lawen and Mair had five children and fifteen grandchildren with number sixteen due in the coming weeks. The princess marveled at the fact that Lawen, who looked younger than her late father, was a grandfather sixteen times over.

Perhaps dwarves don't age the same way humans do, she ruminated.

When they finally reached their destination, Eirwen stopped walking and her mouth dropped open at the sight of the small town. Much like her borrowed clothing, the village of Gallin looked like it was about four hundred years behind the towns and cities that made up her kingdom. The few nicer homes were half-timbered houses while most of the villagers dwelled in smaller wood-framed homes of wattle, mud, and straw. Eirwen had only seen drawings of fifteenth century houses made of wattle, or woven twigs, in history books and paintings. While the homes were larger than many of the apartments lower class Talfryn citizens lived in, they seemed so primitive.

"Come on," Lawen urged. "Frynin's house is the large one with the red tiled roof."

Eirwen swallowed and nodded, following the man's lead as they strolled through the village. Humans and dwarves alike loitered, conversed, and worked in the village while animals roamed freely through the well-worn paths. Lawen seemed to know many of the villagers, who greeted him with waves and shouted greetings from afar. A little boy even ran over to him, nearly knocking the dwarf over with a hug as he thanked him for the story he sent over while he was sick. The people of Gallin loved Lawen, and seeing their adoration calmed some of Eirwen's nerves. However, she noticed that there wasn't a single human young woman roaming about. Only dwarves, little boys, and human men walked the streets.

"Why aren't there any young women here?" Eirwen whispered.

"Most human parents don't let their daughters leave their homes until they've gotten married," Lawen revealed. "The Siren only takes young, beautiful virgins, so they stay inside to avoid catching the reapers' attention. Some women even choose to conceal their pregnancies so the reapers won't realize that a new child is on the way. If the rapscallions found out, they would return when the girl came of age to see if she was fit for the Siren."

"What are reapers?"

"Warriors who fell under the Siren's spell or decided to serve her of their own free will. She sends them out periodically to take girls for her household. The Siren keeps the young virgins around as servants until they've become their loveliest and then feeds on them. She disfigures the ones who don't become beautiful enough for her purposes and sends them home or gives them to her reapers as a reward."

"So she's a cannibal?"

"No, she's far worse. The Siren gives them an apple laced with her special potion to ensure that they sleep deeply. Then, she drains all of their blood into her bath. These baths of fresh virgin blood have kept her young and beautiful for at least two centuries, but many believe they aren't the sole source of her power."

Bile rose in Eirwen's throat as she imagined the bloody scene, but her compassion for the people of Edwig edged out her nausea. They'd been forced to live in fear and to mourn their daughters because of one woman's wickedness. Even if the Siren was simply deranged and not a practitioner of the dark arts, she still had to be stopped.

But am I really the one to do it?

Just as the princess once again began to weigh the prospect of taking on the Siren, she and her travel companion reached Frynin's home. Lawen grabbed the lower of two brass knockers and banged on the heavy door. After several breaths, a man opened the door. Every question Eirwen intended to ask evaporated from her pink lips and tears ran down her cheeks as she gazed into the kind blue eyes that looked so much like her own. Though his brown hair was longer than she'd remembered, his face was partially obscured by a graying beard, and he wore the same old world garb as everyone else, Eirwen would have recognized him anywhere.

He was, after all, her father's double.

"Frynin, I'd like to introduce you to—"

"Snow White," the elder interrupted. "Yes, I know. She's exactly as I imagined, but I didn't expect to make her cry at our first meeting."

"I'm sorry," she croaked, wiping away the tears even as more spilled forth. "I-It's just that you look exactly like my father. He passed away three months ago."

"You poor child," Frynin sympathized. "Why don't you come in and have something to drink while you steady yourself."

Eirwen nodded and followed Lawen into the house, Frynin patting her on the back before disappearing into his kitchen. Lawen sat opposite Eirwen, flexing and contracting his hands in anxiety as he searched for the right thing to say to the princess. For all of his decades as a writer, he couldn't find the words to comfort a young woman who had just seen a man who was the spitting image of her late father. Eirwen, on the other hand, kept her eyes on the window to her left, dabbing away the last of her tears with the edge of her overly long sleeves. When Frynin strutted back into the room with two mugs, the princess forced a smile and the dwarf did as well, thankful for the unruffled man's company.

"I know a lady like you is probably used to wine and mead, but all I have is beer," Frynin apologized.

"Beer is fine," she assured him.

Eirwen took a sip of the beer, which tasted of cinnamon, allspice and honey, and relaxed slightly. Though the princess had never tasted beer before, she enjoyed the spicy, robust drink.

"It's really good," Eirwen praised.

"Thank you. It's my own blend," the elder grinned. "Now, are you feeling any better or do you need to lie down and rest for a bit?"

"I'm fine, but I still can't get over the resemblance. You look just like him."

"Well, when I foresaw your arrival a few months ago, the powers that be told me that I would be as a father to you and you as a daughter to me. I've never been any good with young women—my status as a bachelor is proof of that—but I do feel a strange fondness for you."

"And I you," Eirwen smiled. "I know you're not my father, but I can tell that you're a kind, wise gentleman as he was."

"I don't know if I'm a gentleman, but I'll take the compliment," he chuckled.

"What else did the prophecy say about your Snow White?" she asked, still hesitant to own the name she'd gone by for years.

"That one day a young woman with hair as black as coal, skin as white as snow, and lips as pink as roses would come to Edwig from a faraway land and silence the Siren's call forever using the Armor of G'lau and Sword of Sanbryd."

"As you can see, I don't have a sword or armor. That alone should disqualify me from this prophecy."

"The Armor of G'lau and Sword of Sanbryd aren't like the armor and swords you're accustomed to," Frynin countered. "They are the embodiment of everything that is good and pure in this world: honesty, righteousness, forgiveness, faith, and wisdom. Only the one who is worthy of the items and dedicated to the cause can wield them."

"Who has them now?" Lawen piped up.

"I'm not sure. They were forged in the Valley of Obaith and blessed in the Waters of Garia by the Winter Guard when the Siren first claimed her throne, but they haven't been seen since."

"Who is the Winter Guard?" Eirwen asked.

"A group of men sworn to fight the Siren," Frynin answered. "Having drunk from the salty Waters of Garia themselves, they are immune to her song."

The princess furrowed her brow.

"So they created the armor and the sword before you even had this prophecy?"

"Yes, the original intent was for one of the women from a nearby village to bear the armor, but the Siren heard of their plan and had every woman over the age of twelve killed to ensure that no one in that generation could wear it."

Wrath filled Eirwen's heart as she heard more evidence of the Siren's villainy. She couldn't comprehend how one woman could be so evil. Even as she wished for the evil queen's reign to finally end, the princess couldn't help wondering what had happened to the Siren to make her be so cruel. After all, few people went to such extremes to hurt others without first being hurt themselves. However, no amount of past pain or hardship justified her lust for power and disregard for the sanctity of life.

"If you don't know where these items are or who has them, how can I or anyone else use them to defeat the Siren?" she continued.

"If you commit to the journey, you will be equipped for the journey," Frynin recited. "You will receive the sword and armor after you've been tested at the Waters of Garia."

"Tested how? I don't understand any of this," Eirwen groaned, shaking her head.

Frynin leaned forward and took Eirwen's fair hands in his, making her heart ache as she remembered sitting in that exact position with her father countless times before.

"There are forces at work in this world that we are neither wise enough to understand nor powerful enough to control, but I have complete faith that you will earn the hallowed armor and sword," the elder insisted. "Surely the fact that I, a man who reminds you so much of your own father, had this prophecy is a sign that you are the one sent to save us all."

Eirwen opened her mouth to speak, but a sharp rap at the door caught their attention before she could speak. Frynin abandoned his seat and went to the window, his body tensing as he clandestinely peered through a gap in the shutters. The elder mouthed the word "reapers" and Eirwen's eyes widened whereas Lawen reached for the sword in his belt. Placing a finger on his lips, Frynin gently pulled Eirwen to her feet and ushered her into the kitchen before shutting her in to keep her out of sight. The old man then gestured for Lawen to sheath his sword and the dwarf reluctantly did so, but he assumed a fighting posture, his feet spaced apart and knees bent with his fingertips barely grazing the sharp weapon. Nodding in approval, Frynin finally answered the door to greet the two reapers.

"Hello, sirs! What can I do for you today?"

"We received a report that a young woman came to visit you today," the first man began, his cold, gray eyes studying the elder from under a pair of bushy black eyebrows. "Who was she?"

"Someone reported wrong because I haven't had a young woman in this house since I was a young man. Even then, she didn't stay for long," Frynin joked with a wink.

The second reaper, a towering blond with a beard that reached his chest, grabbed Frynin by his shirt and slammed him into the door, but the elder maintained his composure and shook his head at Lawen, signaling for the dwarf not to interfere yet.

"It's illegal to lie to a reaper," the aggressive henchman taunted. "I could kill you and everyone in this house for—"

"Don't hurt him," Eirwen called, coming out of the kitchen. "I'm the woman who came to visit Frynin."

The blond reaper continued to hold Frynin against the door while his swarthy counterpart walked over to Eirwen, sizing her up and smirking in approval at what he saw.

"And what is your name, milady?"

"Eirwen."

"Where are you from, Eirwen?"

"Talfryn."

"I've never heard of Talfryn," he breathed, standing close enough that the princess could smell that he hadn't bathed in at least a week.

"It's a small island kingdom north of France. My father was the king."

The intrusive reaper began to walk around Eirwen and lifted her braid from her back, inhaling her clean, feminine scent. She shuddered despite her best efforts to stay composed, which inspired a low snicker.

"Which makes you a princess?"

"Yes."

He came back around to look her in the eye, placing a dirty, rough hand on her fair cheek.

"Well, Princess Eirwen of Talfryn, what are you doing in our sunny southern kingdom?"

"Don't bother with her," the blond reaper said, releasing his hold on Frynin to join the two and lift up Eirwen's left hand.

The tanned reaper looked from the ring to the ethereal girl before him.

"Are you engaged or married?"

"Engaged."

"To who?"

"Prince Roderick of Angharad."

"Is it an arranged betrothal or a love match?"

"We love each other very much," Eirwen answered, a familiar warmth filling her as she thought about her sweet betrothed.

"Someone else has already claimed her," the blond insisted. "You know the rules. The Siren would have our heads if we knowingly brought her a girl who already belonged to another."

The first reaper sighed and took a step back.

"Yes, she would," he grieved, reluctantly tearing his gaze away from the wide-eyed princess to look at Frynin again. "We'll leave you in peace, old man, but don't lie to us again."

"Thank you, sir," the elder said with a low bow.

With one final glance at Eirwen, the reaper shook his head and left, his hulking, hostile partner trailing behind and slamming the door after them. The instant the door was closed, everyone let out a collective sigh of relief. Rather than relishing in their privacy, Lawen climbed onto a nearby stool to peer out Frynin's front window and made sure the reapers were truly gone. Once he was satisfied, the dwarf hopped back down and joined his companions.

"What were you thinking?" the dwarf scolded. "You could have gotten all of us killed."

"I'm sorry. I couldn't let Frynin risk his life by lying for me," Eirwen apologized.

"There's no need to apologize, Eirwen. No one got hurt," Frynin assured her, glaring at Lawen as he took his seat again.

"Why did they leave when they realized that I'm engaged? I thought the Siren wanted young maidens."

"Yes, but she also needs a heart that's been untouched by true love and a body that's been preserved in purity. Love and lust make the blood too hot, so a virgin in love is as useless as a wife or a woman of the night."

"The truth may have been enough to save us for now, but reapers report everything to the Siren," Lawen said. "All she'll have to do is hear your name to know who and what you are. We need to leave."

"Lawen is right," Frynin agreed. "Go east to the village of Naroc, and visit the shepherd Hywel. He lives a half day's walk from the village, and he'll put you up for the night. The innkeeper in Naroc, Maredh, will make sure you have food for your journey before you set out for the Waters of Garia tomorrow."

"Then to Naroc we go," Eirwen said.

"Aye," Lawen agreed. "Let's be getting on before those blackguards return."

The dwarf began to set off for the back door, but Eirwen placed a hand on his shoulder.

"If we leave through the back, we'll look like we're doing something wrong," she pointed out. "Let's go through the front door in case they're watching the house."

The dwarf nodded and the pair walked to the door, Eirwen putting her hood on again. When she opened the door, a light brighter than the afternoon sun blinded the trio, but the warm brilliance didn't inspire terror in the princess' heart. The radiance disappeared as quickly as it had manifested and the first thing Eirwen laid eyes on was a glowing sword belt the exact same bright blue shade as her eyes. The colored leather and matching scabbard were covered in an intricate pattern of silver flowers and vines that shone in the afternoon sunlight. Eirwen reached out to touch the shining accessory, but pulled her hand back and turned to the elder.

"Is that …?"

"Yes. It's the sword belt from the Armor of G'lau," Frynin confirmed.

"How did it get here?" she asked. "Surely the reapers didn't leave it."

"The prophecy said that Snow White would be tested before receiving the enchanted items," he reminded her. "I know for certain that one test takes place at the Waters of Garia, but perhaps there are several trials and not just one."

"And you just passed the first one," Lawen added. "I'd put that on if I were you. It's glowing like the sun itself and it'll only attract attention unless you cover it up with your cloak."

Heeding the dwarf's advice, Eirwen picked up the sword belt, and an invigorating spark shot through her body the instant her fingers touched the garment. When the princess fastened the belt around her waist, it stopped glowing and tightened on its own to fit her slender frame. Squaring her shoulders, Eirwen faced Frynin with a smile and gave him a hug.

"Thank you for your help."

"You're welcome, child," he replied. "Have a safe journey."

The princess reluctantly ended the embrace, willing herself not to cry again as she and Lawen left her father's doppelgänger to find the village of Naroc and its hospitable shepherd.

◆　　◆　　◆

Just as the sun began to disappear behind the majestic snowcapped mountains in the west, an exhausted Eirwen stopped and plopped down on a tree stump, wiping sweat from her brow. The merciless sun had been beating down on the princess all day during their trek through the woods, and she wasn't accustomed to traveling so far on foot. Lawen, on the other hand, didn't seem to have any trouble navigating through the woodland and actually had to slow his pace to accommodate for Eirwen's.

"Are we close?" she panted.

"I think so. The last marker I saw on the road said that Naroc was five miles away."

Eirwen nodded, drinking the last of her water. Though there was a road that went straight from Frynin's village to their destination, Lawen had insisted that they not take it. After all, if word got back to the Siren about Snow White finally appearing, reapers surely would have been patrolling the road and setting up check points along the way. Thankfully, the Siren's lair in Afala and the sacred water lie to the east, so it was highly unlikely that anyone would be searching for her west of Gallin. However, Eirwen concurred that caution should be their closest companion, so they traveled off the road using the sun and Lawen's map as their guides.

"Are you all right?" Lawen inquired, noting the princess' flushed face.

"Yes, I just needed a moment."

Not wanting to slow down her athletic counterpart, Eirwen got to her feet and began walking again. The pair walked for another ten minutes before a strange but welcome sound reached their ears.

"Is that bleating?" she whispered.

The two picked up their pace, practically jogging toward their destination until they broke through the tree line and saw a small home where a fenced in herd of sheep grazed peacefully. Eirwen beamed and the pain in her feet suddenly seemed bearable as they strolled through the tall, swaying grass to the shepherd's home. When they reached the house, the black and white collie lazily lying on the porch cocked its head slightly, regarding the two with sluggish curiosity. Seeing the shepherd's pet reminded Eirwen of her lovably languid toy spaniel, and the pup's presence lifted her spirits even as her heart longed for Talfryn.

"Well, you're certainly not a guard dog," Eirwen teased, affectionately scratching behind the dog's ears and earning a lick that pulled a giggle from her lips.

Lawen smiled at the princess' lighthearted interaction with the pup, delighted to see her laugh for the first time since they met in the woods. The news of her significance in Edwig had placed a heavy burden on Eirwen's shoulders, and he hoped that her joy would be multiplied when she defeated the Siren and was able to return home. Unfortunately, that victory seemed so impossibly far away that he wasn't sure when or how they'd accomplish such a feat.

The creak of the door opening stole the travelers' attention, and Eirwen rose to her feet just as Hywel emerged from the house.

"Can I help you?" the sunburnt man yawned.

"My name is Lawen, and this is Princess Eirwen of Talfryn," the dwarf introduced. "Frynin, the elder of Gallin, said that you would give us shelter for the night."

"Why wouldn't a princess stay at the inn?" Hywel asked skeptically. "I've only one bed, and my cooking doesn't compare to Maredh's."

Lawen looked up at Eirwen, and the princess opened her cloak enough for Hywel to see her sword belt. The shepherd's hazel eyes widened, and he covered his mouth with a calloused hand before meeting Eirwen's azure gaze.

"Snow White?" he whispered.

She nodded.

Hywel straightened his posture and opened the door all of the way, frantically gesturing for the two to enter before watchfully peering out at the forest and closing the door behind them.

"This is quite a privilege," he rejoiced. "I wouldn't wish such a hard journey and a poor host on anyone, but I'm so honored to have the legendary Snow White and her companion in my home."

"Thank you for your hospitality," she said. "We truly appreciate it."

"It's no trouble at all," Hywel assured her. "Please sit down. I'll fix you a plate of food."

Once the travelers washed up a bit, the shepherd pulled out the seat at the head of the table and Eirwen sat down, thanking him once more. Lawen took his place on the bench on the longer side of the table and chugged the ale that was offered. Within moments, the princess and the dwarf each had a plate of rye bread, cabbage, and lentil soup, which they eagerly consumed. While Hywel's offerings were nowhere near as refined as the dishes her chef in Talfryn prepared, she still thought the bucolic meal was delectable after a long day of traveling.

"So, are you really going to defeat the Siren?" Hywel asked once his guests came up for air.

"Well—"

"Aye," Lawen interrupted. "Eirwen's going to defeat her all right."

"I'm going to *try*," she corrected. "I don't have any skill as a warrior, but I'm committed to taking this on and doing my best to succeed."

Hywel nodded, chewing thoughtfully on a piece of bread.

"Well, you wouldn't have gotten that sword belt if you weren't the woman for the job," he encouraged. "As far as I know, no one has seen the Armor of G'lau or Sword of Sanbryd for a century."

"Until now," Lawen grinned.

"Until now," the shepherd echoed. "Let me get you both something to sleep in, and I'll wash your clothes while you sleep."

Hywel abandoned his seat and returned several moments later with two nightgowns. Once they were done eating, Eirwen and Lawen took turns changing clothes behind a makeshift dressing screen and Hywel collected their sweaty, soiled clothing. After some convincing, Eirwen slept in the bed instead of on the floor and Lawen curled up on the small couch by the fireplace. As she rested her head on the pillow, Eirwen's mind turned to her loved ones back in Talfryn, and she prayed that they—specifically Roderick—would somehow know that she was all right. With that silent entreaty, the princess drifted into a much-needed night of sleep.

Chapter 3

A rooster's enthusiastic call awakened Eirwen the next morning, and she was surprised to see the two men already up and dressed. Upon noticing the princess, Hywel vacated his seat and immediately began spooning some of the creamy oat-based meal into a bowl for her.

"Good morning, milady," he greeted. "Did you sleep well?"

"Better than I have in weeks," the princess praised, taking the bowl. "Thank you."

"I know it isn't much, but it'll tide you over at least until you get to Maredh's inn. He'll have plenty of food for you to eat and take with you for your journey."

"This is better than any gruel I could make by my own hand," Lawen said. "I'm useless in the kitchen."

"Then it's a good thing you have a wife," Hywel smirked, lifting his ale.

Lawen chuckled, touching his mug to the shepherd's.

"Aye. It's *very* good thing."

After breaking their fasts and changing into their clean clothes, Eirwen and Lawen bid Hywel adieu and resumed their journey. The princess closed her eyes and breathed in the morning air as she pulled on her hood, enjoying the dew's fresh scent and the sun on her fair face. Eirwen had slept peacefully in the shepherd's bed and the spiced oats had warmed her soul, so she felt rejuvenated and ready to face the day.

When they strolled into Naroc, that evening Eirwen again noticed the lack of young women and her spirits fell slightly. Being the heir to the throne, she had lived a sheltered life surrounded by protection at all times, but it had been out of an abundance of caution on her parents' part. On the other hand, the people of Edwig were living in fear and hiding their daughters to keep them from being snatched away to satisfy a nefarious woman's selfish desires for beauty and power.

Ruminating about the state of affairs in the unknown kingdom sobered the princess, so her mood was considerably darker when she and Lawen finally met the innkeeper. Maredh, who stood behind the counter reading an old book, was a man of advanced years with silver hair and a beard that still had a little black coloring to it. Upon noticing his customers, Maredh's dancing brown eyes crinkled at the corners as he greeted them with a grin.

"Hello, sirs," he sang out. "Can I interest you in a room or a meal today?"

"There's only one sir here," Eirwen corrected, lowering her hood.

The innkeeper let out a low whistle when he saw her obsidian hair, pale skin, and pink lips.

"Are you …?" he began.

"Yes," the princess confirmed. "Can we please speak with you in private?"

Maredh nodded and ushered them into his office, a room filled with books, ledgers, and beverages that would have put some hair on both Lawen's *and* Eirwen's chests if they'd been offered a sip. Thankfully, he only offered honeyed ale that was more water than anything and two slices of freshly baked apple cake. Once the two expressed their gratitude, Maredh took his seat and leaned forward, resting his elbows on his knees and clasping his meaty hands.

"So, you're Snow White?" Maredh asked.

"My name is Eirwen, but yes."

"From what village do you hail?"

"I'm from Talfryn. It's a kingdom in the north."

"Well, I've never heard of Talfryn, but I am *so* happy to see you in Naroc," he trembled, tears filling his eyes as he spoke. "That blasted witch took *both* of my daughters. Losing Afanen was difficult enough for my wife, but she never recovered after the reapers took Briallen four years later. To this day, I still think she died of a broken heart."

"I'm so sorry for your loss," Eirwen whispered, placing a hand over his. "I will do everything I can to stop the Siren."

Maredh stood up and gave them his back as he cleared his throat and poured himself a stronger drink. He emptied the first mug of beer into his stomach with one long swig and poured himself a refill. After hastily wiping away his unwanted tears, the innkeeper turned back around and gave the pair a smile that didn't quite reach his weary eyes.

"Will you be needing rooms for the night?"

"No, we're going to continue our journey to Afala. Frynin said that you would give us food for the road," Lawen answered.

"That I can do," Maredh confirmed with a nod. "At least stay until my stew is done. It'll stick to your bones better than salted meat or stale bread."

"That sounds lovely," Eirwen smiled. "Is there anything we can do to help?"

"We can't risk anyone else seeing you, so you should stay in here," the innkeeper said.

"Well, no one will think anything of it if I'm out and about with all of the dwarves I've seen since we arrived," Lawen pointed out. "Will you be all right in here alone, Eirwen?"

"Yes, I'll be fine."

"Perfect," Maredh exclaimed with a clap. "We'll be back within the hour."

The two men left the office and Eirwen let out a sigh, moving a stray lock behind her ear while she reflected on Maredh's tragic testimony. The princess had been quick to assume that the Siren was so cruel to others because of some calamity or hardship in her own life, but seeing the innkeeper's despair quieted some of her pity for Edwig's vindictive queen.

How could a woman prey on innocent young women and break their loved ones' hearts for the sole purpose of preserving her position and beauty? The depths of the Siren's evil seemed unfathomable to Eirwen, but the people of Edwig were suffering whether she could grasp their tormentor's brutality or not.

In an attempt to distract herself, Eirwen rose from her chair to examine the collection of bold brews that Maredh had purchased and fermented over the years. When the princess heard the door open and shut several minutes later, she turned around expecting to see the innkeeper or her dwarf companion. Instead, she saw the two reapers and a male dwarf whose sinister stares made her blood run cold. Not wanting to give into the panic that was already making her heartbeat crescendo in her ears like an approaching steam engine, Eirwen tried to steady her breathing while she glanced around the room for anything that could be used as a weapon.

"I told you she was here," the dwarf boasted, snatching the pouch of coins the blond reaper held in his large hand.

"Hel—"

Before Eirwen could finish her cry for help, the tanned reaper leapt forward seized her, putting his hand over her mouth. Eirwen bit down on his grimy fingers, and he loosened his hold, shouting a stream of obscenities that would have made her turn scarlet had she not been desperate to escape. The princess squirmed free and lunged for the door only to be stopped by the fist of the cursing reaper's blond counterpart. Eirwen stumbled backward and fell to the floor, her head hitting the floor with a loud thud and stars dancing before her eyes as pain like none she'd ever felt before radiated along her jawline and the back of her head. Seeing that their prey was too stunned to put up a fight, the reapers tied a gag around Eirwen's mouth and placed iron shackles on her ankles and wrists.

Eirwen's fair-haired assailant tossed her over his shoulder as if she was nothing more than a sack of grain, and his partner opened the door. Then, as the reaper hauled her into the early morning sunlight, the suddenly blinding rays stung her eyes and Eirwen was powerless to fight the darkness that swallowed her whole.

◆　◆　◆

By the time the princess awakened several hours later, someone had removed her restraints, but she had traded shackles for a prison cell. Eirwen pulled herself to her feet and stumbled into the damp wall to her left as dizziness overtook her. She gingerly touched the sore spot on her jaw and winced, still incredulous that someone had the gall to assault her. Yes, she had bitten her abductor's hand in a moment of desperation, but she had never been punched in her life. As the future queen of Talfryn, she could have someone executed for raising a hand against her.

But she wasn't in Talfryn.

"Good. You're awake."

Eirwen turned to face the source of the nasally voice and saw that her visitor was a man of at least fifty with graying hair that reached his shoulders. His hairline had receded enough that his head was bare from his dark gray eyebrows to his crown, which meant that she had an unobstructed view of his triumphant chestnut eyes and smirking chapped lips.

"Who are you?" she asked.

"My name is Areth, and I'm the elder of Naroc."

"If you're the elder, then do you know Frynin?"

Areth rolled his eyes.

"Yes, I do."

Eirwen moved away from the wall and over to the iron bars that caged her in, gazing at Areth with desperation in her azure eyes.

"I don't know what the reapers told you, but I don't belong in prison. I'm here to help you and—"

"I know exactly what you mean to do, Snow White, and I'm going to be the man who keeps you from bringing your plan into fruition," he sneered, shifting his weight and adjusting the cane he'd been leaning on. "At midnight, the people themselves are going to convict you of your crimes and demand your execution. When I'm finished with you, the people will be picking up stones to kill you themselves."

"But I haven't done anything wrong."

"You came to Edwig and crossed the Siren. That's enough."

Areth turned to go, but he stopped with his back to Eirwen when she spoke again.

"Don't you care about what she's doing to your people?" she shouted.

Instead of responding, the elder wordlessly limped out of the dungeon, his footfalls and cane echoing down the dank corridor ominously with every step he took. Eirwen sank to her feet, hyperventilating and hugging herself as sobs shook her body. Unless Lawen and Maredh were able to free her before the new day began, she would lose her life and any chance she had at seeing her homeland again.

She would also die without having the opportunity to say goodbye to Roderick.

Eirwen had foolishly assured herself that she would be home and reunited with her beloved fiancé in only a matter of days, but the prospect of never gazing upon his smiling face again was too much to bear. So, the forlorn future queen gave in to her anxiety and sobbed until she no longer had the strength to open her eyes.

◆　◆　◆

Midnight came far too soon for Eirwen. Her *magnanimous* host hadn't given her a single meal or even a drop of dirty water, but the fear in her heart was greater than any hunger or thirst she could complain of. When the time came, a guard shackled Eirwen again and snatched her from her cell, slamming the door shut with a clang that made the anxious princess jump.

The two silently marched from the gloomy corridor to the ground floor and outside to the courtyard. Eirwen's gaze immediately passed the group of a half-dozen murmuring men and settled on a wooden frame with a single noose hanging from it. The guard shoved the princess under the frame and looped the rope around her neck. Eirwen closed her eyes and struggled to calm her ragged breathing as the guard tightened the noose, but the loud crack of Areth hitting his cane against the instrument of her demise interrupted Eirwen's burgeoning panic and quieted the babbling crowd.

"I've asked you here at this ungodly hour because we have a criminal in our midst," he began. "This harlot has been traveling through our land preying on good, honest men."

While the lying elder continued pontificating before his captive audience, a sweet melody wafted into the courtyard. The men's eyelids drooped, and all of the tension left their bodies as the dulcet voice's wordless melody grew louder and louder. Only Eirwen, Areth, the guard, and the two reapers who watched from the shadows were unaffected by the song. None of the elder's lies elicited a true emotional response from the jurors. Rather, the men nodded and droned their affirmations as Areth brought forth fabricated evidence. He'd even secured a false testimony from a similarly bewitched dwarf who bore a remarkable resemblance to Lawen and claimed to have been her accomplice. All of the men who held her fate in their hands were loyal to the Siren or under her control.

As Eirwen fought not to accept the hopelessness of her situation, she closed her eyes and bowed her head to pray, but a throaty, seductive voice purred in her ear before she could begin her entreaty.

"Poor, sweet, innocent Snow White," the Siren cooed. *"How do you expect to save these people when your fate is already sealed?"*

"Even if I don't defeat you, someone will," she whispered. "Evil never wins."

When the words left Eirwen's lips, the glazed over green eyes of a dwarf in the front row cleared and he straightened up, looking around in confusion. The princess didn't notice the lucid man, but his newly aware eyes settled on her.

"What is evil?" she scoffed. *"You only call me evil because I'm more powerful than you are."*

"I call you evil because you use your power to prey on your subjects instead of helping them."

Two more men shrugged off the Siren's spell, their attention also turning from Areth to Eirwen.

"I am a queen. It is my subjects' duty to serve me."

"A good queen lovingly leads her people and seeks to serve them instead of being served," Eirwen corrected. "We may wear crowns and live in castles, but we are servants of our people."

A fourth man awakened from the enchantment and shuddered as the villainess' vocals grew louder and her beguiling voice multiplied to create a haunting harmony.

"Serving is a task for the weak."

"Serving others is an honor. It helps them become stronger, and a strong kingdom makes for a strong queen," she countered. "When you use your people for selfish gain, you only succeed in ensuring your own demise."

Another newly awakened juror covered his ears with trembling hands and rocked back and forth as he became aware of the malevolent melody that had ensnared him.

"How can a woman who has no power talk about strength?" the Siren cackled. *"You don't even have a weapon to defend yourself with."*

"I'm fighting on the side of righteousness. If I'm meant to complete this quest, I'll be given everything I need to do so. If not, I've at least paved the way for someone greater."

The final man awakened, and the Siren's song came to an abrupt halt. The only sounds that were heard in the courtyard were leaves skittering across the ground as the cool nighttime breeze carried them and Areth's passionate but counterfeit charges against Eirwen. The elder finished his speech shortly after the song ended and looked up from his carefully written notes to see the six men giving him their full attention and Eirwen standing in chains with her eyes closed and head bowed, finally free to pray without the Siren's intrusive taunting.

"How do you sirs vote?" Areth asked, lifting his chin.

Eirwen took a deep breath and opened her eyes, facing the men who held her life in their hands.

"Not guilty," the dwarf cried.

Areth furrowed his brow and hobbled a few steps forward.

"Excuse me?" he asked.

"Not guilty," a second man added.

Suddenly, the courtyard was filled with shouts of innocence and absolution, and the incredulous elder gaped at his rebellious jury. After several moments, he shook his head and banged his cane against the wooden frame again, but Eirwen didn't jump this time.

"Enough," he barked. "Do I need to read the charges and bring back the witnesses again?"

"No, we heard you," a burly juror with a booming voice answered. "We just don't believe you."

"She's innocent," the man who had been rocking in his seat muttered. "Anyone can see that."

The men all rose from their seats, inspiring the terrified guard to loosen his grip on the rope, give up his keys, and back away as they removed the rope from Eirwen's neck and unlocked her shackles. The instant she was free, the liberated princess gave each of the men a hug.

"Thank you so much," she breathed.

"I have a feeling we'll be the ones thanking you soon enough, Snow White," the dwarf replied.

The sound of a horse neighing stole Eirwen's attention away from the men. When the princess turned to her right, she saw the two reapers riding into the night, the fairer of the two glancing over his shoulder as he went.

"They'll get theirs eventually," one juror said.

"And so will this one," another man added, dragging Areth over to them. "What should we do with him?"

"Let's string him up and give him a taste of his own medicine," the dwarf proposed.

"No," Eirwen said forcefully. "You will give him a fair trial and pass judgment as you see fit, but do not take his life as punishment. Please."

The men murmured their reluctant agreement, and the princess heaved a sigh of relief.

"Thank you. Now, where are we and how can I get back to …"

Eirwen's voice trailed off, and the hairs on her neck stood on end when she noticed a glimmer of light out of the corner of her eye. The princess abruptly broke away from the men and flitted over to the source of the glow, which was obstructed by an unoccupied pillory. The light faded when Eirwen rounded the wooden structure, but the grin that lit up her face was just as radiant. She leaned down and picked up the surprisingly lightweight cuirass, which was adorned with the same blue and silver design as her sword belt. An equally comforting warmth also emanated from the breastplate.

Securing the light but still bulky armor in her arms, Eirwen joined the jurors again, beaming uncontrollably as she addressed them.

"Could you gentlemen please show me the way back to Maredh's inn?"

◆　◆　◆

As soon as Eirwen swung the door to Maredh's inn open, the morose man vacated his seat and rushed over to the princess, who held a bundle swaddled in her cloak. Despite his initial relief at the sight of the grinning girl, the innkeeper's brown eyes darkened when he saw the bruise on her chin.

"Who did this to you? Are you all right? Lawen and I were out searching for you all day."

"I'm fantastic. Don't worry about me," she assured him. "The two reapers we encountered in Frynin's village took me into custody."

"How did you escape?"

"Well, Areth held a trial for me with all sorts of false accusations and witnesses to help the Siren. She exerted her influence over the jurors, but they broke free of the spell and exonerated me," Eirwen explained, unwrapping her cloak from around the cuirass. "I also found this."

"Goodness," he breathed. "You've had quite the eventful day."

"Eventful is an understatement. Is Lawen here?"

"He volunteered to search the woods nearby, but he should be back soon," the innkeeper explained. "I can't believe that Areth, of all people, was responsible for this. He was the first person I went to, and he swore up and down that he hadn't seen you. I thought he was an honest man."

"From what I gathered before I left, the reapers offered him ten bags of silver coins if he held the mock trial. Money can make a man do wicked things if he loves it too much."

"Aye, it can," Maredh agreed. "Now, I know you're exhausted, but are you hungry at all? I can warm up some food for you if you'd like."

"That would be great," Eirwen grinned.

Then, the princess followed the innkeeper out of the foyer and finally got to enjoy some of his famous red stew before settling in for a much-needed night of rest.

Chapter 4

Lawen and Eirwen set out going east the next afternoon after being given supplies and well-wishes from the people of Naroc. Though the Siren's hold on the land was still strong, the six jurors had seen that there was hope beyond their suffering thanks to Eirwen. The princess found their hope and joy encouraging, but her mind kept turning back to Roderick and her kingdom.

Was her fiancé worried about her? How were her people faring in her absence? Had her disappearance created a panic? Would the Siren stretch out her powerful hand and strike them because of her impertinence?

Heavenly Father, please protect them all, she silently entreated, willing herself to trust that God could keep them safer than she ever could.

"Why the long face," Lawen asked. "I don't understand how anyone could look so glum after the *amazing* day you had yesterday."

Eirwen smiled and shook her head.

"I'm just thinking about the people I left behind in Talfryn. I don't even know how I got here, so I doubt they know where I am or that I'm all right."

"They'll know in their hearts," he assured her, "and when you return with a superbly-written account of your adventures in Edwig penned by a certain dwarf, they'll know that you're both safe and heroic."

"Let's hope so," she chuckled. "Do you miss Mair?"

"Of course, but when you've been married for almost a century, a few days to yourself can be kind of nice," the dwarf said with a wink. "On a serious note, yes. I miss her terribly. The only things that make the separation bearable are my faith that I'll see her again and the delightful company I have on my travels."

"You're a great travel companion as well," Eirwen smiled. "Can you tell me one of your stories? I only caught the end of the tale you were telling the children at the inn."

"Well, you're a bit older than my audience back in Naroc, so I'll try to spice things up a bit."

For the remainder of their travels that breezy day, Lawen told the story of a young wolf named Raffus who left his pack to join two jackals. The opportunistic pair promised him freedom and the finest meats in the land only to lead him down a road of dishonor and destruction. They attacked the most defenseless creatures in the forest, which Raffus' pack had sworn to protect, and even fed on the omega wolf of another pack. The misguided wolf's icy blue eyes eventually opened to the destruction and heartbreak his actions were causing and was filled with dread and hopelessness but also a desire to stop the two jackals he'd once thought of as so wise.

As the sun began to set, the dwarf wrapped up the story with Raffus defeating the two jackals in a fierce fight by the light of the full moon and returning to his pack with his head hanging low, ears drawn back, and tail between his bloodied legs. Rather than casting his son out for leaving the pack, Tlaidd welcomed Raffus by licking his face and playfully wrestling with his him before cleaning the blood and muck from his silver fur. At the end of the tale, the pack celebrated Raffus' return with a chorus of howls and yelps heard by every creature in the forest. Though Lawen's fantastical tale was complete fiction, it still warmed Eirwen's heart and helped her cast aside some of her fears and concerns.

When they decided that it was time to set up camp, Eirwen volunteered to start the fire and cook the duck Lawen had snatched during their journey. Despite her best efforts, Eirwen overcooked gamey bird, but the merciful dwarf sang her praises and said nothing disparaging about the slightly dry meat. On the bright side, the pears she'd picked from a nearby tree were ripe and juicy while Maredh's rye bread and honeyed ale made tasty additions to their supper. At the end of the meal, the two were blissfully full and the weight of their fatigue made their eyelids droop and pulled yawns from their lips.

Lawen volunteered to take first watch, so Eirwen slept peacefully by the hearth until her time came to act as the dwarf's protector. With the dagger one of the jurors had given her resting securely in her boot, the princess sat on the boulder across from where Lawen snored softly and studied the creatures of the night. As she watched an owl land in a nearby tree and fix her with an inquisitive golden gaze, something else in the shadows caught her eye.

She was being watched.

A man, his identity shrouded by a hood and shadows, peeled away from a nearby oak and ran away, limping slightly with every step. Without a moment of hesitation, Eirwen took off after the snoop, sprinting through the forest and dodging low hanging branches as she tried to keep the man in her sights. After hearing a grunt and the rustle of leaves ahead, the princess finally caught up to the man, who was scrambling to his feet with his back to her, cursing under his breath upon hearing her footsteps draw near.

Eirwen reached down and pulled the knife from her boot with a quaking hand, praying that she wouldn't have to use it while her breathing calmed enough for her to speak.

"Who are you?"

"You're mighty brave to come dashing after me at night by yourself, Snow White," he said, still refusing to face her as he wiped a bloody hand on his cloak. "Maybe I've lured you away from your camp to kill you for the Siren."

The princess tightened her grip on the knife and took a step back.

"I won't ask again. Who are you?" she repeated.

The spy turned around, and Eirwen nearly dropped her knife as she recognized one of the reapers who had arrested her in Naroc. The colossal blond had a new gash running from his eyebrow to his chin and a rag tied over his injured left eye. Another such scrap was also wrapped around his right thigh as a makeshift bandage, but blood still managed to seep through the tan fabric and run down his muscular leg. Though the reaper was a full two heads taller than Eirwen and had the build of an accomplished warrior, there was no fear or anger in her heart when she looked into his downcast hazel eyes.

All she felt was compassion.

"You're one of the men who arrested me," Eirwen said.

"Yes," he grumbled.

"Is your partner here as well?"

"No, he's lying in a ravine five miles from here with his throat slit."

"By you?"

The reaper nodded, and Eirwen's stomach lurched.

"Well, it looks like he got in a few good licks before you defeated him," she observed. "Why did you kill him?"

He turned away, furrowing his brow while he clenched and unclenched his massive hands.

"After we had left Naroc, Andras wanted to patrol the woods in case you came through on your way to the Waters of Garia, but I didn't feel right about it anymore," he explained. "When I saw you on trial and you challenged the Siren instead of the charges against you, the singing in my head stopped and I was myself for the first time in ten years. *Ten years!*"

The reaper ran his hands through his flaxen hair, shaking his head.

"I didn't think anyone could ever stop her. I didn't *want* anyone to. I wanted to stay drunk on her beautiful voice and gaze upon her face until I breathed my last, but when the song stopped, I realized what she was and what she'd forced me to do," he grieved. "You see, I wasn't just a reaper. I was a *huntsman*—the finest of her soldiers. I spent years plucking young girls from their homes and killing anyone who got in my way or spoke against the Siren, but I had no control over myself. I was helpless."

Tears ran down the man's dirty sallow cheeks and disappeared into his great beard.

"After Andras and I fled Gallin, the Siren told us not to return unless we had Snow White's lungs and liver on a silver platter for her to eat."

Bile rose in Eirwen's throat at the prospect of the evil and apparently cannibalistic queen devouring her organs.

"After the trial, Andras was still under her control. He turned on me when he realized that I was a free man and had no intention of completing our mission, but I bested him," the huntsman continued, wiping snot from his nose with the back of his hand.

"If you don't want to kill me anymore, why are you here?" Eirwen asked softly.

"I don't know … I don't have anywhere else to go. My people have forsaken me, and any number of Edwigian men would be happy to throw a noose around my neck for what I've done."

Eirwen's free hand went to her throat as she remembered her trial the night before.

"I thought about falling on my sword after I killed Andras, but I was too much of a coward to follow through. Maybe that's what I'll do after you leave," the reaper said, but his eye was suddenly alight with hope when he met her concerned gaze. "Or maybe you can do it for me."

The princess' blue eyes widened and she took a step back, shaking her head, but the huntsman fell to his knees at her feet and took the hand she clutched the knife in, holding it to his throat. Sensing Eirwen's dread, the suicidal man wrapped his fingers around hers tightly so she couldn't release the blade even if she wanted to.

"No, I can't kill anyone," she insisted.

"You'll have to take the Siren's life by force when the time comes. At least I'm giving mine up freely," he pointed out. "Do it. Put me out of my misery."

"No," she sobbed, "I can't kill you. I *shouldn't* kill you."

Eirwen gently got on her knees as well so she could look the huntsman in his wild, bloodshot eye.

"I know that you've done terrible things, but as long as there's breath in your lungs, you can change and start anew. The Siren's power no longer has a hold on you. You're a free man. Use your freedom and the skills she refined in you for good instead of evil," Eirwen pleaded.

The tormented man pulled her hand closer, nicking his skin with the knife.

"This is exactly what she wants you to do. She needs you to be lost without her so you'll return to the fold or kill yourself so she has one less adversary," she continued, fighting the anxiety that rose in her upon seeing his blood on her blade. "If you make me kill you, you'll be letting her win by letting her claim another life. Please don't do this."

The huntsman let go of Eirwen's hand and rested his head on her shoulder, his body shaking with sobs. She wept as well out of both sorrow for the poor, guilt-ridden man and relief. The princess threw the detestable knife to the ground, placed her arms around the huntsman, and rubbed his back to comfort him. When the warrior's tears subsided, he pulled away and sat back on his heels, taking in the princess with a new perspective.

"How can you put your arms around a man who would have gladly killed you on any other night?"

"Because I forgive you. You were under a spell, so I refuse to condemn you for what the Siren forced you to do," she answered with a smile, "Now, what is your name, huntsman?"

"Ivor."

"Well, Ivor, what do you plan on doing with yourself now that you're a free man?"

"I don't know … I suppose I could start over in another kingdom, but I can't bear to leave Edwig yet. It just doesn't feel right."

"Would you like to accompany Lawen and me? We could use another man on the journey, and this could be an opportunity for you to give back to the people before you go."

"I'd like that," Ivor said with a nod.

"All right. Follow me."

Eirwen stood, and the huntsman began to do the same, but his eyes fell to Eirwen's feet and widened in disbelief.

"Milady …"

Eirwen looked down and saw a pair of greaves on her feet. The protective shoes perfectly matched the other three pieces from the Armor of G'lau that she'd received, and her joy multiplied at the sight of them.

"You really are Snow White," he breathed, finally meeting her eyes again.

"It would seem so," Eirwen replied. "Let's hope I can live up to Edwig's expectations."

Eirwen extended her hand to Ivor with a smile, and the injured man took her hand. Once she helped the enormous former huntsman to his feet, she gave him another hug and they began their walk back to the camp.

Chapter 5

Before he even opened his hazel eyes the next morning, a grin was on Lawen's lips. The smell of eggs and meat cooking tickled his nose and lifted his spirits, but the smile fled faster than a fox from a hound when he saw the hulking blond ne'er-do-well sitting by the fire as he cooked the aromatic meal. The dwarf slowly reached for his short sword, but his eyes never left his enemy. According to Eirwen's account of her arrest, the fair foe had been the one who gave her the nasty purple bruise on her porcelain face. Any man who would strike such a sweet, innocent woman and deliver her up to be tried and executed for trumped up charges was a man who deserved death. However, the small man nearly jumped out of his skin when Eirwen's voice cut through the silence.

"That smells delicious," she praised from behind him. "I've had cooks my whole life, so I'm absolutely useless in the kitchen."

Lawen sat up, furrowing his dark eyebrows at the princess in disbelief while the man behind him said something he didn't quite care about in response and the maiden laughed.

"Good morning, Lawen," she greeted, noticing her friend was awake. "This is Ivor. He's going to be joining us on our journey."

"He's a *reaper,*" the dwarf hissed.

"Technically he was a huntsman, but yes," the princess cheerily corrected. "The Siren's spell over him lifted during my trial, and he wants to help us defeat her."

Lawen gaped up at Eirwen for a moment while she began to re-braid her hair, but he couldn't quite find the words to voice his incredulity.

"Don't worry, little man," Ivor called from the fire. "If I wanted either of you dead, you never would have seen daybreak."

The princess narrowed her eyes and shook her head at their new travel companion in disapproval before sitting beside Lawen.

"He's a friend," she whispered, thankful that the sizzling food was loud enough that Ivor couldn't hear her. "Ivor wanted me to kill him last night for the deeds he's done, but I refused to do it. He's a changed man through and through. We can trust him. I'd bet my life on it."

Lawen studied the princess' earnest gaze for a moment and then tossed a glance over his shoulder at their unlikely cook. Looking back at Eirwen, he sighed, and a smile graced her lips as some of the tension left his body.

"All right," he agreed.

"Great," Eirwen grinned. "I also have more good news."

"Is Areth joining us too," Lawen teased.

Eirwen walked over to her things and lifted her cloak from the pile, revealing her growing collection of enchanted armor.

"Frynin said that one of the things the armor represents is forgiveness, so this certainly justifies your kindness toward the huntsman," the dwarf acknowledged.

"The Siren has forced him and countless others to do terrible things in her name. Who would I be to condemn him for succumbing to a power that he was defenseless against?"

"Who, indeed?" Lawen agreed, thinking more of his own harshness toward Ivor than the princess. "I'm going to see if our new ally needs any help."

The humbled dwarf, who had been ready to end Ivor's life only moments before, squared his shoulders and walked over to the huntsman. Lawen plopped down on the tree stump across from his new traveling companion and made conversation. Eirwen relaxed as she watched the two former enemies converse, grinning as Ivor laughed at the clever writer's jokes. Seeing that small glimmer of healing in their contentious relationship gave her hope for the Siren's other men.

Recognizing that it was all right to join the two men, the princess crossed the small camp to sit at the fire, praying that the people of Edwig would forgive and accept the other reapers and huntsmen as quickly as she and Lawen welcomed Ivor.

◆　◆　◆

Once the trio filled their bellies with Ivor's cooking, they packed up their few belongings and headed east. Just when the sun was at its highest, beating down on the travelers mercilessly, the sound of running water urged them on. When the greenery became sparser, Eirwen saw a stream just past the tree line and she eagerly retrieved her empty water skin. However, Ivor stretched out his arm to block her way before they could step into the clearing. The burly blond shook his head and pointed north.

Eirwen and Lawen looked to their left and saw two reapers at the bank of the stream. The men appeared to be close to Eirwen's age, but their youth didn't make them any less of a concern since each was armed with a sword and a dagger. However, the way one bald, bearded young man stumbled over to his horse while the other laughed uproariously from where he sat by the water told the group that they'd been drinking something much stronger than water.

"Stay here until I give you the signal and then travel east for at least half an hour," Ivor whispered. "I'll take care of them then come find you."

The huntsman started toward the reapers, but Eirwen grabbed his arm.

"Please don't hurt them on our account."

"I didn't plan to," Ivor said with a lopsided grin.

The princess released his arm, and the warrior crept away from them through the woods before stepping into the clearing twenty yards to the north. The reaper by the stream, whose brown hair was pulled away from his face in a low ponytail, saw Ivor walking toward them and scrambled to his feet, squaring his broad shoulders. His bald companion stumbled around and hastily shoved their empty skin into his sack before standing beside his drunken companion and assuming a similar posture.

When Ivor reached the young lads, he crossed his arms over his barrel of a chest and glowered down at them. The former huntsman was fully aware of the fact that his partially healed scar and makeshift eyepatch made him look even more menacing than he had before his skirmish with Andras.

"What are you two doing?" he asked.

"We just finished our midday meal and were about to fill our skins with water so we could continue our search," the bearded boy answered, keeping his coffee-colored eyes on the ground.

"What are you searching for?"

"Snow White," his friend said. "The Siren said that she was traveling by day and gave us orders to search the woods for her."

"And how is your search going?"

"We don't have any leads yet, but we planned to search west of the stream this afternoon."

Ivor turned around and gave his back to the two reapers while he pilfered the reaper's wine skin from his pack. The massive man opened the skin and sniffed at it before facing the young men again with an expression that would've made even the bravest man tremble in his boots.

"You *imbeciles,*" he bellowed, punctuating his tirade by hurling the skin at the reapers. "How do you think her majesty would react if she knew that you were compromising your mission by working while you're drunk?"

The bald fellow looked up, his eyes wide with fear as he spoke.

"W-We're sorry, sire. W-We were just—"

"Y-You were just putting everything we're working for in jeopardy," Ivor mocked, a sinister sneer gracing his lips. "I've half a mind to flog you both and tell the Siren what you've been up to."

The two henchmen remained silent as they waited for their superior to pass judgment.

"Luckily for you, I don't want to waste my strength on you nitwits, so I have something different in mind."

Ivor pointed to two great stones that were each as large as the reapers' torsos and weighed more than any man could comfortably carry for more than a few steps. However, the huntsman wasn't concerned about his former allies' comfort.

"You're going to pick up those stones and carry them over your heads from here to that large oak about a furlong downstream. Then, carry them back here," he instructed. "I'll be here watching your every step, so don't even *think* about trying to cheat your way out of this."

"Yes, sir," they droned.

The regretful reapers skulked over to the stones and picked them up, hoisting the weighty rocks over their heads. As the two men began trudging toward the oak tree, which seemed torturously far away, Ivor turned toward his travel companions and gestured for them to resume their journey. Eirwen and Lawen furtively darted from the trees and crossed the stream, their eyes on the two reapers. Thankfully, Ivor covered the sounds of their footsteps by barking orders and taunts at the inebriated young men, who were too busy being burdened and berated to notice that the very woman they'd been told to find was only yards away.

Eirwen looked back at the three men once she was concealed by the trees on the east side of the brook and was relieved to see that they still had a ways to go before they reached their destination. So, she and Lawen continued their trek through the woods, careful not to make a sound lest they encounter more of the Siren's loyal men. After what they surmised was a half hour, they sat down and waited for Ivor. Lawen took advantage of his free time to record more of their adventures in his book. Eirwen, on the other hand, picked a few pears and berries that grew in the vicinity for their party to snack on then closed her eyes for a moment of relaxation.

"You two certainly look rested," Ivor said.

The dwarf and princess jumped at the huntsman's unexpected arrival, earning a rumbling chuckle from the surprisingly stealthy giant.

"Are the reapers all right?" Eirwen asked. "Those stones looked quite heavy."

"They're perfectly fine," he smirked, amused by her concern. "They're a little sore, but they'll live."

The princess nodded and stood up.

"Do you need to rest, Ivor, or should we keep going? Lawen and I don't mind waiting for a bit."

"I'll survive, but we need to find somewhere to seek refuge until nightfall," he answered. "Apparently the Siren has her reapers and huntsmen searching for you by day, so our best bet is to travel at night while they're shut up in the village inns."

"There may not be reapers at night, but there are plenty of scoundrels lurking in the forest after sunset," Lawen pointed out.

"Yes, but they won't be looking for me specifically," Eirwen said.

"She's right," Ivor agreed. "Besides, we don't exactly look like we have a lot of valuables to steal. Anyone rich enough to be worthy of robbery would be traveling on the road."

"Well, where do you propose we hide out for the next several hours?" the dwarf asked. "I don't know anyone in this part of Edwig who I would trust with Eirwen's safety."

"I do," the huntsman grumbled. "Come with me."

Eirwen and Lawen let Ivor lead the way through the forest, their afternoon journey considerably quieter than their morning travels. An hour later, they neared another village. Ivor flipped his hood on, and he and Eirwen kept their heads low while they passed through the bustling town. When they reached their destination, a small, unremarkable house in the northeast quadrant, Ivor took a deep breath and knocked on the door. After a few moments, the door swung open to reveal a tiny old woman with graying blonde hair that was tied up in a simple snood. Despite cataracts clouding her hazel eyes, she still recognized him well enough to for anger to distort her aged features.

"May we come in," Ivor asked, his voice sounding oddly strained.

"Do I have a choice?"

The old crone trudged back into the house, allowing Ivor and his dumbstruck companions inside her modest home. As soon as the door shut, a fiery-haired woman about five years Eirwen's senior strolled into the house from the back door holding a basket of newly harvested potatoes in her hands.

"Who is it, moth—"

The woman dropped the potatoes at the sight of Ivor. Luckily, the huntsman caught the basket before it could spill, handing it back to the maiden, who had turned whiter than a sheet.

"Ivor?" she whispered.

"Rhianon would be of no use to the Siren," the old woman said, coming between the two and fixing Ivor with a fierce glare. "What do you want?"

"I'm not here for Rhianon, and I'm not working for the Siren anymore, Nesta," Ivor explained.

"No one leaves the Siren's service," Rhianon disputed, tears evident in her dark eyes. "You're trying to trick us."

"He's telling the truth," Eirwen spoke up, coming from behind her reformed friend and removing her hood. "My name is Eirwen, but I believe the name Snow White carries more meaning in Edwig."

The two women took in the princess' fair skin, dark hair, and rosy lips just as many others had and then shifted their suspicious gazes back to Ivor.

"So you're under *her* spell now," Nesta assumed.

"No, he isn't," Eirwen disputed. "I can't cast a spell any more than I can cook a duck without rendering it bone dry."

"It wasn't *that* dry," Lawen cracked under his breath.

"I don't know how, but I broke the Siren's hold on Ivor and six other men back in the village of Naroc," the princess continued. "He is his own master now, and he's using his freedom to help me defeat her."

"We need your help, Nesta. Reapers and other huntsmen are searching for her by day, so we need somewhere to stay until nightfall," Ivor said, casting a lingering glance in Rhianon's direction. "You're the only people I trust in this village."

"Then we'll help you," Rhianon said, placing a hand on his arm. "What else do you need?"

The huntsman reddened behind his beard but maintained his even tone and rigid posture.

"Just some supper when the time comes and somewhere to clean up. I have plenty of money to pay you—"

"I don't want your money, Ivor," Nesta interrupted. "We'll give you shelter for the day."

"Thank you," he said, bowing slightly. "I'll go fetch some firewood."

The hulking huntsman threw on his hood and vacated the house before anyone could say a word, leaving the three women and the dwarf to get to know one another in Ivor's absence.

"Thank you so much for your hospitality," Eirwen said. "I know it's probably difficult to accept that Ivor has changed after being under the Siren's spell for so long, but I can attest to his transformation. Not long ago, Ivor would have gladly ended my life out of obedience to her song, but he's a different man now."

"I can see that," Nesta said, eyeing her gorgeous guest carefully. "What is your relationship with Ivor? Are you just allies are more?"

"Mother," Rhianon hissed.

"Oh, goodness no," the princess chuckled. "I'm engaged to a man I love very much back in Talfryn. Ivor is only accompanying me so he can make amends for the deeds the Siren forced him to do."

Rhianon and her mother both relaxed slightly, and their two visitors began to grasp at least a small part of Ivor's involvement with their family. Thankfully, the young redhead decided to shed some light on the situation before their minds could wander much farther.

"Ivor and I were engaged before the Siren took him," she explained. "He heard her song a month before our wedding and left in the middle of the night to go to her castle in Afala. I haven't seen him in ten years."

"I thought the Siren couldn't take someone who was in love," Eirwen said.

"Any man can fall under her spell. It's only women who are useless to her when they're in love because their blood is too hot for her," Lawen corrected.

"That's why Rhianon has been safe all these years," Nesta chimed in sadly, kissing her daughter's cheek. "Her love of Ivor has kept her from marrying other men, but it's also kept her from being taken by the reapers."

"I'm so sorry," Eirwen breathed. "I've been away from Roderick for only a few days, and I miss him terribly. I can't imagine the pain of being separated from someone you love for a decade."

"It's not so bad," Rhianon disputed with a smile that didn't quite reach her brown eyes. "I'm free to help my mother, and I can go out and about in ways that other women can't. My heart may belong to someone else, but I'm the freest woman in Wynfor."

"I know you said you didn't want any money, but I'd like to be of some use while I'm here," the princess insisted. "Is there anything I can do to help you, ladies?"

"There is some laundry to be done, and we could use some more water," Nesta answered.

"I'll help with the laundry," she offered.

"And I can go to the well," Lawen added.

With that division of labor, the four eased into an afternoon made less awkward by the tasks set before them. Ivor returned an hour later carrying freshly chopped wood and a few rabbits he'd caught in the woods. Nesta and Rhianon insisted on cooking supper themselves, so their guests sat at the far end of the house by the back door, which they'd opened to allow some fresh air in. Lawen was snoring away nearby, so Eirwen decided to strike up a conversation with her taciturn companion.

"Is this where you grew up, Ivor?"

"Yes."

"Do you have any family here that you'd like to see before we leave?"

"No, a plague killed my mother and father before the Siren called me," he grumbled.

"I'm sorry. I lost both of my parents as well."

"Recently?"

"My mother and the little boy she was carrying died in childbirth when I was six, and my father passed away three months ago."

"I'm sorry for your loss as well."

Several moments of silence passed between them and Eirwen bit her bottom lip, studying the inattentive huntsman before shifting the topic slightly.

"Nesta and Rhianon told me about your engagement."

Ivor narrowed his eyes, which were trained on something outside, and clenched his fists, but he remained silent.

"Do you still love her?"

"Of course. The Siren's magic might have ruled over me for all these years, but love is one thing she can't control," he retorted.

"Now that you're free, would you ever go back to her?"

"She wouldn't have me."

"How do you know that?"

"Rhianon deserves better. What woman would want a man who spent a decade sending her friends and her people to their deaths?"

"A woman who loves you enough to forgive you," she answered. "Rhianon hasn't been able to keep her eyes off of you all afternoon, but you've been so closed off that she probably thinks you're indifferent toward her."

Ivor shook his head with a sigh, running a hand through his hair.

"I'm not trying to pressure you," Eirwen assured him. "I just don't want you to turn your back on love because you're still punishing yourself."

"Supper is ready," Nesta called from the other side of the house.

Ivor leapt from his seat and strode over to the women, more eager to escape the princess' company than to fill his belly with food. With a sigh, Eirwen awakened Lawen and the two joined the others for a tasty but tense meal.

◆　◆　◆

Once everyone had their fill of Nesta and Rhianon's rabbit stew, Eirwen helped the ladies clean up after the meal and the men went to buy supplies. The instant they returned from their evening errand, Ivor abruptly announced their departure. Lawen and the princess awkwardly bid their hostesses adieu, and Ivor grunted in gratitude before they set out into the night.

The huntsman strode several yards ahead of them for the first hour of their travels, not bothering to glance backward at his fellow travelers or say a more than a word or two to them. Watching the agitated blond isolate himself in such a way saddened Eirwen, but she prayed that God would soften and heal his heart whether he and Rhianon found their way to one another again or not.

When the full moon was at its highest in the night sky, Eirwen's eyelids began to droop and she regretted not taking a nap as Lawen had earlier. Ivor, on the other hand, seemed perfectly alert despite not sleeping a wink at his former fiancée's house. However, the princess perked up when Ivor stopped and held up his fist, signaling for them to halt as well. The former foe slowly drew his sword from its sheath and Lawen did the same while Eirwen took her dagger into her trembling right hand.

Ivor lifted his sword and spun around, striking down an arrow that someone had loosed into the night before the projectile could find its home in the back of his head. Eirwen's breathing quickened and she looked behind her to see where the arrow had come from, but Lawen grabbed her hand and pulled her along as he and Ivor broke into a sprint away from their unseen foes. Arrows embedded into trees as they zigzagged through the dark forest, and the princess struggled to keep up with her more athletic comrades. Stumbling over a fallen branch, Eirwen fell to the ground with a yelp of pain. Lawen and Ivor backtracked to help her up and stayed low to avoid the arrows, which had suddenly stopped flying through the air.

"Do I hear a woman with you, huntsman?" a voice called in the darkness.

The trio remained silent, not sure if alerting their attackers to Eirwen's presence would help or hurt their cause.

"We don't mean to hurt the girl," another man called from the opposite direction. "We only want the men carrying her off to the Siren."

"They're not kidnapping me," Eirwen cried.

The grass and leaves around them began to rustle, and Ivor assumed a fighting stance with his sword at his ear as a group of fifteen men wearing black clothing emerged from the darkness and surrounded them.

"I don't know what he told you, but that's what huntsmen and reapers do," a man with a black gray-streaked beard and matching hair scorned. "They take poor, innocent girls and drag them to Afala to be killed by that monster."

"Yes, and marauders like you take poor, innocent girls for their enjoyment then slit their throats when they lose their appeal," Ivor mocked. "I'm not working for that crooning harpy anymore."

"I can vouch for him," Lawen spoke up. "Ivor arrested Eirwen on behalf of the Siren, but he—"

"Eirwen?" he repeated, shifting his green gaze to the princess. "Is that your name?"

"Yes, I'm Princess Eirwen of Talfryn."

"Take off your hood."

Eirwen did as the leader instructed and watched his eyes widen as he took in her distinctive brand of beauty and armor.

"You're Snow White," he breathed.

"Yes, I am, and these are my friends Ivor and Lawen. They're going to help me defeat the Siren."

Eirwen winced at how unsure her voice sounded, but the men didn't notice her lack of confidence. Instead, they grew excited and talked amongst themselves as a sinister grin spread across the man's face.

"Well, isn't this a nice surprise," he chuckled. "I was hoping for another girl to play with, but this is so much better!"

Ivor launched himself at the dark-haired man, who evaded his blow and struck him the face with enough force to break his nose and send him to his knees. Three of the bandits rushed forward and held him down, ripping the sword from his hands as blood trailed down his face.

"Do you want us to kill him, Yorath?" one of Ivor's keepers asked as he held a knife to his throat.

"Please don't hurt him," Eirwen pled, Lawen helping her to her feet.

Yorath crossed his arms and stroked his beard thoughtfully as he gazed down at the earnest girl.

"I won't … for now," he grinned before turning to his men. "Bring them back to the camp!"

Ivor fought against the three men who tried to shackle him, but Yorath hit him in the temple with the pommel of his sword, felling the large man and inspiring a gasp from Eirwen. It took two men to drag the unconscious huntsman through the woods, but Lawen and Eirwen were far more compliant. The two let the bandits shackle them and guide them through the forest, shoving them if they walked too slowly and making crass comments about Eirwen's beauty. The princess held her tongue despite her irritation and embarrassment, not wanting to sink to their level by responding to their inappropriate comments in anger.

Eventually, they reached a small camp of tents where a weary woman tended to the large roaring fire while another plucked feathers from a freshly killed chicken. They regarded Eirwen, Lawen, and Ivor with suspicion and pity before going back their work as if they'd never seen the new prisoners. The men put Lawen and Ivor in one tent, ensuring Ivor was bound wrist to ankle, and Yorath had his other cronies dump Eirwen in a tent at the opposite end of the camp. The princess took advantage of her privacy by closing her eyes and bowing her head to pray.

Lord, please help us through this. Protect Lawen, Ivor, and me from harm so we can continue our journey unscathed and unsullied.

The sound of rustling cloth reached Eirwen's ears and she opened her eyes, her body tensing when she saw that the scoundrels' leader had joined her in the tent. Yorath loomed over her, his arms crossed and head tilted to the side as he studied the prayerful princess.

"So, you're the famous Snow White," he began. "I was expecting a soldier, but you look more like a lady. It's quite a pleasant surprise."

Eirwen didn't know how to respond to his statement, so she remained silent.

"Are you a warrior?"

"No, I've never fought a battle in my life."

"Then why do you think you stand a chance against the Siren?" he asked. "I've seen many men rebel against the enchantress, and even great warriors have lost their lives to the reapers and huntsmen without ever reaching her. I know the Armor of G'lau and Sword of Sanbryd are powerful, but if all you have by your side are a huntsman and a dwarf, you're going to suffer the same fate."

"I have faith that I wouldn't have been chosen for this quest if there wasn't a chance that I could succeed or at least do some good by trying."

"Faith won't protect you from a knife in your back or a morningstar's spike in your skull," Yorath argued. "You need an army, and I'm prepared to give you one."

"On what conditions?" Eirwen asked, sensing a catch to his offer.

"My men and I will help you if you marry me and make me the king to your queen after we defeat the Siren."

"I-I can't marry you," she stammered. "I'm already betrothed to someone else."

"But he isn't here to help you, is he?"

"That's not his fault."

"No, but it *is* your disadvantage," Yorath asserted.

"I'm a woman of my word. I cannot and will not break my promise to Roderick," Eirwen persisted. "Even if I wasn't engaged to someone else, I can't marry a man who spends his time attacking travelers in the woods so he can shackle and intimidate women. You'd make a difficult husband to submit to and a horrible king to share a throne with … a throne that I have no intention of taking. I have my own kingdom in Talfryn. I don't want Edwig."

"Well, aren't you high and mighty," he scoffed.

"I'm not trying to offend you. I only mean that there is more to consider concerning marriage than a militaristic advantage. My conscience won't allow me to marry you."

"Your conscience is a liability. I may make a difficult husband and a horrible king, but I can keep your head on your shoulders," he sneered. "If you don't come to your senses by dawn, you and your friends will pay the price."

With that threat, Yorath swept out of the tent. Before she could begin to process what had just taken place, one of the other men entered to yank Eirwen out of that tent and shove her into the one where Ivor and Lawen were being held. The princess immediately went to Ivor's side, attempting to assess his injury the best that she could with her hands still bound.

"I'm fine," he grumbled.

"You're bleeding," she argued.

"I *was* bleeding," Ivor corrected. "Besides, I've been through worse."

Eirwen furrowed her brow and bit her lip before sitting down and turning her attention to Lawen.

"Are you all right?"

"They never even laid a hand on me," he reassured her. "What about you? Did they hurt you at all?"

Eirwen shook her head, tears stinging her eyes.

"No, but I'm scared of what they might do."

"What happened?" the dwarf asked softly.

"Yorath wants to use me to defeat the Siren and take control of Edwig for himself," she explained, "and he wants to do so by marrying me."

"What a romantic fellow," Lawen breathed. "How did he react when you rejected him?"

"He said we would pay the price if I didn't change my mind, but I don't know if I can bring myself to do it."

Eirwen wept as she imagined returning home and telling her beloved prince that she'd chosen someone else. If she agreed to Yorath's terms, she would be hurting the man she cherished above all others, but if she didn't, two men would probably lose their lives. Either way, she would be forcing someone she cared for to deal with the consequences of her decision.

"You can't do it," Ivor said.

"They're going to hurt you if I don't."

"Let them! I've spent a decade killing countless people in the name of an old evil, and I'd gladly give my life if I can keep a new one from sitting on the throne. Yorath may not have magic on his side, but he's probably just as bad as the Siren at heart."

"Aye," Lawen nodded. "He'd just poison this kingdom with his own brand of venom."

"But what about the Siren? She's the whole reason I'm here."

"Yorath isn't going to kill *you,*" Ivor pointed out. "You're far too valuable for him to dispose of so easily, but I think he's underestimated you because of your pretty face and pampered upbringing. Eventually, he'll do something stupid and you'll be able to escape."

"Don't worry about us," Lawen reiterated. "I've lived a very long, happy life. Mair let me accompany you on this journey fully aware that I may never come back. It would be hard, but she would mourn me knowing that I gave my life fighting for the greater good instead of simply writing about it."

"That isn't something she should have to live with," Eirwen argued.

The tent flap opened, and Yorath stepped into the tent with three other men.

"Well, Snow White, have you changed your mind yet?"

Eirwen looked to her two allies, and they both nodded. Her voice shaking, the princess turned back to Yorath and spoke.

"I can't do it."

As soon as the words left Eirwen's lips, Yorath's three henchmen seized Ivor and dragged him out of the tent. Eirwen scrambled to her feet to follow her friend, but Yorath held her back.

"You don't get to watch this, princess," he whispered. "Your huntsman is going to die alone because of you."

"Please don't—"

A cry of pain echoed through the night, but it ended as swiftly as it began. Eirwen's knees buckled as grief overwhelmed her and Yorath let the princess fall to the ground sobbing. The smirking bandit wordlessly left the tent, and Lawen crawled over to Eirwen, tears wetting his cheeks as he attempted to comfort her. Eventually, mourning gave way to restless sleep and the heartbroken princess spent the rest of the night dreaming of the fallen huntsman and the sweet lovelorn woman he'd never get to be reunited with.

Chapter 6

When Eirwen roused the next morning, her eyes red and puffy from her grief, she remembered the events of the previous night and guilt flowed over her.

"There wasn't anything you could've done," Lawen whispered. "Ivor spent his life killing for an evil like none we've ever seen, but he at least died standing for something good."

"That doesn't make me feel any better about what happened."

"It will in time," the dwarf said. "I know you don't want to think about it, but they're coming for me next. I want you to know that I'm not scared and that I won't regret it."

"Good morning," Yorath greeted cheerfully as he entered the tent with two other marauders. "Did a bad night's sleep help you come to your senses, your snowiness?"

"She's not going to help you," Lawen said, rising to his feet and squaring his shoulders.

"Are you going to let him speak for you?"

"No, I'm not," Eirwen answered, "But he's right. I haven't changed my mind."

"So you're willing to sacrifice the little gnome?"

Lawen's face flushed, and his neck tensed at Yorath's insult.

"The *dwarf* is sacrificing himself," he corrected through clenched teeth.

Yorath sighed and stroked his beard.

"Is there anything I can do to change your mind?"

"No, I will *never* align myself with you," she swore, rising to her feet, "especially after you just murdered one of my friends."

"If killing your friend didn't sway you and this one is ready to throw his life away, then I have no use for you," he said, turning to his companions. "Bring them."

The men seized their steadfast prisoners, dragging them out of the tent and into the early morning sunlight. They forced Lawen and Eirwen to their knees and Yorath walked into view again, unsheathing his sword.

"This is your last chance, Eirwen."

"You don't have to do this, Yorath," she argued. "If you help me defeat the Siren as my *ally* and commit to turn away from this destructive path, I will make sure you have a chance to start a new life. You could have a great career as part of the military or—"

"I want to be a *king*, not a soldier," he seethed.

"Then I can't help you."

"Very well then," Yorath said, raising his sword. "I'd close my eyes if I were you."

Eirwen closed her eyes, a tear wetting her cheek as she waited for Yorath's fatal blow. However, the next thing she felt wasn't the edge or tip of a sword. It was the lightness of shackles being removed from her wrists as applause reached her ears. The princess opened her eyes and furrowed her brow when she saw Ivor standing a few yards away holding a very distinctive shield. One of the men helped Eirwen to her feet and removed the shackles from her ankles as well while another man freed Lawen.

"I don't understand," she said.

"Please forgive me for how I treated you," Yorath beseeched, falling to his knees and lowering his head. "My real name is Mervyn, and my men and I are members of the Winter Guard."

"As in the men who created my armor?"

"Yes, your highness. We have been quietly waging war on the Siren's men for years, but our true mission since the prophecy has been to find Snow White, make sure she is worthy of the pieces of armor our predecessors passed down to us," he explained. "When we saw you in the woods, we truly thought you were just a normal maiden who had been taken by a huntsman, but after hearing your name and seeing your face, I knew our interaction served a higher purpose. Will you please forgive us?"

Eirwen looked around the camp and saw that everyone but Ivor and Lawen had fallen to their knees.

"He's telling the truth," Ivor corroborated, drawing near and handing her the shield. "They explained their plan when they pulled me from the tent last night, and they've treated me like a king ever since."

"The Siren has lured some of the most righteous men away without singing a single note with promises of power, riches, and ease," Mervyn continued, his head still bowed. "We needed to make sure that you had enough faith to be unwaveringly righteous and not to compromise when faced with death. Needless to say, you passed with flying colors."

Eirwen let out a sigh as her mind turned to Areth. The elder tried to have her killed, and he hadn't been under the Siren's spell. Even though the princess wasn't particularly fond of the Winter Guard's methods, she understood their concerns. Keeping that in mind, she stepped forward and placed a hand on his shoulder.

"I forgive you," she said. "Please stand."

Mervyn rose to his feet, and the rest of the Winter Guard did the same.

"My wife and the other women aren't quite finished preparing breakfast, but there's a clean change of clothes and some water to wash with in the tent where I took you last night," he said. "Our plan today was to take you to the Waters of Garia so you can get your sword. Would you be all right with leaving after we eat, your highness?"

"That sounds perfect," Eirwen smiled.

◆　◆　◆

That afternoon, Eirwen donned the rest of her armor, which the warriors had been entrusted with, and rode to the northeast with the Winter Guard and her two friends. Though she had ridden a horse many times, doing so with her legs astride the animal felt strange after riding sidesaddle her whole life. Thankfully, no one in the company was concerned about propriety, so she didn't feel exposed or judged for straddling the horse.

Time passed quickly thanks to Mervyn's wife, Siana, who told the princess all about her husband's adventures. Hearing about how the Winter Guard had saved countless young women from the reapers in addition to protecting other Edwigians from the henchmen's greed made her feel better about aligning herself with the soldiers. Seeing the way they laughed with Ivor and Lawen and treated them as equals also helped her trust the men more.

Two hours later, the smell of salt water joined the earthy scent of the forest as the group rode into a foggy, sparser part of the woodland. Though the mist obscured their vision and the soft light that filtered through the canopy created an eerie but beautiful prismatic effect in the fog, none of the men of the Winter Guard became afraid. Ivor, however, kept his hand by the hilt of his sword and his eyes narrowed, waiting for some hidden foe to attack.

Luckily, no one interrupted their journey, so Eirwen and her plentiful escorts emerged from the forest at the edge of the Waters of Garia without incident. The large lake's shore, which was devoid of any flora or fauna, was littered with small, semi-transparent white pebbles and salt deposits as far as the eye could see, and a small island shrouded in an even denser fog sat in the middle of the lake.

Mervyn and his men dismounted while Ivor helped Eirwen from her steed, and Lawen hopped down from his pony. After walking to the edge of the sacred waters, the men drew their swords and held the gleaming weapons in front of their faces before uttering the words each man had patiently waited to recite since his induction to the guard.

"Humbly we come to the sacred shore. Devoted we are to see good restored. So we raise our swords every day and night until darkness is defeated by the coming of light."

Every member of the Winter Guard knelt and thrust his sword into the water, which bubbled and churned around each blade. Eirwen and her companions, dumbstruck by wonderment watched as the violently tumultuous water receded to reveal a stark white walkway that extended from the shore to the island. Mervyn rose from his place and approached Eirwen while the rest of the Winter Guard stayed in their supplicant positions.

"This is one part of the journey you must make on your own," he said. "On that island, you will face your final test and earn the Sword of Sanbryd. No harm will come to you there."

The princess nodded and pulled on her helmet, which was as inexplicably light as the rest of her armor, praying silently as she set down the path that the men created for her.

God, help me pass this test.

Despite the immeasurable amount of water that had just covered the walkway, it was perfectly dry, so all she heard as she walked toward the island were white stones crunching under her feet and the water roiling against its invisible barriers. For the first minute of her walk, Eirwen eyed the saline surf that flowed on either side of her, waiting for it to unexpectedly wash over her, but that moment never came. Feeling slightly more secure, she picked up her pace and walked with more confidence toward the isle.

When Eirwen set foot on the island, she was surprised to see that it was completely devoid of life. The only fixture on the white isle was a marble statue of a six-winged eagle that was perched on a golden column with a capital decorated with curling acanthus leaves and an elaborate scroll. The sculpture had a beak and talons of gold while brilliant rubies served as its eyes. Eirwen drew near the statue and admired the artisan's craftsmanship, but she realized that the eagle was no sculpture when its sparkling red eyes blinked.

Eirwen stumbled backward with a yelp and the magnificent bird flapped its half dozen wings, hovering just above the priceless pillar and letting out a fierce call that chilled its sole visitor to the bone. The sound of the roaring sea stole her attention from the eagle, and she turned around just in time to see the walkway she'd arrived on covered with water again. Eirwen's heartbeat quickened and her once calm breaths verged on becoming gasps as she realized that she was trapped on the island alone with the formidable, dazzling creature. Thankfully, the bird's deep, resonant voice forced her attention away from her unexpected separation.

"What is your name?" the eagle asked.

"Princess Eirwen Briallen Sayer of Talfryn," she answered, surprised that she was able to respond without her voice quivering.

"Why have you come here?"

"To take the final test and earn the Sword of Sanbryd."

"Then the test you shall take," the eagle said, gracefully landing on the pillar and clutching the scrolls of the capital with its gleaming talons.

"Sharper than steel but no sword in sight. Brighter than fire in the dark of the night. More pure and priceless than diamonds or gold. Sweeter than honey but never grows old. Who or what am I?"

Eirwen bit her bottom lip and looked toward the waters as she processed the unexpected rhyme. She'd mentally prepared herself to perform a task or to face a difficult decision in the style of the Winter Guard, but not to answer a riddle. Eirwen hadn't heard an enigma since her mother teased her with them as a child.

Queen Gwenyth would pull her daughter into her lap and recite rhymes of her own making while she combed her long, dark hair. Oftentimes, the tiny princess would scrunch up her pale face in confusion and throw out the most outlandish guesses she could think of, but the answers were always incredibly simple and sometimes in plain sight … the sapphire necklace around Gwenyth's neck, the king's eyes, or a book sitting on the side table. The clever queen had taught her daughter that sometimes the simplest things could seem majestic if you looked at them with new eyes, but that certain things were too wonderful to be described accurately with man's limited vocabulary.

As Eirwen remembered her mother's lesson, she went back over the creature's riddle. Whoever the eagle described was more powerful, bright, valuable, and sweet than anything than anything in the world, and no one on earth could boast in that nor could anything … at least not anything manmade.

"It's not a who," she realized. "It's a what."

The eagle blinked but remained silent.

"The answer is God's word," Eirwen said.

"You have answered correctly," the bird said, flapping its six wings yet again.

A rident grin lit up Eirwen's face only to disappear as the ground began to shake. The princess fell back onto the white-pebbled ground while the grand eagle sat perfectly still on its golden perch. After the tremor stopped and Eirwen managed to sit up, she was surprised to see a silver hilt with a large glittering sapphire pommel between her legs. The princess scrambled to her knees and seized the incredibly warm grip. When Eirwen pulled, the ground gave up the sword with very little effort.

The expertly crafted blade was slightly longer than the princess' arm and decorated with the same pattern of silver flowers and vines that graced the rest of her armor. It was more breathtaking than Eirwen had imagined, and her muscles tingled in anticipation at the prospect of wielding the wondrous weapon. However, the reality that her success in battle meant having the Siren's blood running down the sword's fuller and soiling her hands sobered the princess. Thus, the levity of success was shadowed by the gravity of death. Her spirits subdued, Eirwen looked back at the eagle.

"Thank you."

"There is no need for thanks," the eagle responded. "You have proven worthy of the calling you've been given."

Before Eirwen could respond, the eagle fluttered its wings, creating a great wind that howled fiercely and yet never touched the princess. Instead, the gust bended around her and cut through the salty lake, uncovering the white-pebbled pathway back to the shore. The princess sheathed the exquisite sword in the scabbard she'd received at Frynin's humble home and gave the eagle a nod before beginning the walk back to her awaiting allies.

As the princess neared the shore, Ivor, Lawen, and Winter Guard scrutinized her form to see whether or not she had received the sword. When Eirwen was about ten yards from the expectant crowd, she unsheathed the sword and held it high with the most genuine smile she could muster up, earning raucous applause and cheers. The instant she was ashore, the water covered her path once more and Ivor grabbed the princess for a hug that nearly knocked the wind out of her, but not so fiercely that she couldn't laugh at his enthusiasm. Mervyn decided that the group should have a celebratory supper, and the men set off into the woods to hunt for an animal worthy of such a feast while the women and a few members of the guard stayed behind to prepare the other parts of the meal and set up camp.

Recognizing her lack of culinary skill, Eirwen elected to help erect a few tents and let Ivor take her through several drills so she could become acquainted with her sword. The series of movements he showed the princess were designed to help her learn different positions and facets of sword fighting, but her body seemed to know every defensive and offensive technique the instant her hands grazed the hilt. Once the former huntsman was satisfied with Eirwen's proficiency, she gladly retired her sword for the night and approached Siana, who was tending to her assigned dish by the fire. The herbaceous aroma of potatoes caused a smile to spread across the princess' face, and she marveled at how she'd once disdained the tasty tuber and dismissed it as being too provincial.

"Is there anything else I can help with?" Eirwen asked.

"No, you've done more than enough, and you need your rest for tomorrow," Siana declined, patting the space next to her. "Have a seat."

Eirwen sat down beside Siana, smiling at the sight of the woman's two young boys and several other children throwing the smooth white rocks into the salty sea, cheering with every skip and splash.

"The children really love it here," the princess observed.

"Yes, they do," Siana confirmed, a grin crossing her bronzed face. "It's one of the few places they feel completely safe."

"Why is that?"

"No one who's under the Siren's control can pass through the fog that surrounds the Waters of Garia. If a reaper, huntsman, or some other foe tries to reach the lake, he becomes disoriented and loses his way," she explained. "Since only those whose hearts haven't been infected by evil can reach the waters, this is the only place where none of her minions can find us."

Siana's five-year-old twins, Cadel and Iago, came running over to their mother, nearly knocking her over with their hugs. Eirwen loved seeing how Siana kissed and doted on her rowdy sons, but her good mood waned as her mind turned to the women in her own family.

Since Queen Gwenyth died when Eirwen was so young, she'd grown up with governesses who tried to fill the beloved queen's role. Alas, for all of their lessons and wisdom, they'd never been able to replace her mother. As much as she cherished the few short years she had with the benevolent queen, Eirwen had been ecstatic to learn that King Rhys was remarrying and giving her a stepmother to guide her into womanhood.

Though she and Nerys were only a decade apart in age, Eirwen looked up to the beautiful blonde at first. She'd hoped that the new queen could at least be a friend to her, but Nerys had always been cold and aloof, only deigning to spend time with Eirwen when forced to and enduring the princess' company for as little time as necessary. When the new queen gave birth to Ifan, Nerys was more generous with her time, but only because Eirwen relieved some of her motherly duties. The affectionate princess calmed Ifan when he was upset, cared for the prince when he was sick, and played with him until they were breathless from laughter. However, despite that freely given help, Nerys' treatment of her stepdaughter had gone from cold to cruel with every passing year. After King Rhys' death, Eirwen prayed that Nerys' spite and scathing criticism would abate so they could comfort and love one another in the wake of their shared loss, but her derision had only increased.

As Eirwen reflected on her strained relationship with her stepmother, she resolved to make more of an effort to repair their bond. Though she had fretted and prayed about Nerys' animosity toward her, the princess felt as if she hadn't done enough to pursue peace with her. When she returned to Talfryn, she would devote herself to doing everything in her power to restore and build up her relationship with the grieving woman so there could finally be harmony and joy in her home.

Chapter 7

After the men returned with a large deer and several rabbits, the women quickly prepared and cooked the meat. The lakeside camp was filled with music, dancing, and laughter that lasted late into the night, but Eirwen left the celebration early to ensure that she had enough rest for the next day. Thankfully, she was able to drift off despite the noise around her and slept through the night without waking up once.

By the time her blue eyes opened, Eirwen had slept six hours. Much to her dismay, that physical rest hadn't done anything to lift the heaviness from her soul. The princess rose from her mat feeling unease that verged on nausea, but she knew that her discomfort had nothing to do with the delicious food she'd eaten the previous night or the salty air she breathed.

Today was the day she would kill the Siren.

While Eirwen knew she would eventually have to face the melodic monster, she had willfully put the fact that she was tasked with ending the Siren's life out of her mind. The princess had never killed anything more than a fly or spider, but now she had to kill a *woman*. Seeking to clear her head, Eirwen hastily threw on her clothes and went for a walk down the shore.

Once the princess was nearly a quarter mile from the camp, she sat down on the white pebbles and hugged herself as the cool breeze picked up and caused her to shiver. Eirwen gazed out at the water, which lapped against the shore and moved some her windblown hair out of her face so she could watch the sunrise. The cornflower blue sky blazed orange and yellow and the reflective water took on the same beautiful, glowing palette, but the radiant sunrise did nothing to chase away her fears and reservations.

Lord, help me through this.

The sound of pebbles crunching underfoot reached the princess' ears, and she looked away from the sun to see Mervyn approaching with her cloak.

"Siana saw you leave and thought you may need this," he explained, putting the cloak around her shivering shoulders. "It can get pretty cool here in the morning."

"Thank you," Eirwen replied, giving him a smile that stopped just short of her weary azure eyes.

The warrior lowered himself onto the ground beside Eirwen and rested his elbows on his knees, fiddling with one of the hoary stones as he studied the princess.

"You look awfully pensive for someone who just woke up," he observed. "I can barely form a coherent thought before I break my fast."

"I'm just thinking about what I have to do today," she confessed. "Have you ever killed someone before?"

Mervyn nodded, averting his eyes for a moment.

"Yes, more times than I'd care to admit."

"Do you feel at peace about it?"

"I don't think anyone ever feels truly at peace after killing someone. Yes, there is a time for war and a time to kill, but there is a weight that comes with carrying out those tasks even when a life is taken for the noblest reasons," he explained. "I've killed many reapers and huntsmen over the years to protect the people of Edwig, and even when I see the people I've saved, I wonder if the men I saved them from could have been redeemed somehow."

Mervyn tossed the rock he'd been holding at the lake and watched it skip twice before sinking.

"When I realized that you'd somehow broken the Siren's spell on Ivor, I remembered all of the reapers and huntsmen I'd ever killed and questioned my decision to end their lives. Then, I thought about Siana," Mervyn said. "I rescued her from a reaper ten years ago, and we fell in love shortly thereafter. If I hadn't killed that reaper, she would be dead, we wouldn't have our sons, and many of the men she's nursed after battles would be in the ground as well. Do I wish that I could have saved her without claiming the reaper's life? Yes. Do I regret saving her? Never."

Eirwen gazed at a bird thoughtfully as it soared over the lake.

"The Siren has killed thousands of Edwigians since she began her reign. If I had the power to kill her and spare the people of this kingdom from her oppression and cruelty, I would gladly deliver the killing blow," the warrior continued. "Now, I hate to cut our talk short, but the cloak isn't the only reason Siana sent me over here. Breakfast is almost done, and she'd have my head if I let Snow White go off to fight without something sticking to her ribs."

Eirwen smiled despite herself as Mervyn stood up and helped her do the same. Then, the two eased into a lighter conversation about the soldier's energetic sons as they walked back to their camp.

◆　◆　◆

After a hearty breakfast, everyone prepared for battle. Afala was four hours from the Waters of Garia, so they would face their enemy just as the afternoon began. Ivor, who had gladly traded his huntsman's uniform for armor once worn by a fallen member of the guard, helped Eirwen don her armor and inspected her sword, finding it sharper than any blade he'd ever wielded. Unfortunately, there hadn't been a suit of armor small enough to fit Lawen, but the dwarf was able to wear a breastplate and helmet, which gave him added protection without making it more difficult for him or his borrowed pony to bear the extra weight.

Before the group set out, they gathered in a circle and everyone, even the women and children, took a knee and bowed their heads as Mervyn prayed over them.

"Lord, be with us today as we finally battle our nemesis face to face. Give us the wisdom to be merciful when our hearts rage for blood and the conviction to raise our weapons against those who will not turn from their evil ways. Lastly, God, help us all to return not just unscathed but victorious. Edwig has been groaning collectively under the weight of the Siren's oppression, and I pray that today would be the day when her reign comes to an end so healing can finally begin in the land. I pray all of these things in Jesus' name. Amen."

Everyone in the camp echoed the affirmation and rose to their feet. Wives and children wished their men well while the rest of the guard tried to dispel the tension and fear with humor and conversation. Alas, the reality that they would all soon face their greatest enemy cast a grim shadow over the Winter Guard and their new allies that no joke or pun was clever enough to lift.

Once the warriors said their goodbyes, everyone mounted their horses and left the camp to round the lake and cross into Afala. The fighters traveled in silence long before secrecy necessitated it as a somber mood fell upon them. Lawen didn't even share his witty writings as he normally did despite spending most of the ride putting pen to paper to chronicle their journey.

After reaching the other side of the Waters of Garia, the group set off through the countryside's swaying golden grain, pausing only briefly to eat the bread and cheese they'd been given for the journey before they approached the stone pillars that marked the beginning of the Siren's territory. When Eirwen passed through the pillars, she shuddered and noticed that the sun seemed to dim in the evil queen's domain. Not even the sweet scent of the apples that hung from the multitude of trees around them brought the uneasy princess comfort. Her eyes scanned the apple trees, looking for any indication that an attack was imminent, but Eirwen didn't see a single soul until they emerged from the orchard and reached the clearing that surrounded the Siren's home.

Despite its malevolent mistress, the castle looked no more frightening or majestic than any of the other royal residences Eirwen had visited. However, the hundreds of fearsome, scowling men before her more than made up for the palace's unremarkable appearance. The reapers and huntsmen, who stood between them and the lifted drawbridge, glowered at the Winter Guard with undisguised derision. The princess could sense their thirst for blood all the way from her place in the center of the group. Even if they hadn't been horribly outnumbered, Eirwen still would have been nauseated with fear.

"Look," a man wearing an impressive suit of black armor taunted. "The Winter Guard has finally come out of whatever hole they've been hiding in to be exterminated like the rats they are."

"I've killed quite a few rats in my day," a reaper piped up. "These sorry fellows will be much easier to slaughter."

"No one has to be slaughtered today," Mervyn spoke up, riding to the front of the vanguard. "If you surrender, we will allow you to keep your lives."

The Siren's men laughed uproariously at Mervyn's offer, which only added to the sinking feeling in Eirwen's stomach.

"Why should we surrender when we can trounce you without a thought?" the man called once the laughter subsided. "You're outnumbered and outclassed."

"That's the Siren's general, Cadoc," Ivor explained. "He's also her mate."

"So he's with her willingly?" Eirwen asked.

"No, but he's the most fervent, handsome man she's bewitched."

"Then Cadoc isn't her mate," the princess corrected, her eyes darkening with anger. "He's her victim."

Without warning, Eirwen broke away from her protectors and rode to the front of the Winter Guard, Lawen and Ivor cantering after her.

"Eirwen, you need to stay in the back," Mervyn directed. "It's not safe for you to be so exposed."

"I need to speak to them, Mervyn," Eirwen insisted. "Please just give me a few minutes. If they don't relent, I'll go right back to where you had me."

Mervyn held her insistent gaze for a long, silent moment before letting out a reluctant sigh.

"All right," he conceded, "but if I see them so much as *reach* for an arrow, I'm starting the attack."

The princess nodded and turned to face the army. As she scrutinized the bewitched men, many of whom were impossible to look in the eye because of their helmets, Eirwen realized that speaking to them through her own armet even with the visor lifted, made her seem cold and distant. With that in mind, she pulled the helmet from her head and balanced it on the pommel of her saddle. Alas, before Eirwen even spoke, the Siren began her song yet again. Instead of the men becoming drowsy with indifference as the haunting melody filled the air, they became more bloodthirsty than they'd been when the Winter Guard arrived, shifting their weight impatiently and glaring daggers at the princess as they imagined her innocent blood running down their freshly sharpened blades with every word she uttered.

"Sirs, I have no doubt that you could defeat a small group such as ours if this were simply a fight that could be won with impressive numbers and physical skill, but this is not such a battle," Eirwen began. "These valiant men have been fighting on the side of good ever since the Siren began her reign. Though I have only recently joined their company, I am of the same mind. The light will prevail over the darkness whether five hundred men lift the banner of righteousness or a paltry fifty."

The singing grew louder and Eirwen raised her voice, determined to be heard over the melodic manipulation that filled everyone's ears in an attempt to harden the reapers' and huntsmen's hearts. However, the princess remained steadfast, assuring herself that the Siren wouldn't work so hard to keep the men under her spell if she wasn't in danger of losing them.

"While we are prepared to wage war today, our wish is not that you would perish fighting for a woman who has manipulated you because you are just as *blameless* as the people who have died at her hands. You are just as *precious* as the girls you've been bewitched into stealing from their homes. You are just as *beloved* as the men you've struck down to accomplish the mission she's forced upon you," the princess shouted. "There has been enough death in this kingdom to last centuries, and I don't want a single drop of blood spilled today in defense of her wickedness. Yes, our goal this afternoon is to end the Siren's sinful reign and bring peace to the people of Edwig, but my heart's *true* desire is that you would find peace and freedom. Break the yoke of slavery that she has placed around your necks, reclaim the years she's stolen from you, and return to your families so they can have their sons, fathers, and husbands back. If you want freedom, and I know you do deep in your hearts, *wake up!* Lay down your weapons, renounce the Siren, and lower the bridge!"

The princess' uncharacteristically powerful voice echoed across the clearing, but she received neither cheers nor jeers response. The only sound on the still battlefield as Eirwen waited for the men's response was the Siren's seductive song fading into silence and the raspy calls of the vultures that circled above, eager to scavenge the flesh of fallen warriors after the highly anticipated battle ended. After nearly two minutes of stillness, Mervyn sighed and turned to Eirwen.

"I'm sorry, Eirwen, but it didn't work. Please return to the rearguard. I'll send for you when—"

Mervyn drew his sword and whipped around, the Winter Guard doing the same as the sound of metal clanging reached their itching ears from across the field. Eirwen turned her gaze back to the Siren's army expecting to see the enthralled men marching forward, but instead she watched the reapers and huntsmen drop their swords and shields on by one, filling the afternoon air with a beautiful but dissonant symphony of metal hitting grass, rock, and dirt. Even Cadoc released his longsword and ripped off his armet, hurling the helmet into the dirt and spitting on it contemptuously.

"Lower the bridge," the young general barked, running a hand through his shoulder-length black curls and avoiding eye contact with the tearful Eirwen.

"My God," Mervyn breathed, observing his agitated but nonaggressive former enemies. "You broke the spell."

"Yes, but these men have a long road to travel before they've fully recovered," Eirwen replied, directing her horse to move forward as the rest of her company did the same. "Would you mind leaving some of the Winter Guard out here to tend to the Siren's army? If they're anything like Ivor, guilt and self-loathing are their closest companions right now. They'll need someone to be compassionate toward them and keep them from harming themselves."

"Lawen and I can stay," Ivor volunteered, "I can understand their plight better than anyone."

"Thank you," Eirwen said, giving her two friends a warm smile. "They're lucky to have you both right now."

"Take the men you need, Ivor," Mervyn instructed. "I trust your judgment."

Ivor nodded and circled back, recruiting several men to minister to the downtrodden former combatants as the bridge loudly lowered before them. Once the bridge was securely in place, a gust of wind swept down the pathway and knocked everyone from his horse, leaving only Eirwen sitting on her steed. When the princess opened her eyes, she saw that the gale-force winds hadn't been a product of nature.

The Siren had emerged from her castle.

The deadly songstress stood on the doorstep of the castle, her blonde spirals trailing after her on the ground with every step she took but never entangling her bare feet. The beauty was nearly six feet tall with a gracefully thin neck and a pair of impossibly red eyes that matched her gown as well as the glowing amulet that adorned her neck. Her immaculate, porcelain skin had a luminescence that left Eirwen speechless with awe, and her full, crimson lips were slightly upturned in a confident half-smile. Though the princess associated the evil sovereign with bloodshed, the Siren had an air of serenity about her that even the most peaceful people didn't exude. However, as Eirwen took in the Siren's unparalleled allure, the blood red eyes that examined her from across the bridge reminded the princess of the true source of the queen's beauty.

Death.

Eirwen remembered that countless young maidens had been drained of their life's blood so that the vain vixen could continue to enchant and beguile men from her ill-gotten throne. As Maredh's tale of his lost wife and daughters came to mind and she recalled Ivor holding her knife to his throat begging for her to end his life, Eirwen saw the Siren's beauty as the wickedness that it was. In an instant, her wonder turned to ire.

"Welcome to Afala, Eirwen," she purred. "As much as I would love to entertain the men you've brought with you, this is a women's war. Prove that you're not a coward and face me alone."

Eirwen bit her tongue, forcing herself not to strike out at the deadly seductress as she collected her thoughts and Mervyn came to stand beside her, poised with his sword in hand.

"You don't have to do this," Mervyn pointed out. "It would be an honor to go into battle with you."

"I know," Eirwen sighed, dismounting from her horse, "but it wouldn't be a fair fight if I brought the whole Winter Guard with me."

"Forgive me for being blunt, but she's worse than any witch I've encountered, and you've never even raised your sword in battle. I've seen seasoned fighters fall to weaker opponents, and I don't want to see you suffer the same fate."

"I don't know what this battle holds for me, but we've already seen that I can overcome her magic and the Sword of Sanbryd practically wields itself," she reminded her friend. "I'll be fine."

The princess moved to cross the bridge, but Mervyn seized her arm.

"Please be careful," he warned. "Her tricks aren't limited to melodies and harmonies."

Eirwen nodded, and Mervyn reluctantly released her arm. With a deep breath, the princess squared her shoulders, unsheathed her sword, which vibrated with power, and began the lonely walk down the drawbridge to meet her foe. The sky darkened to a menacing gray hue and the clouds above churned more violently the closer she drew to the smiling, stunning sorceress, causing her to grow more guarded with every step. When Eirwen stepped off the bridge ten feet from the Siren, it abruptly rose and slammed shut with a loud bang, making the princess jump and her enemy chuckle.

"Aren't you a jittery little thing," she teased. "Come with me. Dinner should be almost ready."

"Dinner?"

"Yes, I haven't eaten since dawn, and I'm starving. I'm sure you are too," the Siren called over her shoulder as she sauntered into the castle. "Come along."

Eirwen tightened her grip on the Sword of Sanbryd, swallowing the lump in her throat while she trailed behind her unexpectedly hospitable adversary. As the princess walked through the castle, her blue eyes inspected every nook, hallway, and room she passed for fear that someone or something would jump out at her. Surprisingly, all Eirwen observed was beautiful artwork and exquisite craftsmanship at every turn.

Finally, the Siren sashayed into the great hall and Eirwen's mouth watered at the sight and smell of the roasted turkey, fresh bread, exotic fruits, and other delectable dishes. The murderous monarch gracefully lowered herself into the ornate chair at the head of the table while Eirwen stood at the entrance to the room, vacillating between hunger and hesitation.

"Please sit down, Eirwen. I just want to have a civilized chat."

The princess finally sheathed her blade before sitting at the only other place setting at the table. The beautiful blonde began her meal. Eirwen, however, simply tapped her fingers on the sword's sapphire pommel. Her blue eyes fell to the impressive spread before her, but something told her not to partake in the Siren's mouthwatering meal. Instead, Eirwen studied her enemy for several silent minutes while she nibbled on her meal with unparalleled grace.

"Why are you being so nice to me?" Eirwen finally asked.

"Because power demands respect, and you've proven to be very powerful," she answered plainly. "Now, please eat. I hate taking my meals alone."

"Is it respectful to have someone arrested and tried for false charges?"

The Siren filled the hall with a laugh that rang more brightly than wind chimes on a breezy summer day, but Eirwen wasn't distracted by the woman's deceptive charms.

"Yes, you're right. That wasn't exactly kind of me."

"Neither is kidnapping innocent girls so you can bathe in their blood."

"A woman does what she must," she shrugged. "You're about to be a queen as well. I'm sure you'll understand in time that it's a heavy burden to wear a crown."

"The kind of burden you're bearing is one you created yourself. I didn't win my crown with murder."

Before Eirwen could react, a gust of wind swept her chair away from the table, slamming it into the wall as the Siren rose from her seat, pulled the sword from her belt, and sauntered over to her.

"I wanted to resolve this matter calmly, but you seem determined to condemn and insult me," the Siren seethed, looming over her stunned adversary with her crimson eyes and amulet aglow. "You don't deserve to die peacefully."

Eirwen stumbled to her feet and freed her own sword, earning laughter from the Siren that was closer to a cackle than music.

"I've eviscerated men who have triumphed over kings with little more than a thought," she taunted. "Do you really think *you*, a pampered, sheltered little princess, can defeat me?"

The Siren leapt forward and brought her sword down on Eirwen's, beginning the battle that would decide the fate of Edwig. Despite her lack of training, Eirwen found herself lunging and fading with the strength and skill of a warrior twice her size and thrice her age. However, the Siren's magic afforded her the same deadly proficiency.

Eirwen deflected her foe's every blow and struck back with fierce determination that she didn't realize she possessed, but the Siren's sinister song rose like an unwanted mist and filled Eirwen's mind, distracting the princess long enough for the queen to give her a powerful kick to the chest. Eirwen flew across the room and slammed into the banquet table with a bang, knocking over the wine and food. The formerly mouthwatering meal, which was suddenly rotten and riddled with maggots, tumbled to the floor and burned holes in the expensive carpet. Before Eirwen could recover from her fall, the Siren descended on her with a blow that made the princess' arms quiver.

Unfortunately, the Siren didn't relent, forcing Eirwen to defend herself against an onslaught of attacks that left it impossible for her to go on the offensive. However, as their blades clanged against each other and joined the Siren's increasingly loud song, the princess noticed her enemy's crimson amulet glowing more brightly. Rather than deflecting the Siren's next strike, Eirwen took a chance by rolling out of the way. With nothing to stop her blow, the queen stumbled forward and fell into the ransacked table.

By the time the songstress regained her footing, Eirwen was on her feet again. The Siren advanced and Eirwen let her enemy's blade slide off hers so she was free to spin to her right, snatch the chain holding her assailant's amulet, and tear it from her neck. A glaring light filled the room and the force of the blinding blast threw the women apart. Eirwen crashed into the wall and the Siren flew into the hallway, landing on the floor with a sickening thud.

The princess pulled herself to her feet, wincing in pain and wondering if her whole body was black and blue underneath her hard-won armor as she grabbed her sword and staggered out of the great hall. Disgust joined Eirwen's discomfort when she looked down and saw that the dull amulet was bleeding onto her stark white hand. Fighting the urge to vomit, she chucked the necklace onto the ground and stomped on it, earning another resplendent flash as she shattered the bleeding jewel. Satisfied with the fruits of her gruesome labor, the unsettled royal went to find the Siren.

She didn't have to search long.

When Eirwen stepped out of the room, she saw her enemy gazing into a mirror several yards away with her back to the princess. Even without seeing the Siren's face, she knew that the amulet's spell had been broken.

The queen's blonde ringlets, which had once been long enough to dust the floor, were reduced to brittle, graying waves that barely reached her mid back and the veiny, crepey hand that clutched her sword trembled as she gaped in horror at her altered reflection.

"Mirror, mirror, upon the wall," the Siren quaked with rage, "look how far she's made me fall."

"This fight can be over now if you surrender," Eirwen called softly. "I don't want to kill you."

"You may not have killed me, Snow White, but you've stolen the only thing that ever mattered to me," she sneered.

When the Siren turned around and Eirwen finally saw her true appearance, the princess swayed slightly, steadying herself against the wall as the breath went out of her overworked lungs.

"Nerys?" she gasped. "I don't underst—"

The Siren charged at her again, determined more than ever to kill her young adversary. Eirwen tearfully tried to defend herself, but with every attack she deflected, she realized that her opponent had lost the supernatural strength and speed that the amulet had afforded her and that her unfocused animosity made her perilously sloppy.

Nerys' life was hers for the taking.

"Please stop," Eirwen shouted between blows.

Blinded by rage, the bloodthirsty Siren let out a primal yell and increased the intensity of her attacks, but she took even less care with her stance than she had before. Eirwen's heart sank when she recognized that her stepmother had no desire to relent. With grim resolve, the princess decided to end the battle. Once again using the enhanced fighting ability and might that the Sword of Sanbryd had given her, Eirwen drove Nerys back foot by foot until the enraged woman tripped over a buckle in the rug below and tumbled to the ground.

Eirwen stepped on Nerys' sword and poised the tip of her blade inches above her stepmother's heart, too fearful that she would inadvertently draw blood to actually touch steel to silk.

"Just surrender," she panted. "This doesn't have to end with one of us dead."

The winded princess loosened her grip on the enchanted blade and reached out her free hand.

"You can come back from this," Eirwen continued. "I'll do everything I can to help you, and I won't let them lay a hand on you."

Nerys' grimace softened, and she reached up to take Eirwen's hand. Just before her fingers grazed Eirwen's, the defeated woman grabbed her stepdaughter's sword, not caring that the sharp steel cut into her hands, and thrust the blade into her chest. Eirwen screamed in wordless horror, and her legs gave out. She fell to her knees, tears streaming down her flushed cheeks while blood bubbled from her stepmother's lips. The princess yanked the sword from Nerys' chest with unsure hands and applied pressure to the mortal wound in a futile attempt to save her enemy's life.

"You may have taken my place, but I've taken your innocence. Now, you'll have to live the rest of your life knowing that my blood is on your hands," she rasped weakly, blood trailing from her smiling lips. "Goodbye, Snow White."

Nerys' dark eyes rolled into the back of her head, and she went limp as her black heart shuddered to a stop. Eirwen pulled the cooling corpse into her arms, not caring that her stepmother's blood soiled her armor as she shook with violent sobs. Edwig was finally safe from the Siren's reign of terror and greed, but at what cost?

Chapter 8

Eirwen woke up with a blood-curdling scream and wept uncontrollably, her tears wetting the pillow before Roderick could leap from his chair and come to her side. The prince pulled his frenzied fiancée into his arms and smoothed her wild dark locks off her sweat-slicked forehead, attempting to comfort her as concern for her emotional state overshadowed his joy over her long awaited awakening. When Eirwen's tears finally subsided several minutes later, she opened her eyes and saw that she wasn't in the antiquated, medieval kingdom of Edwig but in her own bed in nineteenth century Talfryn.

"How did I get here?" she sniffled. "I don't remember leaving Edwig."

"Edwig?" Roderick repeated. "You've been unconscious for days. You fell ill at dinner on Friday evening and have been in bed ever since. Whatever you think happened was only a dream."

"What day is it?"

"Sunday."

Eirwen furrowed her brow and let Roderick's words sink in while he wiped away her tears.

"I felt perfectly fine all day on Friday. How could I have been so sick that I would be in bed for three days?"

The prince heaved a deep sigh while he took her hands in his. Rather than answering Eirwen right away, Roderick searched his beloved's expectant eyes as well as his own soul as he struggled to form the words he knew would break her heart.

"Nerys poisoned you," he revealed. "She had the footman inject your apple with poison when he served the Eusebian cider at supper. She wanted to kill you so she could rule Talfryn."

Eirwen pulled away from Roderick, stumbling to her feet and shaking her head.

"No, Nerys would never do that. She—"

"She confessed," Roderick interrupted. "I knew that something was wrong that night, so I went to question the footman. He was so racked with guilt that he gave Nerys up before I could even say a word. When I confronted your stepmother with the footman's accusations and the syringe of poison he turned over, she too confessed. Nerys told us what poison she used, so the doctor was able to procure the antidote just in time to save your life."

Eirwen shivered as she remembered her dream, which suddenly seemed just as real as it had while she slumbered. Roderick rose from the bed and came to her side, his brow furrowed in concern at the sight of his fiancée's torment.

"Where is she now?"

"Nerys is in the tower awaiting her execution with the footman."

"But what about a trial?"

"Considering her confession and the evidence against her, the judge passed sentence early yesterday morning. Nerys didn't even defend herself. I tried to talk the judge into giving her a life sentence or at least waiting until you were well to pass judgment, but he thought her offense was too grave. She's to be hanged within the hour."

Eirwen pushed past Roderick, grabbed her purse, and sprinted out of the room in her nightgown, nearly running into the doctor who had come to check on her. The princess bolted through the castle, ignoring Roderick calling her name and the curious stares of servants as she ran out of the front door. The doctor's coach was still sitting at the bottom of the steps, and his coachman bowed low at the sight of his barely dressed, barefoot future queen.

"Take me to the tower as fast as possible," she commanded, climbing into the coach without the young man's assistance.

"Yes, your highness," he said.

The coachman took his seat and whipped the horses, causing the animals to gallop wildly back down the road and away from the castle just as Roderick and the doctor emerged from the castle. Sensing his ruler's urgency, the young man pushed the animals to their limit. Rather than watching the passing countryside, Eirwen bowed her head and prayed fervently with every moment that she wouldn't be too late to say her peace to Nerys and her accomplice.

The coach came to an abrupt stop just outside of the tower, throwing the princess forward in her seat, but Eirwen braced herself by grabbing the window. Her flustered subject promptly jumped down from his perch and opened the door.

"I'm sorry for the rough journey, your high—"

Eirwen flew out of the coach and sprinted as quickly as her legs could take her to the Tower Green. As the panting princess drew near, she saw her proud stepmother and the weeping footman standing on a raised platform with nooses around their necks. The hangman walked up the steps to do his grim duty, but unlike most executions, no one shouted jeers in his direction. Instead, the statesmen and noblemen in attendance glowered at the condemned criminals in spiteful silence.

"*Stop!*"

Eirwen's cry from just behind the crowd shocked everyone out of their silence, and the hangman stopped just short of pulling his lever. The men in the crowd bowed hastily then murmured amongst themselves, regarding their ragged ruler with curiosity as the winded, perspiring young woman climbed the wooden steps and walked over to her stepmother. Nerys, who had begun to quake in the presence of her victim, kept her eyes trained on the horizon and refused to look Eirwen in the eye even as she stood right in front of her.

"I know exactly what you did, Nerys," she whispered. "I know that you poisoned me, and I know that you admitted doing so, but I want to know why."

The former queen's dark eyes shone with unshed tears, but she remained silent.

"Answer me. Why did you do it?"

"Because with you as queen, there would be no place for me in this castle," she admitted through clenched teeth. "I didn't want to spend every day watching you grow in power, joy, and beauty while I wasted away into nothing."

"Do you regret what you did?"

Nerys nodded, and tears moistened her cheeks, but with her hands tied, the former queen couldn't wipe them away.

"What about you?" Eirwen asked, turning to the footman. "Are you sorry for what you did?"

"Yes," he sobbed. "I'm so sorry, your highness. She offered me money, and I just couldn't say no. I—"

The princess held up her hand to silence the blubbering criminal and walked over to the hangman.

"Please let them down and untie their wrists," she ordered.

The judge raised his voice to be heard over the crowd as he pushed his way through the bewildered men to the gallows. At the same moment, Roderick arrived on horseback and dismounted before running to the platform as well.

"Your highness, I have already passed judgment on these two villains. They have committed the worst kind of treason, and the punishment for their crime is death."

"If you kill them, they won't be the only ones who suffer. My half-brother Ifan would be an orphan, and their families would mourn their deaths for the rest of their lives," Eirwen argued. "I too would suffer knowing that someone I love and one of my subjects were dead because I was too hard-hearted to be a merciful ruler."

"With all due respect, no one can overturn a conviction of this magnitude especially when we have *two* signed confessions."

"I'm not overturning your conviction, your honor. I'm changing the sentence."

The princess turned to the conspirators, relieved to see that Nerys, who rubbed at her newly freed wrists, was finally willing to look her in the eye.

"You are both forthwith banished from Talfryn and stripped of all of your titles, duties, and possessions," the princess proclaimed, emptying her purse and handing each offender a handful of priceless coins and jewels. "Use this to buy your way onto a ship and be gone before dawn tomorrow. Nerys, there should be enough here for you to travel to your brother's estate in Wolstan, but you may go wherever you like."

"What about Ifan?" Nerys croaked, her voice barely above a whisper.

"He needs his mother, so he will join you once you're settled with Ferdinand. Just send word once you've arrived, and I will make sure he arrives safely," Eirwen answered. "Ifan will maintain his current place in the line of succession and keep his inheritance, which is yours to manage until he comes of age."

Nerys covered her face and began to weep, but she sobbed even harder and the crowd gaped at the women in awe as Eirwen wrapped her arms around the woman who had almost succeeded in ending her life.

"I forgive you," she whispered. "Please learn from this and do better wherever God takes you."

Nerys nodded and wiped her tears, unable to speak in response to her stepdaughter's unexpected, undeserved clemency.

"You may both use the carriage I arrived in to travel to the shipyard," Eirwen continued. "Please have a safe voyage."

The two outcasts hurriedly climbed down from the platform in solemn silence and Eirwen trailed after them, the crowd too stunned by their leader's actions to argue with her or prevent the criminals from boarding the carriage and leaving the tower. Only Roderick had the presence of mind to speak to his astonishingly serene fiancée.

"Eirwen," he breathed, looking at the woman he loved with new eyes, "that was amazing."

"I couldn't live with the guilt if they died because of me," she explained, "and I couldn't let bitterness infect my heart as it had hers. A resentful woman makes for a poor ruler."

"Then you're going to make a brilliant queen," he complimented before kissing her on the cheek. "But first, you need to come back to the castle and be examined by the doctor."

"You can use my coach, your highness," the humbled judge offered. "I'll make sure your horse is returned to the castle as well."

"Thank you, your honor," Eirwen replied with a smile.

Roderick placed his hand on his beloved's back and led her away from the crowd to the judge's coach, his heart swelling with love and pride for his future wife. The fiery haired prince helped Eirwen into the horse-drawn vehicle, and their new coachman closed the door behind them while she leaned her head on Roderick's shoulder. Eirwen laced her fingers through his with a smile, feeling more prepared than ever to ascend to the throne and rule the kingdom she cherished with love, compassion, and newfound wisdom thanks to a poisoned apple and a fantastical dream.

The End

Ingrid's Engagement

How A Beauty Tamed A Beast

Chapter 1

When the King of Villriket's devastating war reached Anselm that frigid December, no one was more prepared than Edmund Kappel. The Count of Anselm became intimately acquainted with combat's destruction and uncertainty ten years before when he saved his king's life during their last war with the Villriketians. As a reward for his gallantry on the battlefield, King Ansgar promoted Edmund from landgrave to count. The ruler also gave him the wealth, land, and responsibilities that came with his new title. In spite of all his riches, Edmund had something far more precious than his sprawling estate to protect that winter.

His three beloved children.

Ansgar's unabated abhorrence for his neighbor to the north had come back to haunt him and Edmund's family as Villriket's vengeful king, Viggo, invaded Schlagefilde and drew perilously close to the castle where he and his cherished children resided. Despite Edmund's past loyalty to King Ansgar, the ruler didn't lift a single pampered finger to defend the people of Anselm from Viggo.

Instead, he ordered every able-bodied man under fifty in the kingdom of Schlagefilde to defend his palace. This egregious act left the commoners and any noblemen who didn't live at court utterly defenseless. Depriving his people of protection from a foreign army was the latest in a long line of offenses committed by the profoundly selfish king. Unfortunately, Edmund's family was mere hours away from suffering the retribution Ansgar had inspired with his relentless thirst for Villriketian blood.

"Is visiting the Villriketians' camp yourself truly necessary?" the count's eldest daughter, Ingrid implored, wringing her porcelain hands. "Can't you send a messenger or guard to contend with the king?"

"I could, but a warrior like Viggo will never respect a man who won't speak with him eye to eye. Dietrich tried to communicate with him through an emissary only to receive his rejected offer ripped to shreds with greater demands from the king," Edmund said. "Facing the man may not be ideal, but King Ansgar abandoned us. Dealing with Viggo myself is the only way to save the men and women God has placed in my care."

Ingrid lowered her hazel eyes to the floor and fought back the torrent of tears threatening to burst forth. When her mother, Carina, passed away five years ago, she grieved deeply and still lived with the pain her untimely death inflicted. Albrecht and Doris were too young to remember their mother, but each room in their home held both joyful and painful memories of the kindhearted countess that haunted Ingrid daily. If Viggo expressed his dislike for her father's terms by ripping his body open with a bayonet or dagger instead of ripping up a mere message, living in the beautiful castle without him would be *unbearable*.

After fastening the shiny buttons of his scarlet military jacket, Edmund finally looked at his flaxen-haired daughter, and the sight of her despair made his heart ache. The count took her hands in his and she met his gaze, a stray tear snaking down her flushed cheek.

"I *will* come back to you," he swore. "You have nothing to fear today."

Ingrid nodded, too afraid of unleashing the sobs she struggled to hold back if she spoke. Edmund gave her a kiss on the forehead and pulled her into his arms. Though he prayed for the Lord to give her strength and comfort in his absence, he knew the gravity of his departure weighed heavily on her tender heart. Since her childhood, the young beauty always giggled at the tickle of his moustache, but laughter had abandoned her long before that melancholy moment.

Instead, Ingrid pulled away and blotted her glistening eyes and cheeks with a handkerchief while she walked to the dresser and picked up her father's Pickelhaube. After placing the black and gold spiked helmet over his graying blond locks, the nineteen year-old maiden kissed her father's cheek.

"I'll be praying for you, Papa."

Before Edmund could respond, his rambunctious twins came tearing into the room to wish their father farewell. Ingrid envied their blissful blindness to the chaos surrounding them. Nevertheless, she greeted her brother and sister with a smile while they clung to their father's legs to prevent him from leaving. Alas, their sweet, innocent faces failed to chase away the sinking sensation in her stomach that none of their lives would ever be the same again.

◆　◆　◆

For the next six hours, Ingrid paced back and forth in their foyer, her eyes watching the old grandfather clock and her hope waning with every resounding chime. In the event that the vicious Viggo proved to be as beastly as the rumors said and the bloodthirsty king killed her father in a fit of rage, Ingrid would be the new Countess of Anselm. For all her years observing Edmund's hard work and leadership, she was no more ready to take up her father's mantle than she was to assume her mother's

Furthermore, her position wouldn't be secure until she found a husband to oversee the county with her. Few men would respect her as the county's leader without a man by her side, but she couldn't think of a single man in Anselm who she could bear to spend her life with … or one who would tolerate her.

The sound of a door opening distracted Ingrid from her frantic thoughts two chimes after the clock announced the twelve o'clock hour. The young maiden whipped around to greet her father only to see one of his men instead. While the aged former soldier looked unharmed, the panic in his wide brown eyes stirred more apprehension in Ingrid's thundering heart.

"Your father is on his way with King Viggo to sign off on the terms of their truce. They will be here in five minutes," Franz wheezed. "He wants you to take the twins into the tunnels and not to come out until he says to."

"Thank you, Franz."

Ingrid picked up her skirts and sprinted to the twins' playroom, where their nurse, Gerda, watched over them.

"Is Papa home?" Doris asked.

"Not yet, but let's play a little game until he gets back," she suggested with a smile. "Have you ever played in the tunnels before?"

The twins shook their heads.

"Well, when you play in the tunnels, the goal is to be as quiet as possible. If we play the game exceptionally well, we'll force Papa to come find us when he returns! Doesn't that sound fun?"

"Yeah!" Albrecht exclaimed.

"I want to play," Doris added, abandoning her doll as she climbed to her feet.

"Great! The game starts now, so don't make a peep and walk as quietly as possible," Ingrid whispered.

Ingrid placed her index finger to her lips then took her siblings' hands while Gerda gathered her belongings … including the gun Edmund gave her before his departure. Upon leaving the playroom, the foursome crept down the hall to the library. Once inside, Ingrid glided over to the bookshelf to the left of the roaring fireplace. She slid the miniature bronze globe on the third shelf to the right until the tell-tale click reached her ears.

The bookshelf moved forward two feet, and Ingrid pushed it to the left to reveal the dark, chilly passageway. After seizing the two lanterns hanging from the back of the bookshelf, the young maiden lit them and handed one to the nurse.

Gerda ushered her charges into the tunnel and Ingrid filed in after them, turning the crank in the wall until the bookshelf slid back in place. Without the fire's warmth to chase away the winter cold, the four began to shiver, but Doris and Albrecht remained silent. A fierce determination to win the game spurred the children on as they set off down the stone tunnel. Though the dank corridor descended below the estate and led to the old, unused well several yards outside its walls, they stayed within fifty feet of the entrance.

For five minutes, the twins played a game during which they took turns trying to slap each other's hands while their nurse made sure they didn't giggle too loudly. Pacing mere inches from the entrance to the tunnel, Ingrid eagerly waited for her father or some other messenger to come bearing peaceful news.

When the low grumble of masculine voices reached her ears, Ingrid's eyes widened and she strained to listen to their conversation. Once the speaking became louder, she recognized her father's voice and determined that the accented growl mingling with his belonged to King Viggo. While most people from Villriket tended to over pronounce certain consonants if they learned English through the written word, Viggo's pronunciation was perfect. Alas, neither his fluency nor his deep, velvety voice comforted the count's daughter as she eavesdropped on the men's exchange.

"I'm sorry we don't have more to welcome you with, Your Majesty. We were preparing for war not a royal guest," Edmund said.

"I don't need a wasteful banquet or dancing. As soon as we've settled everything, I'll be on my way to that coward's palace in Bjartyra," Viggo seethed.

Ingrid heard the rustling of papers as the men began discussing the terms of their agreement. The people of Anselm would not stand in Viggo's way as he traveled to the capital. In return, Edmund would pay him tribute after the Villriketian king triumphed over Ansgar. If Viggo lost the war, Edmund would burn the agreement lest King Ansgar discover their truce.

Once Edmund finished penning the document, he read it aloud to ensure he accurately recorded every detail they discussed, but Viggo interrupted him halfway through the reading.

"What a beautiful painting," the king said, his voice softening a bit. "Is she your wife?"

"No. Now, you'll receive three hundred—"

"So she's your daughter?"

Several moments of uneasy silence passed between the two men before Edmund answered curtly.

"Yes. Three hund—"

"What is her name?"

"Ingrid."

"Ingrid is an excellent name," he approved. "Has she been claimed by someone?"

Edmund hesitated.

"Well … I—"

"Don't lie to me," Viggo snarled.

"The king's youngest nephew mentioned courting her, but nothing is set in stone."

"She's far too exquisite for one of Ansgar's sniveling kinsmen," he muttered to himself. "I'll take her."

Ingrid nearly stopped breathing, but she leaned closer to the wall, determined not to miss a single word of the conversation.

"I beg your pardon?"

"Keep your money, land, and harvest. Give me Ingrid's hand in marriage, and I will spare your county."

"Your Majesty, I doubt she would consent to marrying you."

"Then *command* her to do it!" he roared. "You are the master of this house, aren't you?"

"Yes, but my daughter's happiness means the world to me. I won't force her to marry a strange man from a foreign land."

"Do I look like some common merchant's son? I'm a *king*, and I want her to be my queen," he insisted. "If you'd rather keep her happy and save her charms for someone who will likely be dead before the week's end, go ahead. However, I won't promise to show your little county mercy if she isn't by my side."

"Your Majesty, I—"

"Wait," Ingrid shouted, frantically turning the crank and opening the tunnel wide enough to slip back into the library. "Please don't hurt any of our people. I'll marry you."

Ingrid's heart boomed louder than a steam engine as Viggo turned his glare from her father and gave her the full weight of his icy blue eyes.

Even though he kept his long, dark mahogany locks back in a low ponytail, she still found the foreign king's age impossible to discern. Viggo's unkempt, graying beard, which stopped an inch above of his uniform's third brass button, obscured most of his face. The king's wild facial hair would have held her rapt attention if not for a long-healed scar, which split his left eyebrow in two. The little Ingrid could see of his face was peeling and sunburnt from spending countless days waging war in the merciless winter sun. While she couldn't tell whether the king was handsome or not, the wild look in his eyes sent a chill down her spine that had little to do with the drafty tunnel behind her.

Edmund clenched and unclenched his jaw, fighting the urge to berate his daughter for placing herself in such a precarious position. Of course, he couldn't chastise her with the scornful King of Villriket standing a yard away, so he remained silent.

"I guess you don't know your daughter as well as you thought. She clearly realizes it's better to be a foreigner's queen than a countryman's duchess."

"I'm not marrying you because of your title, Your Majesty. My people's safety is my only concern."

"Well, at least you're honest. That's more than I can say for King Ansgar."

"Am I to come to the palace after you capture it?" she asked, her voice trembling more the longer she bore the weight of Viggo's unflinching stare.

"No, you'll leave with me now."

"A respectable lady like Ingrid doesn't belong in a war zone. Her accompanying you now is neither proper nor convenient," Edmund broke in. "She needs accommodations fit for a woman of her caliber, and you would sully her reputation if you forced her to travel with you unsupervised before your wedding."

"Then you'll come as well. I won't have you going behind my back and putting her on a ship to Eusebia as soon as I leave," the king decided. "One of my men will supervise you in my absence, so pack whatever you need. I'll send additional escorts to bring you to the camp after sunset."

When neither the count nor his daughter could muster up a single word to say in response, the gruff royal turned on his heel and stalked out of the room, his heavy footsteps echoing in the hallway until he slammed the front door shut moments later.

"Ingrid Carina Kappel, what were you thinking?" Edmund shouted.

"I'm sorry, Papa. I couldn't let him hurt you or anyone else. Please don't be cross with me."

The count shook his head, berating himself for lashing out at his inconveniently selfless daughter.

"I'm sorry. I'm angry with *myself*, not you," he sighed. "I should have lied to him when he asked about your painting. Now, if he's victorious, you'll be married to that beast for the rest of your life."

"Maybe it won't be so bad," Ingrid said with a slight smile, flicking a bit of dust off his shoulder. "A man who recognizes Ansgar's corruption must value uprightness and justice to some extent."

"Yes, but Viggo is not known for having an agreeable personality. He has a frightening temper and a vengeful spirit. This isn't what I wanted for you."

"But it's the hand God dealt me. Besides, don't you always tell me that what others mean for evil, God frequently uses for a much greater good?"

Gerda and the twins emerged from the passageway before Edmund could reply. Ignoring his breaking heart, he crouched down to greet Doris and Albrecht with kisses and smiles when they ran to him.

"Is it true, Papa? Is Ingrid getting married?" little Doris asked. "I heard you talking in the tunnels."

Edmund blew air out of his nose and his chin quivered as grief suddenly overwhelmed him. Thankfully, Ingrid spoke on his behalf and spared him the pain of having to confirm the distressing news.

"Yes, you'll both have a new big brother soon," she beamed, turning her eyes back to her father. "I'm going to help the staff pack our belongings. Please let me know if you need anything."

The count nodded and further explained their family's future to the twins while Ingrid left the library with a soul too burdened by her fear of the future to muster up the hope she so convincingly feigned to assuage her guilt-ridden father's conscience.

◆　◆　◆

When Viggo's men reached the castle moments before sunset, Edmund and Ingrid had been packed and waiting for hours, silently counting the minutes until their arrival. Asking the Lord for strength, she stopped biting her nails—a detestable childhood habit that reemerged hours before—and jumped to her feet. The taciturn father and daughter departed their estate and boarded the carriage, both praying they would have the chance to see the their beloved home and family again.

The ride from the Count of Anselm's home to Viggo's camp on Castle Hill lasted an hour. Ingrid used the time to scrutinize the passing countryside with new eyes. She searched the forest for any indication that King Ansgar's men were lying in wait for their enemy rather than appreciating the majestic old trees and the cloud-shrouded mountains in the distance. As the camp came into view, Ingrid couldn't decide whether or not she was relieved that her self-seeking king hadn't somehow intervened and ended her marriage before it could begin. Edmund's mind, however, was focused on the younger king.

Despite his unfavorable opinion of the foreign ruler's demeanor, Edmund mentally commended King Viggo for choosing to set up camp on the hill. He even had men standing at each corner using spyglasses to watch for enemy soldiers from their elevated vantage point. The amount of advanced weaponry the army had both terrified and impressed the count as he and his daughter stepped out of the carriage. Their own king failed to equip his soldiers with the latest inventions as Viggo had because of his own pride and penchant for wasting the crown's money on luxury items.

Out of concern for his people's safety, Edmund ensured his aged protectors each had Colt Revolvers as well as a few cannons. Yet nothing they possessed rivaled Viggo's multitude of lethal Gatling guns and

Congreve rockets. With the artillery the Villriketian men possessed, they wielded the power to cut down anyone who approached long before they reached the summit.

Their escorts, Espen and Johan, steered them through the camp to the large tent beside the king's cabin, where the blue, yellow, and white Villriketian flag whipped proudly in the wind. Holding the flap open, the men gestured for their uneasy guests to enter. The moment the father and daughter stepped inside the tent, Viggo stopped scrutinizing his map of Schlagefilde. The king's younger companion, who shared his dark hair and cold blue gaze, did as well. The man swept his eyes up and down Ingrid, shook his head, and crossed his arms while the king abandoned the table to greet the count and his daughter.

"Welcome to our camp. My men erected tents for both of you, and some of my most trusted men will guard you around the clock," he explained. "You can trust Espen and Johan with your lives."

"Aren't you going to introduce me to your new bride, brother?" the man at the table taunted.

"Prince Halvard, allow me to introduce you to The Lord Edmund Kappel, Count of Anselm, and his daughter Lady Ingrid Kappel. Your lordship, this is my brother and the leader of my army, Prince Halvard Lund."

"It's a pleasure to meet you, Your Highness," Edmund said with a bow as Ingrid curtsied.

"My brother gave up a hefty tribute and much needed supplies to marry *you?*" Halvard said, ignoring the count.

"I suppose so," Ingrid replied.

"Did you at least sample the goods first to make sure she's worth it, Viggo?" the prince asked, a smirk gracing his full lips.

Ingrid's cheeks reddened and she cast her eyes downward. Edmund, on the other hand, had no trouble maintaining eye contact. The count glowered at the ribald royal, his nostrils flaring as he fought to keep his temper and maintain his distance.

"Of course not," Viggo rumbled.

The prince chuckled to himself, turning his attention back to the map.

"Well, I hope she gives you enough sons to make up for everything she's cost you."

Luckily, the unapologetic king segued into a new topic as if Halvard didn't just offend his future bride and father-in-law with a brazen statement that was more appropriate for a common crook than the king's brother.

"Follow me. I'll show you to your quarters."

The king trudged outside with his unenthusiastic guests a few paces behind.

"Lord Edmund, I know you've been at war before, but your daughter has not. Keep her nearby or in her tent. My men are honorable, but I won't ask them to adjust their behavior or language because a lady is in the camp," he warned. "At least one of your primary guards and another soldier will be with you at all times."

"Thank you for your generosity, Your Majesty," Ingrid jumped in, sensing that her fuming father was still too cross to tame his tongue. "We appreciate it."

Viggo gave a quick nod and plodded forward wordlessly until they reached the two tents. Ingrid lifted the flap to one tent and furrowed her brow as she took in her temporary home.

The fabric dwellings were smaller than a servant's room. A rubberized mat served as the floor and a cot half the size of her bed was positioned on the left with a folded wool blanket on top. Ingrid told herself to be grateful that the king had the decency to respect her maidenhood. Having a separate place to stay while she waited out their unforeseen betrothal was a blessing.

The men had placed her trunk in the corner along with a lamp, which meant she could read at night to soothe her troubled soul. Keeping those benefits in mind, the count's daughter let the flap fall back in place and faced Viggo with a smile that would have warmed even the most frigid of hearts.

"Thank you," she grinned.

"We march on the capital in three days. After we're victorious, I will send for you," the king said. "Camp life is not as glamorous as what you're accustomed to, but you will have living quarters fit for a queen soon enough."

Ingrid nodded and prayed for the next few days to pass as slowly as possible. While she would have preferred the palace to her tent, she wasn't eager to begin her life with Viggo either.

"I don't mind," she said.

"I'm going to return to my brother and finalize our strategy. Edmund, come with me. I could use your knowledge concerning Ansgar's army."

Viggo turned to walk away expecting Edmund to follow him. Instead the count turned to his daughter.

"Will you be all right by yourself for a bit?"

Ingrid perceived Viggo's quiet exasperation as he crossed his arms, so she gave her father a small smile.

"Yes, don't worry about me."

The troubled father studied his oldest child for a moment before giving her a kiss on the forehead and striding after the king. Ingrid exhaled slowly and ran a hand through her hair as her eyes swept across the camp. Strange men in uniform filled her vision for as far as the eye could see. While many were uninjured, others were wrapped in bandages, limping on crutches, or pale from pain and illness.

As she took in her surroundings, Ingrid locked eyes with a handsome young man playing cards with his friends across the way. Despite his dashing, rugged good looks, the way the brunette's green eyes traveled up and down her body as he gave her an appreciative yet lecherous grin made her skin crawl.

Ingrid hardened her expression and turned around to retreat into her new home, but she caught a brief glimpse of another woman walking through the camp. The redhead sat down with the soldiers, and Ingrid remembered stories from her father regarding women who sometimes lived at the war camps to handle laundry and cooking. Since the older woman had joined her tactless admirer, Ingrid opted to duck into her tent instead of introducing herself. There, she spent the next hour reading and turning to prayer when the tale she chose failed to distract her from her mounting restlessness.

When Ingrid at long last reached the heartbreaking account of the protagonist's mother dying—a sorrow she could relate to all too well—a familiar voice reached her ears.

"Ingrid," Edmund called, "are you in there?"

The young woman awkwardly rose from the unstable cot and opened the tent flap so her father could enter.

"How was your time with the king, Papa?"

"As well as can be expected," Edmund muttered. "Viggo is a smart man, but it's easy to exasperate and anger him unintentionally."

"Well, I'm sure being at war in a foreign land can bring out the worst in people."

"Yes, but his brother is no help. He encourages the king's cruelty rather than grounding him. I could've wrung his neck for the remark he made about you earlier!"

"If you had, you would've given him what he wanted. You behaved like the better man, and I'm proud of you for it."

A weary smile crossed the count's lips and he smoothed a stray lock of Ingrid's fair hair out of her face.

"Not as proud as I am of you. Most women wouldn't willingly sacrifice their happiness as you did today. While I'm disappointed in myself for not protecting you better, I recognize that you agreed to marry Viggo out of love for our family and the people of Anselm. I just hope you won't come to any harm because of this."

"I won't," she said, her voice exhibiting a level of faith and confidence her anxious heart lacked.

♦   ♦   ♦

After an uneventful, unsatisfying supper of hard bread and salted pork, Ingrid and Edmund parted ways to spend their first night at Viggo's camp. Ingrid fell asleep with surprising ease, but a scream tore through the night and abruptly ended her brief bliss. Opening her eyes a crack, she wondered if the sound had been part of her dream. Once a few ragged breaths passed through her lips, the cry sounded again only to be followed by cursing in the foreigners' language.

Ingrid sprang from her bed and stepped into her shoes before shooting out of her tent and following the sound of the woman's cries. She sprinted down the hill, causing several men to awaken from their places on the ground. When Ingrid reached the bottom of the slope, she found the brazen soldier she spied earlier on top of a young woman close to her age.

Ingrid identified her as a slave because of her caramel-hued skin and plain clothing, but the woman's status did nothing to deter her. Edmund had freed his father's slaves the instant he became the Count of Anselm and employed them at a fair wage, citing that as people made in God's image, their lives and work were worth as much as any man's. As someone raised by one of a dozen abolitionists in the kingdom, Ingrid abhorred the institution of slavery and the harm it caused with a passion.

"Get your hands off her!" she roared with surprising ferocity.

The man, who stopped short of striking the young woman, looked away from his prey long enough for her to weasel out of his grip and run toward Ingrid, standing behind her as she adjusted her ripped dress.

"What's going on here?" Viggo barked as he joined the trio with Edmund, Halvard, and several other men trailing behind.

"One of your men was planning to violate this woman!"

"She's a *slave* and her owner sold her to me for the night," the soldier argued.

The young maiden's face and neck reddened with rage.

"Just because someone in his *flawed* logic made it legal to label her as property doesn't mean you should treat her as such," Ingrid shot back.

"She's a human being!"

"We're at war, little girl. It isn't all afternoon teas and croquet."

"War doesn't give men the excuse to behave like animals. If you fight this war without honor, you might succeed in winning Schlagefilde, but you'll lose your souls in the process," she countered, turning her eyes to the king. "While King Ansgar hasn't abolished slavery yet, I know you have in Villriket. I don't know what your reasons were for doing so, but *please* don't let your men reap the benefits of my country's folly."

Viggo held his betrothed's earnest gaze with a stony look of his own for several heartbeats before glancing from the cowering slave girl to his soldier.

"Leave the girl alone, Arvid. My standards for your behavior aren't different just because we're in a foreign land."

Arvid's nostrils flared, and he glared at Ingrid before bowing to his king in reluctant submission.

"Yes, Your Majesty."

Viggo turned to leave, but Ingrid took a step forward and touched his arm. The king instinctively whipped around with a glower that made the count's daughter shrink back in fear.

"I-I don't feel right sending her away. Can she stay with us as a free woman? I can't let her go back to her owner … especially if he would take money so someone could abuse her. I have enough money at the estate to buy her freedom tomorrow. I could go to her master's home myself or—"

"Keep your money," he grunted. "She can stay in your tent and she has my protection. No one will harm her."

"Thank you," Ingrid breathed, placing her hand over her heart for a moment.

The king trudged back to the camp, his watchful brother and the ireful soldier not far behind. Only Edmund remained as Ingrid turned to address her new acquaintance again.

"Are you all right? Did he …"

"No, I gave him a swift knee to the groin, so I hurt him more than he hurt me," the girl said in an accent similar to hers, which meant she was likely born into slavery and not stolen from her homeland like others had been.

"I'm glad to hear that! My name is Ingrid. What's yours?"

"Liesel."

"Well, Liesel, my home is your home," Ingrid welcomed with a smile. "This is my father, The Lord Edmund Kappel, Count of Anselm."

Edmund, who looked considerably less regal than usual in his nightgown and housecoat, bowed in greeting.

"We should head back to the camp. It's five minutes until midnight, and I'm not leaving you two out here alone."

"Of course, Papa."

Ingrid placed her arm around the shivering girl to keep her warm as they walked back to their shared shelter. Though the tent and cot were hardly large enough for Ingrid let alone her *and* a guest, the young lady thanked God both for blessing her with feminine company and for showing her the flicker of goodness burning within the sullen sovereign's heart.

Chapter 2

The next morning, Ingrid yawned herself awake and opened her eyes to the wall of her tent. She furrowed her delicate brow in confusion, forgetting the prior day's events until the sound of men laughing in the camp reached her ears. As the future Villriketian queen recalled her hasty engagement, she also remembered the young woman she met the previous night ... a young woman who no longer slept beside her in the cot.

Her pulse roaring in her ears, Ingrid rolled over and sat up. Thankfully, her fleeting panic dissipated as quickly as it developed when she saw Liesel. The freedwoman was perched on Ingrid's trunk reading the novel she'd flipped through the previous day.

"Good morning," Ingrid said. "I hope my snoring didn't keep you awake."

Liesel jumped slightly and put the book away.

"I slept through worse in my master's home, my lady," she placated.

"Don't stop reading on my account. There are plenty of other books for me to thumb through."

"Thank you."

"You're welcome. So, what duties did you perform for your former master?"

Sadness briefly flickered in Liesel's dark brown eyes.

"I was my mistress' lady's maid and my master's secretary."

Ingrid tilted her head and furrowed her brow, flabbergasted that a young woman highly regarded enough to hold such a place in a man's house was given to a strange soldier so carelessly. Yes, many men saw their slaves as little more than chattel, but most masters would value and protect someone with Liesel's skill set and obvious intelligence at least for their own sakes. Either he was extremely careless or he feared the Villriketians would retaliate if he refused to give up the beautiful, curly-haired girl.

"I know what you're thinking. You're wondering why he gave me to that," Liesel pursed her lips for a moment as she tried to rein in her tongue, "soldier."

"Yes, I was, but you don't have to say a word if telling the story is too painful for you."

Liesel shrugged.

"My master was also my father. There was no love between him and my mother, but he treated me better than the others because of it and didn't whip me as often."

Ingrid's heart ached at the thought of any man—let alone her father—abusing Liesel with the leather scourge. She'd seen the scars previous owners left on the freedmen her father employed and knew the whip was an instrument of torture. Even if Liesel's father seldom whipped her, once was still too much in Ingrid's opinion.

"He married a baron's daughter ten years ago, but not being able to have a child of her own eats her up inside," the young woman continued. "She had my mother sold two years ago because she was so bitter. For all her complaining, my master wouldn't part with me … until last night. I don't know how that soldier knew about me, but he showed up on our doorstep with an obscene amount of money asking to purchase me for the night. My master said yes before the money was halfway out of his pocket."

A memory of the woman Ingrid saw in the camp the previous day flashed in her mind.

"What does your father's wife look like?"

"She's a plain woman in her late thirties with fiery red hair."

"I think she was here yesterday speaking with Arvid and some other soldiers. Perhaps she mentioned you to them."

"Well, I bet she's satisfied with herself."

Ingrid seized Liesel's hand, causing the young woman to tense at her unexpected touch.

"I'm sorry people have treated you dreadfully. I swear your life will be different now."

"How can you promise that?"

"I'm engaged to King Viggo. Despite his surly disposition, I think he has a sense of honor. Why else would he have allowed you to join us?"

"I don't know …"

"What would you like to do with your freedom?"

A sigh escaped Liesel's lips as she tucked a dark mahogany curl behind her ear.

"I never expected to be free, so I never thought about what I'd do if I was."

"That makes sense," Ingrid said, silently deriding herself for asking such an impractical question hours into her friend's life as a free woman. "Well, there's no rush! You can stay with me as long as necessary. My father is friends with most of Schlagefilde's abolitionists, so I'm sure he could find a new place for you after this madness ends."

Liesel studied her unlikely champion for a moment before speaking.

"May I ask you a question?"

"Of course! Ask me anything."

"Why are you marrying the king? You seem like a virtuous woman, but he's … well … your personalities seem very different."

"The story is quite romantic," she began with a wry grin. "He promised to leave Anselm in peace if I married him. Now, I'm engaged to a man from a strange land who I've barely had a full conversation with."

"Then I guess we have something in common."

"What?"

"Our fortunes were both decided by men who have more power than we do."

◆　◆　◆

After Edmund, Ingrid, and Liesel ingested a meager breakfast of coffee and pears, which they picked from the surrounding woodland, Viggo called the count to his side once more to provide his insight. Much to her surprise, Ingrid too received a summons from her betrothed. Despite Ingrid's invitation to accompany her and Edmund, Liesel elected to stay in the tent and spend the morning reading. Before receiving her freedom, she only had the privilege of reading at length when her master and mistress were in town and her chores were done. Thus, the count and his daughter met with the king without their new friend.

When they stepped inside the tent, Halvard turned his attention away from his brother and frowned at the sight of his future in-laws.

"Good morning, Your Majesty and Your Royal Highness," Edmund said. "How can we be of service to you today?"

Viggo didn't even look up from his documents when he answered the count.

"We need more information about Ansgar's army."

"And Ingrid?"

"My future wife needs to understand my duties and become accustomed to being by my side."

Edmund glanced at his daughter, who thoughtfully chewed on her bottom lip. From what the young lady knew about other marriages, the men in her kingdom rarely involved their wives in more male dominated aspects of their lives or businesses. After all, their duty was to remain in the home and make sure their households ran without incident. Having a front row seat to a king planning the final phase of his invasion was strange and a bit unnerving. Judging by Halvard's icy glower, Viggo's decision was as abnormal to the Villriketians as it was to them.

Ingrid was raised during an era of relative peace in her homeland. What little she knew about war came from romanticized accounts of it in novels and the few censored anecdotes her father told her. Hearing how Viggo, Halvard, and her father planned the deadly deeds ahead wasn't her idea of a fun morning … especially since the talk of death brought her soul a grave sadness she regularly experienced since her mother's passing.

"Do you have any objections, Ingrid?" Edmund whispered.

"No!"

Ingrid's unusually chirpy voice earned a concerned look from her father. She avoided his scrutiny by turning her gaze to the maps covering the table.

The men discussed guns, cannons, missiles, and explosives for the next hour while Ingrid watched their interaction. Edmund proved the most polite of the trio, Viggo barely passed as civil, and Halvard failed to display anything resembling grace or patience. As expected, the king's bluntness and cantankerous disposition often added to his boorish image, but his brother was far worse. Throughout the meeting, the young prince made snide remarks and underhanded insults about Edmund and the people of Schlagefilde, which the count graciously ignored and Viggo failed to correct.

By the time Viggo was satisfied with their session, Ingrid's stomach was rumbling rather loudly. Of course, she knew expecting or requesting her usual lunch or afternoon tea would've made her a laughing stock at the camp. Nevertheless, the count's daughter hoped Viggo would provide some food to tide her over until supper. Sadly, she was forced to live with her nagging hunger until their evening meal.

To take her mind off her feral stomach, Ingrid walked on the outskirts of the camp with Liesel while Edmund hunted with a few soldiers. The Count of Anselm had the right to hunt anywhere in the county, so he allowed the men to do so providing that they didn't kill more than they needed and bleed the area dry. Considering the pervasive tension haunting the men in anticipation of the upcoming battle, they would have been happy to hunt even if Edmund only permitted them to pluck a few rabbits from the countryside let alone a deer or boar.

"What did you do as your father's secretary?" Ingrid asked.

"I wrote letters, helped manage his finances, purchased supplies, and whatever else he needed at the time."

"Those are advantageous skills to possess. I hate that you gained them under such unpleasant circumstances, but they may help you find a well-paying job when the war is over."

"Maybe. What does a count's daughter do with her time?"

"Help run the household and learn how to become a respectable wife," she answered, feeling silly as she explained her life of ease to Liesel. "My father spent a pretty penny on my governess, but I don't have any artistic talent, and I don't care to. *Science* is my passion. After she convinced my parents that my voice is tolerable at best and that I possess the drawing ability of a six year-old, Papa hired a tutor who could teach me about astronomy and physics. We even had the privilege of seeing William Parsons' telescope on a trip to Ireland a few years ago."

"What's a telescope?"

Ingrid's eyes lit up as a smile graced her rosy lips.

"A telescope is a large tube-shaped device that helps you see the stars! The Earl of Rosse's telescope is six feet wide and over fifty feet long. We were able to see a spiral nebula Charles Messier categorized almost a century ago during our trip."

"I don't know what a spiral nebula is, but it sounds wonderful," Liesel chuckled.

"Nothing stirs my affections for the Lord like gazing at or reading about the stars. Seeing how magnificently he created the universe and realizing that the same God who hung the stars and planets took the time to create and love us takes my breath away," she sighed.

"That reminds me of Psalm 8. I usually feel the closest to God when I'm reading the psalms. In spite of the pain my master and mistress caused, I'm grateful he taught me how to read. Now, I can study scripture and experience God's comfort for myself. My mother couldn't read, so she heard the gospel through word of mouth. She only knew a few verses before I started reading the Bible to her."

Liesel's quiet voice cracked and tears filled her dark eyes, prompting Ingrid to place her arms around her new friend.

"She was very fortunate to have you, and she'll be *ecstatic* to have you again once we're all settled," she said. "I'll do everything I can to help you find her."

"You don't have to do that."

"I know, but I *want* to! I understand how difficult being separated from your mother is. Even though I'll never see mine again on this side of Heaven, I want to help you reunite with yours."

"Thank you."

The newly freed woman pulled away and wiped her eyes, which widened and promptly lowered when she noticed something behind her unlikely friend. Ingrid turned around and froze for a moment upon seeing Viggo standing several yards away. The count's daughter dropped into a clumsy curtsy and wondered how long the king had been listening in on their intimate conversation.

"Good afternoon, Your Majesty," Ingrid greeted. "Can we be of some assistance?"

"You and I will be having a traditional Villriketian supper tonight in my cabin at seven o'clock. Don't be late."

Ingrid opened her mouth to respond, but the king turned and marched away before she could say a word. The young maiden frowned at his rudeness and shook her head.

"I'm sorry, Liesel," Ingrid said once Viggo walked out of earshot.

"I'm used to worse," Liesel said with a half-smile. "Are you scared of him?"

"I can't decide … I'm relying more on faith than sight now," she joked.

"On a lighter note, I think some rhubarb was growing back near the bottom of the hill. Come help me get some!"

Ingrid grabbed Liesel's hand and took off in search of the desired shrub, earning a laugh from her companion as they ran through the woods with their guard only paces behind.

◆　◆　◆

Several minutes before seven o'clock, Ingrid and Johan crossed the camp to the mundane cabin the king called home. Edmund had scowled upon learning that Viggo extended his invitation without consulting him first and that he'd requested a *private* supper with his daughter. However, the count reluctantly consented to the meal when Johan pointed out that with the cook serving the meal and him guarding the pair, the king and his fiancée wouldn't be alone.

Even with the young soldier's assurances, Ingrid's heart still hammered noisily in her ears and her mouth went dry when she reached the doorstep. The maiden had *never* shared an unsupervised meal with a man other than a relative before. The prospect of being alone with the grizzly king made her palms perspire in a most unladylike manner. Without Edmund there to act as a buffer, she would have no one to take the focus off her and anything she may say to offend Viggo.

Let the words of my mouth, and the meditation of my heart, be acceptable in thy sight, O Lord, my strength, and my redeemer, she prayed, remembering a psalm she memorized after an argument with her father years before.

When the cook opened the door, Ingrid stepped inside the cabin. Her knuckles blanched as she clutched her dish and made eye contact with her betrothed. Viggo rose to his feet and remained standing until she sat across from him. A long minute of silence passed between the future husband and wife before Viggo finally spoke.

"What did you bring with you?"

Despite her brief prayer for courage, Ingrid's voice was little louder than a whisper when she answered.

"I'm not quite sure what to call it, but my dish is something between rhubarb pie and summer pudding. You've probably had much better desserts in Villriket, but I saw some rhubarb on my walk today and thought you might enjoy having a sweet dish to eat tonight."

"Well, anything is better than hard biscuits and salted meat."

"I take it we're having something different?"

"Yes, we are. Having a red meal before going off to face your enemy is good luck in our culture. They say the more red food you have in your belly, the less blood you'll lose on the battlefield. I don't know how much I believe the old wives' tale, but I like having an excuse to eat *real* food," the king explained, averting his eyes for a beat. "I wanted to share this meal with you."

"Thank you for thinking of me. I guess it's fitting that I made a dish with rhubarb."

"Yes, it is," he said, the corners of his lips turning up in a hint of a smile.

The cook filled their glasses with red wine and set plates of medium-rare steak, beets, and red cabbage before the king and his fiancée. When Viggo bowed his head and closed his eyes to pray over their supper, Ingrid's jaw dropped. Fortunately, she recovered her wits and did the same as he said grace.

"Lord, thank you for this meal and for the loyal men you placed by my side during this war. Give them the strength, rest, and courage they need to stand against our enemy and be victorious on the battlefield tomorrow. I pray this in Jesus' name. Amen."

"Amen," Ingrid chorused, marveling at the ruler's eloquent prayer as she began eating.

"I overheard some of your conversation with your new friend earlier," Viggo said. "You like astronomy?"

A grin spread across Ingrid's lightly freckled face.

"Yes, I find it so fascinating! What do you enjoy doing?"

"I joined the military when I was fifteen and became king when my parents were murdered five years later. With those two increases in responsibility, I haven't had time to live for my own enjoyment in the past ten years."

"Well, hasn't something warmed your heart or made doing your duty less taxing."

The king chewed on his steak, studying his future wife as he ruminated on her question.

"I took up painting as a child and spent some of my free time during the war against Aspasia sketching what I saw around me. The mountains between the coast and King Tresillian's palace are quite splendid," he confessed.

"Have you had much time to draw since becoming king?"

Viggo's eyes darkened and he looked away, taking a swig of his wine.

"No, I have more pressing matters to tend to."

"Well, you should make sketching or painting your first act of leisure after the war ends! The gardens at the palace in Bjartyra are exquisite. King Ansgar had flowers and shrubbery imported from all over the world and artisans sculpted them into a variety of shapes. A marble fountain with unbelievably realistic cherubs sits in the middle of the garden, and it's hard not to imagine them giggling and playing their little harps!"

"You sound awfully familiar with Ansgar's palace," Viggo remarked coolly. "Your father gave me the impression that he and the king are on bad terms."

"They are. Their convictions and opinions differ far too much for them to be friends as they were in their youth. We've only visited the palace as necessary to pay our respects to the king."

"Lord Edmund told me one of Ansgar's nephews wanted to court you. Are you two already acquainted?"

"Yes, Einar and I have met several times."

"Under what circumstances?"

"Papa first introduced us at the king's ball last year."

"Did you dance with him at the ball?"

"A few times."

"A few times," he repeated, bristling with irritation. "It sounds like you were quite taken with each other."

"Hardly," Ingrid laughed. "Most unmarried men at the ball were at least twenty years older than me or insufferably pompous. While Einar was the most agreeable man my age, we never exchanged a single letter after that night, and he never called on me in Anselm."

Viggo relaxed somewhat, and the young maiden realized he was *jealous!* While she knew men could be territorial at times, the concept of a man being wary of her past potential suitor was so foreign. After all, no man ever expressed interest in pursuing her. Yes, men praised her beauty, but they often found her tolerable at best and tiresome at worst.

To their dismay, she had no intention of amusing them with songs and delightfully shallow conversation. Rather, she wanted to discuss the stars or discover if they were abolitionists like her father and wanted Schlagefilde to follow the examples set by Villriket and Eusebia. Though no gentleman would dare tell her to her face, they likely found her too progressive and uncompromising to be a proper wife who valued the status quo.

But Viggo was different.

"Please don't worry about my past. I never came close to giving my heart to him or anyone else," Ingrid said. "You're the only man who has had any interest in marrying me."

"That's ridiculous! A girl your age should have had some suitors or admirers by now."

"My opinions are too strong and unpopular for most men in my social class to admire me."

"Like your father."

"Yes, I inherited his fair hair and fair ideas," she chuckled.

"He's an abolitionist, correct?"

Ingrid nodded as she chewed on her food.

"Hence you defending the girl last night."

"Yes, but you're doing far more for the slaves' plight than I ever could. Your first act as King of Villriket was to abolish slavery."

"My father began the work by changing the people's hearts. I only had to change the law."

"Well, you're both more enlightened than King Ansgar. It took arm-twisting from twenty lords before he would consider *reading* a law granting freedmen the ability to own property. Even then, he refused to enact it. He said that he doesn't see slaves as people and that letting them amass wealth and property is like throwing pearls before swine. His attitude disgusts me."

Ingrid realized how tightly she clutched her fork and placed it on the table, taking a moment to calm herself as Viggo admired her refreshing compassion for their darker brothers and sisters.

"My grandfather held the same twisted beliefs. His wife, God rest her soul, had enough of an influence to combat his narrow-mindedness and raise my father to be an unbiased man."

"And her legacy is still living in you."

"I suppose."

As they continued their meal, Ingrid's heart warmed upon finding she actually *enjoyed* Viggo's company! The king came off as abrasive during their initial interactions, but he was gentler than his rough exterior and demeanor let on. However, as the maiden grew accustomed to meeting his steely blue eyes as opposed to casting her gaze downward in fear, she recognized a deep sadness in him. His quiet despondency matched the heartache she often struggled with, and she felt a strange kinship with the foreign king.

Their lives had both been touched by profound, life-changing loss.

The two grew more comfortable around one another with every passing minute. Though the king never laughed and his lips were seldom set in anything but a hard line, Ingrid sensed a new lightness in him. He even suggested venturing outside to watch the stars as they ate Ingrid's crimson dessert.

"This is delicious," Viggo praised. "What did you make it with?"

"Rhubarb, a little honey, and some of the hard biscuits we've been eating."

"I never thought anyone could make that rock hard rubbish taste delicious," he marveled. "Did your mother teach you how to cook?"

"No, but when I took over as the lady of the house, I spent some time shadowing the men and women my father employ. I wanted to learn what their duties were and how best to support them in their roles. The cook fascinated me the most, so I still help her from time to time. I think it's because I can see the science behind baking and cooking."

Viggo nodded, finishing off his dessert and savoring the last bite. After a long, contented exhale, he turned to his betrothed and spoke again.

"What advice do you have for me regarding tomorrow's battle?"

"I don't know. I'm not well-versed in war like you, your brother, or my father."

"You may lack our strategic knowledge, but you're a sensible, intelligent woman with a good heart. My father saw my mother as his equal and included her in his major decisions. I would be a fool not to treat you with the same respect."

Ingrid looked away for a moment, chewing on her bottom lip while she asked God for the right words. During this moment of introspection, Viggo studied the count's daughter. His keen eyes noticed the sprinkling of freckles across her delicate, pointed nose and cheeks and that her upper lip was a touch larger than her lower one. The artist who rendered the portrait in Edmund's library altered the maiden's features a bit to make her skin spotless, minimized her upper lip, and changed her locks from their honey blonde shade to a brighter hue all in an effort to make her closer to his standard of beauty.

In Viggo's eyes, the features the painter perceived as flaws in need of an artist's correction only made Ingrid more beautiful … as did her spirit. While it was unwise to demand her hand in marriage without so much as a conversation purely because of her beauty and her name reminding him of his father, King Ingvar, God had been merciful in using his recklessness to give him such a woman … A woman who already had the power to make or break him with little more than a look or a word.

No wonder his brother had called him a fool when he announced his engagement.

"All right," Ingrid finally said, turning her attention back to her surprisingly rapt fiancé.

"What is your advice?"

"I know death and war go hand in hand, but don't take a single life out of anger or vengeance. If someone surrenders or can be spared, show him mercy in the moment and resolve to execute true justice later … even King Ansgar."

Viggo's eyebrows lowered and a crimson flush spread from his dark beard to his hairline. The king sprang into a standing position and began marching away. Ingrid scrambled to her feet and followed, abandoning her borrowed cast iron skillet in the grass.

"Your Majesty, please don't walk away. I didn't mean any offense."

The king spun around and faced Ingrid, his blue eyes blazing with rage.

"Do you know what that monster did?"

"I know he executed your parents, but—"

"He didn't simply *execute* them. The rat served their entire traveling party supper one evening and poisoned every Villriketian in attendance with tainted wine. Instead of being satisfied with killing their countrymen as a so-called show of strength, Ansgar dragged them into the dungeon. There, he forced my father to watch as he beat my mother to death with his own hands. After slaughtering her, he decapitated my father. I received his head wrapped in my mother's bloodstained dress weeks later."

Viggo's chest heaved and his eyes burned with unshed tears while Ingrid's face blanched in horror.

"Ansgar plotted this betrayal for *years*. He wanted revenge against my father for leading the charge against him for the Anderike massacre and alienating him from the other kingdoms," the king continued. "He massacred a village of innocent people for being unable to pay his exorbitant taxes. Then, he took my parents' lives because my father had the strength of conviction to condemn his actions and sway the other kings to do the same."

"I-I'm sorry. I had no idea. My father never told me the details …"

"Do you understand why I can't spare him?"

"I understand your fury. Anyone with a heart of flesh would be enraged, but you can't end Ansgar's life out of a desire for revenge. If you do, you'll be committing the same sin you hate him for … and you'll be doing to his children what he did to you and Halvard."

Viggo scowled at Ingrid and turned to leave, but she seized his arm and he reluctantly stayed put.

"I know you can't let him go free because of his crimes, and I'm not saying you should. Ansgar *must* be brought to justice. I'm only asking you to spare his life on the battlefield so he can stand trial," she pleaded.

"What if he's acquitted?"

"Considering the atrocities he's committed in the past few years, I think you'd be hard pressed to find anyone who wouldn't convict him. If they don't, you can rest knowing that you honored God by being more virtuous and merciful than he ever was. Please don't let Ansgar blacken your heart after he's already broken it."

The seething sovereign glowered down at his betrothed for the longest five seconds of her life before Ingrid felt some of the tension leave his rigid body. The hard lines anger etched in his face also visibly softened.

"I know that your counsel comes from a place of concern, but I will do what I feel is right when the time comes," he said. "I suggest you make peace with my decision. I don't want to begin our marriage on a sour note."

Viggo ripped his arm from her grasp and continued to stalk back to his cabin, leaving his fiancée alone in the night. Ingrid wrapped her arms around herself and shivered as she walked back to the site of their brief, bittersweet dessert under the stars. After picking up the skillet, Ingrid lifted her glistening eyes to the sky, her soul filled with worry instead of wonder as she gazed at the heavens.

God, please help Viggo do what is right. If I spoke wrongly, make him forget every word I said that was not of you. Close his ears to those whose whispers inspire vengeance, and heal the damage and pain that Ansgar wrought in his broken heart.

Chapter 3

Edmund awakened Ingrid and Liesel an hour before dawn the next morning to tell them Viggo and his men were preparing to leave. The sleepy young ladies pulled on dresses and cloaks then emerged from the tent. A somber mood had fallen on the camp, and the only subject on the men's lips as they prepared their guns and other equipment was the battle ahead. Viggo, of course, was reconvening with his brother and a few officers in the tent. There, he and his men discussed strategy and received updates from the men waging war in other parts of Schlagefilde.

When Ingrid and Edmund stepped into the tent, Viggo cast his fiancée a fleeting glance before addressing her father.

"Do you need something from me, Lord Edmund?"

"No, Your Majesty. We wanted to wish you well before you departed for Bjartyra."

The count nodded for Ingrid to proceed, and she hesitantly stepped forward, shivering under Viggo's chilly gaze. She extended her hand to reveal a small brooch featuring an enamel angel studded with diamonds, emeralds, and rubies.

"My mother gave me this brooch the day before she passed away as a reminder that someone far greater than her watches over me, and I've worn it every day since then," she said. "I'd like you to wear it today and remember that the same God who kept you safe your whole life will be with you on the battlefield. I know it isn't terribly masculine, but—"

"I would be honored to wear it," Viggo interrupted, his voice softer than its usual gravely tone. "Will you pin it on me?"

"Of course."

Ingrid wordlessly prayed she wouldn't stick the king as she tried to fasten the brooch with shaking hands. The maiden exhaled in relief when she succeeded in attaching it to his blue uniform without pricking him. She looked up at her betrothed, and gratitude filled her heart when some of the stiffness left his face and body. However, the indifference in his eyes had been replaced by sadness she could relate to all too well.

By mentioning her mother, Ingrid had called to mind Viggo's own parents.

While bringing his pain to light wasn't her intent, she hoped the king would remember the pain death left in its wake and show mercy whenever possible during the last phase of his campaign. Of course, Ingrid knew the inevitability of death during war, but she prayed commands driven by justice and righteousness over rage and vengeance could reduce the number of casualties on the battlefield.

"Thank you," he whispered.

"You're welcome. You'll be in my prayers today, Your Majesty."

"King Ansgar needs your prayers more than anyone," Halvard spoke up. "Then again, why pray for a man whose head will be wrapped in his wife's best dress by sunset?"

Ingrid bit her tongue and remained focused on Viggo.

"Please consider what we discussed last night. I know—"

"I will leave men here to protect you while I'm away," he cut off, stepping away to pull on his gloves. "They will guard you with their lives."

"Thank you, Your Majesty," Edmund replied. "We'll leave you to your preparations."

Edmund gave a slight bow and guided the women outside, lowering his voice as they walked to their tents.

"I don't know what you two spoke about last night, but he's certainly on edge today. What happened?"

"I encouraged him to show mercy … specifically to King Ansgar. I didn't realize the extent of his crimes against Viggo's parents, but I still stand by what I said. Even if a judge sentences Ansgar to death for what he's done, Viggo can at least keep his hands clean by not spilling his blood in vengeance."

Edmund sighed and shook his head as they entered his tent.

"I'm sorry, Ingrid. I should have told you about Ansgar's actions as soon as you agreed to marry Viggo."

"I forgive you. I know you were only trying to protect me."

"Yet I failed to protect you from the predicament we're in now," he said. "Based on the stories my Villriketian friends have shared, I have full confidence that Viggo will make a better king than Ansgar, but I never wanted you to have such a disagreeable husband."

"He isn't so bad," Ingrid defended. "He's just lost. Grief and anger have consumed him for years, but I saw a glimmer of the man he once was and could be again. I'm sure he thinks the victory he's relentlessly worked for will give him peace, but being victorious today won't change him. God will."

"Your faith is greater than mine, but I hope it proves true. My plans for you did not include a cantankerous foreign husband with fire in his veins and vengeance on his mind."

"He didn't become this way on his own, Papa."

"No, his brother is more spiteful than any man I've ever met, and it troubles me that Viggo trusts him and heeds his advice."

"Perhaps they'll both have a change of heart."

"Perhaps."

♦　♦　♦

Ingrid busied herself for the remainder of the day. She rolled up her sleeves to do laundry for the men and cleaned everything she could get her hands on. Though Liesel would have preferred to spend her unprecedented amount of leisure time reading, she abandoned their tent to join Ingrid in her quest for distraction by working alongside her and making conversation when the future queen seemed especially distressed. By the time a messenger returned late in the afternoon, they were both exhausted. Their fingertips were shriveled after hours of cleaning, and sweat dripped from their brows despite the frigid winter air.

A soldier approached on horseback, and Ingrid stopped chewing on her nails, which were translucent after being submerged in water all day. Without haste, she sprang to her feet and interrupted her father's card game with Johan.

"Papa, the messenger is here!"

Standing up and displaying greater calm than his frazzled daughter had, Edmund strode across the camp to the young man with Ingrid on his heels. Mud and blood soiled his bright blue uniform, but he looked well despite the telltale stains. He gave the two nobles a hasty bow and Ingrid's mouth went dry as she waited for the news.

"King Viggo is victorious."

"Is he hurt at all?" Ingrid asked.

"No, my lady."

Ingrid heaved a sigh and took a step back, relaxing for the first time in almost twelve hours. The young maiden turned away and tuned out Edmund and the soldier as they discussed the day's events in detail, thanking God for protecting Viggo.

"Are you all right?" Liesel asked.

"Yes, I'm perfect," she replied, wiping away a tear with a smile. "I'm just happy he's safe."

"Safe and eager to have you by his side, my lady," the soldier continued. "The king ordered your protectors and I to escort you to the palace at once. Someone will pack your belongings and bring them along tomorrow. Are you ready to leave?"

Ingrid's smile faltered as she imagined the once beautiful capital littered with the corpses and devastation that came with war. Despite the unsavory nature of camp life, she preferred a lack of proper bathing facilities and a cloth roof over her head to a luxurious palace tainted and surrounded by death and destruction. Her pulse quickened at the prospect of beholding the bloody aftermath.

Lord, help me through this.

"Ingrid?" Edmund prodded.

"I'm sorry," she answered, smiling sheepishly. "May I have five minutes to pack a handful of my belongings?"

"Of course, my lady," the soldier said.

"Thank you. I'll let you know when I'm ready to leave."

The soldier nodded and Ingrid turned to go with her father and Liesel by her side.

"How are you feeling?" Edmund asked, echoing Liesel's earlier concerns.

"I don't know if I'm ready to see the devastation Viggo left in his wake."

The count lowered his voice as he stepped into her tent, Liesel opting to linger outside rather than encroaching on their conversation.

"What else is troubling you?"

A sigh eased from Ingrid's lips as she began collecting a few key belongings.

"I'm terrified, Papa. I've known for longer than I can remember that I'd marry someone one day, and I trusted you to arrange a marriage between an honorable man and me whether I loved him or not. I never imagined marrying someone like Viggo."

"When you say 'someone like Viggo,' do you mean a king or an unpleasant, grisly fellow?"

"Both! Most women would do anything to have the power, pampering, and prestige that come with being a queen, and their parents groom them for such aspirations. How will astronomy and physics help me support a king?" Ingrid gasped. "And how will I be a good wife to a man whose heart is full of vengeance? I will be a useless queen and a displeasing wife. Viggo will regret marrying me one day if he doesn't already regret our engagement."

Edmund embraced his panicking daughter and his heart broke as she wept in his arms, tears pouring from her eyes as her worries had poured from her heart. The two stood in that position for several moments and Edmund searched his soul for the right words to reassure his distraught daughter. As her brief outburst subsided, he prayed to the Lord that the words on his lips were true and comforting before breaking the silence.

"I never raised you to have the airs and accomplishments expected of a queen. I raised you to be a woman after God's heart. Despite my bumbling, you're a patient, kind, gentle, faithful, and humble young woman who seeks the good of others over her own comfort. You agreeing to marry Viggo is a testimony to your selflessness. The qualities that led you to accept his proposal and treat him with kindness and deference during your brief acquaintance are the same qualities that will help you be a fair, righteous consort and a wife any man would be blessed to have."

"But what use are those qualities when Viggo can't see past his desire for retribution?"

Edmund pulled away a bit and wiped the tears from her cheeks.

"Even if vengeance blinded Viggo, God can remove the scales from his eyes, and he could use your gentle heart, pure conduct, and respectful behavior to do it. Viggo has noticeably softened since we joined his party, and I can only imagine how God could transform him with you by his side. I can't pretend to know God's plans for you, but perhaps he in his sovereignty raised you up to be the queen our kingdoms crave and the wife Viggo never knew he needed as we come out of these dark, tumultuous times," Edmund said. "You were just trying to convince me of this earlier today. Rediscover the faith you had this morning and be the woman your mother and I raised you to be."

Ingrid took a deep, ragged breath and tucked a wild strand of flaxen hair behind her ear.

"You're right. Thank you, Papa."

Edmund kissed his daughter on the cheek, earning a chuckle as his mustache tickled her.

"You're welcome. Now, let's finish packing and be on our way. We don't want to keep the king waiting."

◆　◆　◆

As Ingrid, Liesel, and Edmund traveled to the royal residence, the maiden tried to pass the ride by reading a novel. Despite its riveting plot, the book only served as a visual distraction from the passing countryside. With no details regarding how Viggo had achieved his great victory, she dreaded seeing corpses strewn about her beautiful homeland and other disquieting devastation. It took her at least fifteen minutes to read each page, and her hands trembled more from anxiety than the carriage's rhythmic rocking and bumping when she turned each one.

Prayer also accounted for much of her slow progress. Each time her mind conjured up images of blood and violence, she would close her eyes for a moment and turn her heart to the Lord, begging for the strength, character, and iron stomach required to endure his plan for her with gentleness, courage, and self-control.

When the carriage crossed the bridge over the Dagmar River, Ingrid realized they were less than ten minutes from the palace. Chancing a glance at her homeland turned kingdom, her breath caught in her throat upon seeing that nothing much had changed. Of course, the boots, hooves, and wheels of Viggo's army, horses, and equipment had matted down the grass and created new paths in the snow-dusted landscape. Yet they had left the countryside otherwise unaffected.

Though Ingrid couldn't muster up the joy to smile at this unexpected development, she relaxed her grip on the book in her lap and lowered her hunched shoulders. Considering the terrifying artillery Viggo had at his disposal, the maiden anticipated seeing the mighty oaks and towering pines turned into splinters by cannons or torn in half by Gatling gun bullets. Feeling a bit more brave, the soon to be queen kept her hazel eyes on the scenery for the remainder of the ride. Much to her relief, she didn't see a single corpse or any signs of warfare.

It was as if Viggo had won the war without spilling a single drop of blood.

Upon their arrival, the guards escorted Ingrid, Edmund, and Liesel to their rooms in the palace's east wing. A grin graced Ingrid's lips upon witnessing Liesel's incredulous joy over her gorgeous, forest green and gold room. Alas, her delight waned when the freedwoman mentioned in passing that she never slept on anything nicer than a straw-filled mat in her master's home.

Ingrid's accommodations were also more luxurious than her room in her father's castle, but she couldn't fully appreciate the extravagance. After all, she only had unrestricted access to it because Viggo removed the palace's former master from his throne.

And he'd possibly removed Ansgar's head from his body as well.

Rather than clinging to her father and friend, Ingrid took advantage of her solitude and lowered herself to her knees. She inhaled and exhaled slowly several times to calm herself and clear her mind before uttering her quiet entreaty.

"Heavenly Father, I kneel in a palace of unparalleled splendor in the wake of my betrothed's victory, yet I can't find any peace in my heart. Knowing my countrymen lost their lives so I could be here disquiets my soul, and the thought of marrying the man whose vengeance inspired the violence in question terrifies me. I've had moments of tranquility and seen glimpses of the good that the war and our marriage could bring, but being this much closer to my wedding day and living in the shadow of Ansgar's defeat have all but obliterated the little serenity I found. Please don't let my fear steal my ability to honor you during this time. Help me to be bold when you call me to, quiet when my words would be fruitless, and confident in you no matter what each day brings. Amen."

Rising from the floor, Ingrid freshened herself up and ventured out of her room to find Edmund. When the young beauty opened the door, she saw Johan standing in the hallway poised to knock. Ingrid jumped at the sight of her stern protector but quickly regained her composure.

"I'm sorry for frightening you, my lady. His Majesty would like to see you."

"And my father as well?"

"He finished meeting with the king a few minutes ago."

"All right. I'll follow you."

Ingrid trailed behind Johan and marveled at the palace's bizarre stillness. Whenever she visited the former king with her father, laughter, music, and other merry noises always filled the beautiful home, but now only their footsteps echoed in the corridor. Ansgar's visiting ambassadors and courtiers either fled before Viggo's army reached the regal residence or they were expelled from their luxurious lodgings. Ingrid prayed they were unharmed wherever they were.

Johan led Ingrid to the library, where she'd spent many hours listening to stories and poetry read aloud by various courtiers and even King Ansgar himself. Upon seeing the brusque king with his wild mane, thick beard, and uniform sitting where her perpetually polished sovereign had once lounged, the maiden froze in shock. Fortunately, she recovered and curtsied in greeting before he noticed her astonishment.

"How was your trip to the palace?" he asked.

"Peaceful. I was happy to see so much of the country untouched by the war."

"Well, you have Ansgar's poor judgment and your sage advice to thank for that."

"What do you mean?"

The king rose from his chair and walked over to Ingrid with an unreadable look in his icy eyes.

"Last night, you told me not take a single life out of anger or vengeance and to show mercy to anyone who surrendered," he reminded her. "Before the battle began, I offered clemency to anyone who defected and vowed not to imprison anyone who laid down his arms and came forward. Much to my surprise, all but twenty-three of Ansgar's men surrendered. The rest have been given leave to return to their families."

"What about the men who remained loyal to Ansgar?"

"They tried to fight against us and took down a few of my men and their own brothers in arms, but they lost their lives in the process."

"I'm happy you spared so many lives," she said, hoping Viggo wouldn't be offended by her next inquiry. "Where are Ansgar and his family?"

"The children have been confined to their rooms with armed guards for their protection. King Ansgar and his wife are in the tower awaiting his trial."

Ingrid threw her arms around the king in excitement before she could stop herself. When Viggo stiffened at his fiancée's unexpected embrace, she pulled away and cast her dancing eyes downward. Ingrid's cheeks burned with embarrassment even as her heart sang with joy. Viggo was sparing Ansgar's life and pursuing justice instead of vengeance. Perhaps the beastly man's heart of stone was softer than she originally assumed.

"I'm sorry for throwing myself at you, Your Majesty. I-I was so happy … I forgot myself for a moment. Will you please forgive me?"

Seconds stretched on without Viggo responding, so the maiden looked up. The king's face was flushed as well, and he stared at her with anguish in his blue eyes.

And unshed tears.

The king turned his back on Ingrid and walked over to the desk again, hastily calming himself as the lady averted her gaze. While she waited for Viggo to address her again, she wondered how long it had been since anyone showed the king affection. Ingrid had observed in her short life how men tended to be less affectionate with one another than women were, and his brother didn't exude anything resembling warmth. Viggo's similarly rough façade also surely put off most people and forced them to regard him with fear and respect instead of tenderness and love. He'd also lost his father and mother, and Ingrid knew better than most the heartbreak associated with losing your mother's loving embraces and sweet kisses.

"I take it you approve of my decision," he said after the longest half-minute of silence in Ingrid's life.

"Yes. I'm sure their wives and families will be ecstatic as well."

"Hopefully they won't fly at me as you did. I don't think I'd survive the blow."

Hearing the amusement in Viggo's voice, Ingrid chanced a glance at the king again. Though a hint of a smile graced this face, she could still detect sorrow in his eyes.

"Is there anyone in Ansgar's court who you would trust to help plan our wedding? The ceremony should take place before Christmas if possible and before the New Year at the latest. Considering the brevity of our betrothal, we won't need the pomp most royal weddings require."

"Yes, my friend Lady Marlene would be perfect."

"I'll send for her tomorrow morning."

"Thank you," Ingrid smiled. "Do you want to incorporate any traditions from your homeland into the ceremony?"

"I don't care about the ceremony's specifics, but I think my men would be disappointed if we didn't serve an *overflødighedshorn.*"

"A what?"

"A cornucopia. It's an edible sculpture of sorts made of pastries, and we usually have it at weddings. Do you think the cook here can make it?"

"Considering the elaborate desserts served at court, I'm sure she can manage it."

Viggo nodded, stroking his grizzly beard.

"Perfect. Now, I also summoned you to give you something."

"Oh?"

Viggo reached into his pocket and pulled out a polished gold ring with a modestly-sized ruby flanked by two smaller diamonds. Though it wasn't as grandiose as a future queen's ring should have been, Ingrid's heart still warmed, and her hazel eyes misted over.

After all, it *was* her mother's ring.

"I met with your father today, and he entrusted this to me," he explained. "I know we haven't been acquainted for long, but I promise to prove worthy of your commitment just as your father proved worthy of your mother's."

Ingrid wiped the wetness from her cheeks and smiled, but she couldn't muster up the strength to speak yet. Instead, she extended her hand and Viggo slipped the memento on her ring finger, his eyes never leaving her face. Anxiety gnawed at him as he wondered how best to address Ingrid, but his apprehension couldn't overshadow the tenderness in his heart as he gazed at his uncommonly breathtaking yet flustered fiancée.

Recalling her earlier faux pas and reminding herself to show restraint, the future queen looked up at Viggo and simply grinned at him with genuine, undisguised elation.

"Thank you," she managed to say.

Viggo cleared his throat and walked to the desk.

"You're welcome. We also need an actual location for the wedding. Do you have one in mind?"

"What's wrong with the cathedral?"

The king's once tender gaze hardened into a baleful stare and he took a deep swig of his wine before grumbling in response.

"That's where Ansgar had his men dump my parents' bodies. Their graves still haven't been found."

"I'll find another location. Is there anywhere or anything else I should avoid that would cause painful memories?"

"No. Even the palace's chapel would be acceptable if you aren't able to find something to your liking."

"Well, I'll do my best to find somewhere that will inspire more happy memories than sad ones."

"Brother," Halvard called, strutting into the room unannounced. "Are you ready?"

"Yes, I am," the king said, turning his eyes back to Ingrid. "I will join you for supper this evening."

Ingrid dropped into a curtsy as Viggo and his brother vacated the room. Once their footsteps faded into near silence, the emotional young lady flitted to her father's room. She found Edmund reading his well-worn yet beloved Bible by the evening sunlight. Not wanting to interrupt his time of reflection, Ingrid crept away, but Edmund caught a glimpse of her as she disappeared from the doorway.

"Ingrid?"

She stepped into view again.

"I'm sorry. I didn't mean to disturb you."

"Don't be silly! You could never disturb me," he disputed with a smile as he rose from his chair and beckoned for her to enter. "Besides, I was expecting you. Have you seen Viggo yet?"

Ingrid closed the distance between them with a hug and Edmund chuckled as he smoothed his daughter's flaxen hair.

"I'll take that as a yes."

She pulling away enough to meet her father's smiling eyes.

"Thank you so much, Papa. When did you find the time to get Mama's ring?"

"I packed it with my belongings before we left for Viggo's camp and gave it to him today. With his victory secure and your marriage imminent, I wanted you to have a piece of your mother with you. I hope it gives you strength and courage as you move closer to your wedding day. Do you remember what's inscribed on the inside?"

"Proverbs 31:10."

"'Who can find a virtuous woman? For her price is far above rubies,'" the count quoted. "You, my dear, are more valuable than any jewel, and I hope Viggo realizes that."

"Well, we already know that he thinks I'm more valuable than the tribute you agreed to pay him," she said, the corners of her mouth turned up in a slight smile.

"And as he sees more of your kind spirit, he'll realize his hasty decision was the wisest investment he's ever made."

Ingrid took off the ring for a moment and studied it affectionately.

"Did you show him the inscription?"

Edmund grinned as well.

"Yes, he actually recited the verse the moment he saw the engraving. I think he had a faith at some point, but the hardships he's endured all but snuffed out the fire in him."

"I think there's still a flame there. I've seen it flicker once or twice, but maybe it will burn more brightly now that we're at peace."

"Let's hope so."

♦ ♦ ♦

Supper after nightfall was unexpectedly lighthearted, and Halvard's absence likely accounted for some of the levity. Viggo displayed more playfulness than Ingrid and her father had ever seen. He even told jokes and stories about his homeland, which had Ingrid, Edmund, and Liesel in hysterics! Of course, Edmund chimed in with an anecdote or two detailing his daughter's childhood and encouraged her to elaborate on his accounts of the amusing events. Of all their stories, Viggo found the tale of Ingrid's obsession with roses the most captivating.

One day during a walk through the garden, little Ingrid discovered and fell in love at first sight with Lady Carina's scarlet roses. Each day, she would snip a new bloom from her mother's prized rosebush to add to her growing collection. The disappearing flowers puzzled the groundskeepers and the lady of the house herself.

Following a month of confusion, Carina accidentally uncovered the rebellious rose thief's little scheme. When the lady came to play with her daughter one afternoon, she discovered a pile of rose petals under Ingrid's bed! Though she was upset and perplexed by her vanishing roses, the countess gently chided her daughter with a small smile on her lips and said no more of it.

After Ingrid succeeded in leaving her beloved blooms in peace for three months, Carina took her daughter on a walk through the garden. There, she revealed that the groundskeeper had planted a brand new rosebush just for Ingrid! The gracious countess taught her enamored daughter the art of caring for the plant daily. The day the first rose bloomed, Ingrid was far too invested in her work to snip the fragrant flowers and doom them to die unseen in her room. Rather, she spent many an hour pruning the plant and reading in the shadow of her mother's gift long after the countess passed away.

Just as Edmund and Ingrid ended the story, the clock gonged to welcome the nine o'clock hour, and a servant entered to deliver a message for the king. Viggo tore his eyes away from his fascinating fiancée and read the note. As he skimmed the unexpected epistle, some of the light left his previously joyful eyes, but he returned his attention to his guests without delay. Instead of sharing the message's contents, Viggo playfully asked what other mischievous tendencies his future bride and her newfound friend possessed.

The conversation concluded when the king noticed their mirthful laughter at his own story turning into uncontrollable yawning. Realizing midnight was less than an hour away, Viggo decided to bring their jovial evening to a close and wrapped up the tale of his childhood fantasy that invisible servants worked in their palace. The king walked the three to their rooms, remaining silent lest he weary them further with conversation but also unsure of what to say to the woman who he was growing more fond of with every syllable that eased from her lips.

"Do you have anything pleasant planned for tomorrow, Your Majesty?" Ingrid asked.

"No, why do you ask?"

"I know you have a lot of duties to honor, but men with great responsibilities need great rest. Since the war is over, you've certainly earned a day of peace."

"Well, tomorrow will be anything but restful, but dinner this evening was incredibly refreshing," he answered as they reached her door. "Good night, Ingrid."

"Good night."

With a bow and a curtsy, the two parted for the evening.

Though he'd given Ingrid zero cause for concern and continued down the hallway beside her father without any anger or abruptness, the young lady still suspected that something was amiss with the softened king. Unsure of what could be the source of her disquiet, she entered her room. Once inside, Ingrid uttered a brief prayer for him before retiring for her first evening in the Schlagefilde royal palace.

Chapter 4

The next morning, Ingrid awakened and joined her father for breakfast, where she learned of Viggo's plan to spend his day surveying the palace, Bjartyra, and other neighboring cities. Uneasiness still gnawed at her spirit, so she prayed for the unavailable king as she passed her time reacquainting herself with the palace and looking for any other occupants. Ultimately, she ventured into the library to study Ansgar's impressive collection of books.

After finding a copy of Giovanni Santini's book *Teorica degli Stromenti Ottici,* she strolled into the garden to read about telescopes, microscopes, and other fascinating tools. Thanks to the cold weather, Ingrid found a place to read undisturbed without any trouble.

The young lady lowered herself onto a bench near the fountain of cherubs she adored. Once she was comfortable, Ingrid began the challenge of reading the Italian book, enjoying the chance to practice a language few spoke in Schlagefilde. An hour into her slow progress through the book, the familiar sound of a horse-drawn carriage approaching the palace tickled Ingrid's ears.

Recognizing her fiancé's brusque voice, Ingrid rose from her seat and scampered to the entrance of the garden closest to the palace's front steps to greet him. Sadly, she missed Viggo by only a second as he marched into the palace with Halvard without noticing her presence. Despite the niggling urge to catch up with the two brothers, Ingrid resolved instead to continue her reading until the time came for tea with Liesel and Marlene, who would arrive within the hour.

Ingrid took her seat again and attempted to resume her labor of love through the Italian book. Alas, her racing heart refused to slow, and concentrating on reading the foreign language proved impossible. After five minutes of struggling to give the once fascinating book her full attention, she rose and entered the palace.

As she passed the library, Ingrid spied Halvard opening the door to let one of Viggo's military officers exit the room. When the prince made eye contact with Ingrid, he gave the maiden a shudder inspiring smile. Halvard closed the door and cloistered himself away with his brother once more, squelching any hopes Ingrid had of approaching the king before her visitor arrived.

Profound disquiet rose in Ingrid's heart, inspiring a brief prayer as she returned to her room. Despite her earnest efforts, the lady's silent entreaty and the primping she did to prepare for Marlene's visit did little to settle her soul. Once Ingrid decided that she looked presentable enough to accept company, she knelt before her bed to pray for her fiancé one final time.

"Heavenly Father, please protect Viggo from his brother's influence. I know both men have been hurt by Ansgar's grievous sins, but close Viggo's ears and heart to Halvard's wrathful whispers lest they inspire him to sin in his anger and do something he cannot take back. Help him to examine his ways and test them and cling to you instead of sinking deeper into his heart's darkness. Amen."

Though the sense of foreboding didn't lift from her spirit, Ingrid set her anguish aside and walked to the drawing room early. She hoped to distract herself from her inexplicable affliction by appreciating the priceless artwork Ansgar had purchased and commissioned during his reign with a fortune in unjust taxes.

Not long later, Lady Marlene arrived. The future queen wrapped her arms around her dear friend in a warm embrace. Liesel entered shortly thereafter wearing a beautiful burgundy gown trimmed with cream lace, which Ingrid procured for her that morning. Marlene studied Liesel for a beat, astonished by the girl's presence and elegant dress. Despite her initial shock, Marlene greeted Liesel with the same genuine affection she showed Ingrid.

For the next fifteen minutes, the three discussed the story of Ingrid's unexpected engagement as well as her new friendship with Liesel. Once the planning commenced, Marlene walked them through how she planned her own wedding two years before. Though her husband was one of Ansgar's many wealthy cousins, the duchess' nuptials had been a relatively simple yet still elegant event, which made her the perfect person to seek counsel from. Despite acting as the lady of her house since her mother's death, Ingrid still had little experience in hosting events since Edmund only entertained guests when he felt obligated to.

Liesel shared Ingrid's inexperience in the art of wedding planning, but she also felt odd being a guest at a tea instead of the help. Rather than wallowing her discomfort, she distracted herself by volunteering to record the details that the women discussed. Writing down the arrangements for Ingrid's wedding dissipated some of her uneasiness as the afternoon pressed on. The former slave even found herself enjoying the fragrant tea and buttery biscuits, which she never had the pleasure of enjoying in her master's household. Two pots of tea later, the women confirmed the merchants they would employ and guests they would invite to the modest affair, which they scheduled for December twentieth.

Ingrid would be a married woman in five days.

Once the trio reached a consensus about the royal wedding and divvied up the work, Ingrid and Liesel walked Marlene to the door. As the duchess departed, she gave both women warm hugs and invited them to join her for supper at her estate in the New Year. After Marlene began her journey home, Liesel and Ingrid walked back into the palace and continued chatting about the young lady's upcoming nuptials.

Although Ingrid loved her life with her father and siblings dearly, she had been trying to fill her mother's shoes for years. This meant being the mistress of the home Lady Carina left behind because of her untimely illness and showering her brother and sister with the love and care their mother would have given them. Now, Ingrid was stepping into a role that was hers alone and embarking on a new adventure … One she never could have imagined for herself.

Ingrid's growing conviction that God wouldn't have orchestrated her unexpected betrothal if he didn't intend to guide her through it helped assuage some of her lingering anxiety about being permanently bound to the grisly King of Villriket. However, her heart immediately ached and her disquiet returned when they ascended to the second floor and the sound of weeping reached Ingrid's ears.

It was Ansgar's daughters.

Rather than retiring to her room as planned, the maiden walked to the girls' room and addressed the soldiers protecting them.

"May I see the princesses?" Ingrid asked.

The two men exchanged an uneasy glance.

"I'm not sure if that's wise, my lady."

"Since when is comforting children who are obviously in pain unwise?"

The soldier on the right took a deep breath and pushed the door open, allowing Ingrid and Liesel to enter. Without a thought, the future queen rushed over to the two girls and placed her arms around them.

Albrect and Doris had laughed and played with Ava and Annette many times on their visits to the palace, so seeing the six- and eleven-year-old princesses sobbing uncontrollably shocked Ingrid and broke her heart. Closing the door behind them, Liesel joined Ingrid in consoling the girls, whose weeping didn't subside for half an hour.

"What's wrong, Ava?" Ingrid asked the youngest daughter, who'd chosen to curl up in her lap.

"P-Papa's d-dead," she stammered, tears spilling down her chubby pink cheeks, "and Mama too."

"They're not dead, sweetheart. They're … living somewhere else," she assured the girl, smoothing her ebony waves.

"That's not what he said."

"He who?"

"Prince Halvard," Annette croaked from her place in Liesel's arms. "He said King Viggo was going to put them to death tomorrow. They arrested Anton too."

The color drained from Ingrid's face as she turned her hazel eyes to the door.

"It can't be true," she whispered to herself.

"Are they going to kill us too?" Ava sniffled.

"No! I'm not going to let anyone hurt you," Ingrid swore, kissing the princess' forehead as a protective fire sparked in her heart. "Liesel, can you stay with the girls for a bit? I'll be back as soon as I can."

"Of course."

Lifting Ava from her lap, Ingrid rose to her feet and vacated the room. Once the maiden closed the door behind her, she rushed down the stairs as swiftly as her feet could take her, picking up her skirts to keep from tripping on the suddenly cumbersome garments.

Upon reaching the first floor, she darted over to the library and found both the pernicious prince and his churlish brother poring over maps of Schlagefilde. The triumphant smirk gracing Halvard's lips heated Ingrid's blood until she felt as if she was cooking from the inside out. Alas, the joy radiating from Viggo's eyes when he turned his eyes to his betrothed did nothing to abate her fury.

"Ingrid, I wasn't expecting you until supper," the king said, coming from behind the desk to join his fiancée.

"How could you?" she quaked. "Ansgar was supposed to receive a fair trial."

"I changed my mind," the king said, the warmth gone from his gaze and deep voice.

"But you said—"

"I know what I said," he snapped. "That blackguard dishonors my parents and the hundreds of others who died at his hands with every stolen breath he takes."

"What about Ansgar's children?"

"What about them?"

"I just came from comforting two sobbing little girls because your brother callously told them that they're going to be orphans! Losing their father to prison or an execution is traumatic on its own, but having their whole family ripped away so swiftly and mercilessly *broke* them!"

"Don't lecture me about the pain associated with losing one's parents! Halvard and I know it better than you ever will. Besides, I did those girls a favor."

"Cruelty is never a favor! My mother may not have been murdered as your parents were, but I know the pain of loss. If you kill Ansgar and Bettina like this, you will be no better than him. You'll leave his brokenhearted, traumatized children in your wake on your quest for power and vengeance!"

"Do not compare me to him!"

"Then don't *act* like him! When I first heard about your war against Ansgar, I was terrified, but I also felt hopeful. I prayed for you to somehow bring healing to this broken kingdom, but you're continuing Ansgar's legacy of violence. You just deposed one despot and replaced him with another!"

"How can you let her insult you?" Halvard barked, coming to stand beside his older brother. "I know you think she's beautiful, Viggo, but you can't afford to marry a disrespectful foreigner. She'll undermine you as your queen and be a thorn in your side until she drives you into an early grave."

"I'm sorry for speaking so severely, but I'm not undermining you, Your Majesty. I'm *warning* you," Ingrid corrected, forcing herself to calm down but also refusing to address the prince directly. "I don't know what happened between last night and this afternoon, but *please* listen to reason. Yes, you're a king with the power to do whatever you desire with Ansgar and his family, but you must remember who gave you your crown. God didn't entrust you with this power and give you this victory so you could throw away what could be your greatest gift to this land by satiating your thirst for revenge. If you begin your reign by administering the justice everyone has been craving, you will win the people of Schlagefilde. If you take vengeance, you will rip this kingdom apart and soil your hands with blood in the process."

Viggo clenched and unclenched his jaw with his hands balled into fists at his side as he took in Ingrid's passionate plea, but he remained silent.

"Your Majesty, please—"

"I will not reverse my decision to execute Ansgar, Bettina, and their teenaged son, but I'm seriously rethinking my decision to marry you. If you cannot support me in this, I may have to look within my own borders for a queen who will give me the respect I deserve. Either find it in your *sweet* little heart to apologize by sundown or consider the engagement off."

Before Ingrid could say another word, Viggo stomped out of the library, leaving Ingrid with his infuriatingly smug brother.

"It looks like Viggo is coming to his senses in more ways than one," the haughty prince smirked.

"Don't you love your brother at all?" Ingrid asked, her voice hoarse with emotion.

A frown crossed Halvard's lips.

"Of course I love him."

"Then how can you set him on this destructive path and let him blacken his soul with hatred and murder? Don't you realize Viggo can't come back from this? Once they're dead, he can't reverse his decision."

"Exactly."

Following his older brother's example, Halvard made a hasty exit and left Ingrid trembling alone in the library. Resisting the temptation to wallow in her anguish, the young lady trudged back to the princesses' room, where Liesel still embraced the two children.

The former slave shifted her focus away from the girls to meet Ingrid's eyes with a questioning gaze. Not confident that she could speak without sobbing, the forlorn young lady shook her head and lowered herself on the bed, pulling little Ava into her arms again. With every beat of her anguished heart, she begged God to comfort the princesses and to grant her the strength necessary to persevere no matter what the future held.

◆　◆　◆

After the children fell asleep, Ingrid and Liesel crept into the corridor to return to their rooms. Upon seeing the stars shining through the large windows at the end of the hallway, she realized dusk had come and gone without her apologizing to Viggo.

Their engagement was over.

Ingrid's chin quivered and unshed tears shone in her eyes as she suppressed the unexpected grief welling up in her soul. The two continued their silent trek until they parted ways with a wordless hug outside of Ingrid's bedroom. The instant she stepped inside and saw her equally bereft father, Ingrid let herself fell the full weight of her agony for the first time all day.

She wept not only for her broken engagement and Ansgar's family, but also for the man whose actions inspired her lamentation. Viggo was drowning in his rage and refused to seize the hands of those who only wanted to save him from himself.

Edmund let his distraught daughter take solace in his fatherly embrace for the longest five minutes of his life. Once her weeping gave way to silence, which she punctuated with occasional sniffle, he finally spoke.

"I'm so sorry, Ingrid. I could have prevented this by being more careful or more bold when Viggo came to Anselm."

"Even if you did, those little girls would still be in this predicament. It *kills* me that Halvard swayed Viggo to commit this travesty. What happened to the conviction he had yesterday?"

"When a man is standing on the edge, it doesn't take much for him to fall. Viggo and Halvard were both the victims of a horrible crime. If their present behavior is any indication, they didn't receive the guidance necessary to overcome it. We are all completely lost apart from the Lord and face temptation to commit grievous sins, but not everyone takes the way of escape God provides."

"I'm such a fool. I actually believed he was capable of changing. Now, I fear he's so lost in his thirst for vengeance that nothing will bring him out of it."

"He *was* changing, but if you could influence him, someone else could easily sway him as well. Godly sorrow is what leads to true repentance, not worldly affection."

Edmund left his daughter's side for a moment to fetch her Bible, which lie open on the small desk to the left of her bed. The count flipped through the holy book until he came upon a passage from the Bible's book of wisdom.

"Do you know Proverbs 22:24-25?"

Ingrid shook her head, wiping her eyes.

"'Make no friendship with an angry man; and with a furious man thou shalt not go: Lest thou learn his ways, and get a snare to thy soul,'" Edmund read. "So long as Viggo is in deeper fellowship with his vengeful brother than he is with God, he will be susceptible to Halvard's influence. Viggo must realize his need for the Lord's guidance and stop walking in the counsel of his wicked brother."

"I agree, but I doubt he'll listen to anyone but Halvard after our argument this afternoon. I was so angry with him that I lost control and scolded him like a child when I should have spoken to him like a king."

Edmund flipped back one chapter to quote another verse.

"'The king's heart is in the hand of the Lord, as the rivers of water: he turneth it whithersoever he will.' Our Lord is bigger than your lost temper, so let's pray for God to do what only he can and change Viggo's and Halvard's hearts."

Edmund extended his hand, and Ingrid clasped it before the two knelt on the ground and prayed for the enraged king and his spiteful brother. Ingrid listened to her father's prayers and prayed beside to him without uttering a single word aloud. The father and daughter lost track of time as they inclined their hearts to God and asked for his perfect, divine intervention.

Shortly after the nine o'clock hour, Espen knocked on Ingrid's door and summoned her father for an audience with the king. Giving his daughter a hug and kissing her cheek, Edmund left Ingrid for the night. Without her father's comforting presence, she continued pouring her heart out to God.

As much as she loved the count and hoped that his words would sway the king, only her Heavenly Father could prevent the evil that the Villriketian royals had their minds set on and heal their broken hearts.

Chapter 5

Ingrid arose and resumed her prayers to God an hour before dawn the next day, and she resolved to fast in honor of Ansgar's children. Each time her stomach churned during their time together, Ingrid remembered the greater lack the somber princesses faced and prayed for them all the more. When the girls distracted themselves from their sorrows by playing with dolls after lunch, Ingrid left them in Liesel's care to search for her father. Much to her dismay, she couldn't find the Count of Anselm anywhere. Though Ingrid was tempted to fear the worst for her beloved Papa, she forced herself to remain calm and added his safety to her desperate, earnest prayers to God.

At six o'clock, Johan appeared at the door to the princesses' room, prompting Ingrid to leave the children reading with Liesel and join the soldier in the hallway.

"His Majesty has sent me to tell you that supper will be held at seven."

"Does he still plan to execute Ansgar, Bettina, and Anton?"

"Yes, my lady," he sighed.

"Please send my apologies. I cannot dine with him this evening."

With a nod and worry in his weary eyes, Johan marched back downstairs to his awaiting king and left Ingrid with an even heavier heart. Though she only rejected the supper invitation to continue her fasting and silent prayer, she feared Viggo would take offense to her refusal. Was it better for her to accept the invitation that could have been a peace offering or to honor her conviction?

Recalling her father's words from the previous night, Ingrid decided that if Viggo's only anguish came from losing her instead of offending God, it wasn't enough. With that in mind, she resolved to abstain from supper and prayed her absence would do more good than harm. However, she still urged Liesel to go downstairs for supper an hour later and read Ava's favorite book to the girls while she was gone.

The seven o'clock hour and the princesses' meal passed without any incident, and Liesel checked in on the trio after she finished eating. She had little news to report other than that the king's surly disposition had returned with a vengeance, and Ingrid convinced her weary friend to retire for the evening. The young lady continued entertaining and comforting the princesses until the time came to put them to bed. Ingrid helped them change into their nightgowns and tucked them in before singing a lullaby her mother had often sung her to sleep with as a child.

"Good night, good night,
Sweet children of light.
Embrace the love
Of your Father above
Who holds you safe in his arms.

Good night, good night,
Sweet children of light.
Let sleep come in
And sweet dreams begin
To carry you to His kingdom.

Good night, good night,
Sweet children of light.
Don't fear at all
There within your walls.
His angels will protect you
From harms and frights
That creep in the night
Because you are his children.
Because you are his children."

Before the final dulcet note eased from Ingrid's lips, Ava and Annette had fallen asleep. The maiden leaned over to kiss their foreheads, praying for the old lullaby's lyrics to prove true and for God to protect them from Halvard's and Viggo's wrath. Once she finished her silent entreaty, Ingrid rose from the bed and turned to leave. A gasp escaped her lips, and she dropped Annette's discarded doll when she beheld Viggo's imposing form darkening the doorway.

Tucking a fair lock of hair behind her ear with a shaking hand, she placed the doll in the girls' chest, crossed the room, and curtsied to the taciturn king, whose rapid breathing was all she could hear in the quiet palace. Though the room was completely dark, Ingrid could still make out Viggo's furrowed brow and slumped shoulders as he studied her with bloodshot eyes.

"I'm sorry I couldn't join you for supper tonight. I meant no offense, Your—"

Viggo turned and walked away without a word, leaving Ingrid standing in the doorway and gaping after him in bewilderment. Casting her confusion aside, she resolved to find the king rather than leaving him to his own devices. Ingrid closed the bedroom door behind her and rushed to catch up with Viggo, who had already fled to the first floor.

Once downstairs, Ingrid followed him outside to the garden, and a blast of winter air chilled her to the bone. She mentally chided herself for not grabbing her cloak before chasing after the boorish sovereign, but she pressed on. The lady found him in the gazebo surrounded by Ansgar's rosebushes, resting his hands against the railing as he hung his head in silence.

"Your Majesty, I—"

"Go away, Ingrid."

"Forgive me for being impertinent, but I can tell that you're upset. I won't say a word if you don't want me to, but I don't think I should leave you alone."

Ingrid patiently waited for him to speak and steeled herself for a harsh response. The maiden halfway expected him to bark at her to leave or rail against her for rejecting his supper invitation. Either way, she was determined to stay the course. She had to let the king air his grievances so she could calmly address them in an attempt to be reconciled. If his enmity toward her prevented him from doing what was right, she had to pursue peace with him.

But how could she make amends if Viggo remained silent?

When several ragged breaths passed without him saying a word, Ingrid moved toward the king with some hesitance, but she froze when she drew close enough to look past Viggo's mane of dark hair and see his face in the moonlight. Tears streamed down the king's cheeks and disappeared into his thick, wild beard as he fought whatever emotions waged war inside of him. Viggo glanced in her direction for a moment, but he promptly averted his tormented gaze.

"My mother sang the same song to me as a child," Viggo said, his voice shaking with every word. "Even though I had a nurse as a young boy, she still insisted on tucking me in each night. She would sing the tune before kissing and praying over me exactly as you did. You were praying, correct?"

Ingrid nodded.

A cheerless smile crossed Viggo's lips, but the sorrow never left his piercing eyes.

"You're very different from my mother in many ways, but you remind me of her at times. She was an incomparably artistic, graceful woman. More importantly, she clung to her faith as fiercely as my father did. They were both willing to compromise when they could do so without dishonoring God, but they never yielded when it came to fighting for righteousness. Their convictions are why they're both buried somewhere at the cathedral in Bjartyra."

Ingrid's soul ached for Viggo as she witnessed his profound distress, but she felt powerless to give him the comfort he needed.

"Halvard and I spent our afternoon there two days ago. I only intended to survey Bjartyra and the surrounding area, but he went behind my back and gave our driver the order to take us to the cathedral," Viggo revealed. "At his insistence, we stopped and watched the soldiers attempt to find and exhume my parents' remains so I could give them a proper burial in Villriket. I had no desire to see the men's work and be reminded of what

Ansgar did to them, but that's exactly what Halvard wanted. My sadness turned into anger with every passing second, and he fanned the flames … breathing hatred in my ear like the devil himself until my rage consumed me. I wanted to send Ansgar to hell for the pain he inflicted on my parents, so I gave the order for his execution the moment we returned to the palace."

"Anyone in your position would be angry with Ansgar," Ingrid commiserated.

"Yes, but a wise man wouldn't let his fury control him as I have. My anger is why I sought you out tonight. I was livid when you refused to come to supper, and I came to officially end our engagement. When I heard you singing, my heart stopped."

Viggo gripped the gazebo's railing so hard that Ingrid feared he would snap the delicate wood.

"I remembered what Ansgar took from me, but I realized I was committing the exact same transgression against him and his children. God should have struck me down for my hypocrisy," he trembled. "I'm just as wretched as Ansgar, and maybe even worse. You tried to turn me from my sin *twice* and I lashed out at you instead of heeding your counsel. I should have rebuked my brother for inciting me to violence, and begged God to forgive me. I started breathing vengeance and violence the moment I learned of my parents' deaths, and it has to stop!"

Much to Ingrid's surprise, Viggo wept, and she instinctively pulled him into her arms, letting his hot tears moisten her shivering shoulder as she stroked his back. Though witnessing the king's most intimate expression of his pain grieved Ingrid, his astonishing vulnerability inspired her to hope more than she dared to before their unforeseen encounter.

"I'm so sorry," she whispered several minutes later.

"I should be apologizing to you. You're only here because I threatened your father and your people. I disrupted your life because of my greed, and I treated you poorly when I should have cherished you. I'm not worthy of you, and you certainly shouldn't be condemned to a lifetime yoked to a beast like me."

"You're not a beast, Viggo. You're just in pain. Anyone grieving a loss as profound as yours would be angry or disillusioned in some way. God no doubt placed people like my father and I in your life to help you carry this burden and to comfort you. This is too grave a loss for you to heal from alone."

Viggo ended their embrace, and Ingrid's soul ached at his withdrawal. Despite the tugging of his heart, the contemplative king refused to look into her eyes. If he met her compassionate hazel gaze, he feared he'd lose the nerve to voice the weighty words sitting on the tip of his tongue. In that same stillness, Ingrid asked God for the wisdom to respond to Viggo's next statement or action. Whether his repentant attitude persisted or died away as quickly as it surfaced, she needed to reply based on her faith instead of fear or anger.

"I'm releasing you from your commitment to marry me," he said. "A carriage will take you back to your home in Anselm tomorrow, and I will richly compensate your family for the trouble I caused. A better man than me will see what a beautiful woman you are body and soul and treat you with the kindness and love you deserve."

Before Ingrid could say a word, Viggo trudged away, but he stopped at the bottom of the gazebo's steps and spoke one last time without looking over his shoulder.

"Ansgar, Bettina, and Anton still live. The former king and queen will remain prisoners until enough time has passed for a fair trial by their peers, but I will release the boy tonight. No more blood will be shed in my name."

After his final proclamation, Viggo disappeared into the darkness, leaving Ingrid alone to contemplate their unanticipated interaction. The young lady stared after her former fiancé in shock for several breaths, incredulous that God had answered her prayers for the deposed royal family so quickly … and he also freed her from her hasty engagement to the once barbarous king. Alas, even though elation and praise over Viggo's repentance filled her heart, she couldn't bring herself to feel true joy over her dissolved betrothal.

Two days ago I was preparing to spend my life as his queen, and now I'm a free woman again. I simply need time to adjust, she assured herself as she slowly retraced her steps through the fragrant garden.

Taking a deep breath, Ingrid entered the palace and searched for her father, eager to tell him the news they had both been praying to hear since they first learned of Ansgar's condemnation.

◆　◆　◆

As Ingrid prepared for bed and packed her few belongings two hours later, she praised God for changing Viggo's heart. While she didn't know what the future held for her homeland, her spirit sang with joy. For the first time in decades, her people had a ruler who could see the error in his ways and turn from his iniquity. Just as the maiden sat down to brush her hair, an unexpected sound ripped through the night and shattered her equanimity.

A gunshot.

Dropping her brush, Ingrid shot out of her room. Relief filled her soul when she saw her father and Liesel also stepping into the hallway unharmed. However, the respite only lasted for a brief moment when she realized that one person in the palace had far more enemies than allies in Schlagefilde.

Viggo.

Breaking into a sprint, Ingrid tripped over the hem of her nightgown almost a dozen times as she flew down the stairs to the library. Edmund followed not far behind, shouting at his daughter to stop for fear she was running into a situation he couldn't protect her from. Unfortunately, his less than agile, aged body and her brief head start prevented him from stopping her.

Edmund and his daughter reached the library only moments apart, and the panting count immediately snatched Ingrid away from the door. Though she only had a second to look past the soldiers in the doorway and into the room, dread weighed down the young maiden's heart as the haunting sight replayed before her eyes. Ansgar's fourteen-year-old son, Anton, stood next to the bookcase, which was open to reveal a secret passageway much like the one in her own home. Viggo on the other hand lie motionless on the floor with blood on his shirt.

The king had been shot.

Ingrid tried to pull away from her father to rush to the king's side, but

Edmund held fast to his trembling, tearful daughter and kept her out of sight.

"His men are with him now, Ingrid. Anton would be a fool to try anything more. Let them handle this."

"But, Papa—"

The sound of Viggo's strained voice silenced Ingrid and her heart leapt in anticipation as she tried to discern how badly the prince hurt him.

"I understand your anger, Anton," the king grumbled. "I know what it's like to hate someone for shattering everything you loved, but if you try to blot out destruction with destruction, you'll only succeed in destroying yourself. When I learned of my parents' deaths, I didn't just become angry, I became anger itself. Revenge ruled my every thought and consumed me until nothing remained of me but a bloodthirsty beast in a man's body. I was an unlovable wretch and held my wrath so dear that I came close to committing the sins I detested and lost the person who has meant the most to me since their passing. You would've become another of my many victims if someone didn't show me the error of my ways. Please don't repeat my mistakes."

"What about *my* parents? I'd rather die trying to save them than live as a poor orphan begging on the streets while *you* sit on their throne."

"What if those weren't your only options?" Viggo countered. "What if I let your parents live?"

"You wouldn't."

"I would if it meant keeping you from becoming a monster like me. Don't let me blacken your heart after I've already broken it."

Recognizing her own words pouring from Viggo's mouth, Ingrid waited in wordless anticipation for Anton to respond or make his next deadly move. A loud, metallic thud reached Ingrid's eager ears followed by sobbing and a flurry of movement as the soldiers seized the blubbering teen.

Ripping her arm away from her father, Ingrid finally looked through the doorway. A soldier held Anton's hands behind his back while another tended to Viggo, who rose to his feet holding the discarded gun. The king set the weapon on his desk and walked over to the shamefaced prince, who refused to meet his remorseful blue eyes.

"No matter what verdict the court brings against your parents, I will not allow them to be executed," he promised. "If you prove yourself to be a virtuous man in the next few years, I will place this kingdom back in your hands. Either way, I won't hold your actions tonight or your parents' misdeeds against you. God has forgiven me for much, so who am I not to forgive you for a moment of weakness that I inspired with my own sinful ways."

Viggo glanced at the soldier who had detained the prince.

"Take him to his room."

"Yes, my king."

The two plodded out of the library, and Viggo instructed three guards to explore the tunnels and make sure they were properly monitored. Just as Ingrid stepped inside the room, a medic from the king's army breezed past her with his supplies. The young man went to work cutting off Viggo's bloodied white sleeve to reveal that the teen's bullet had only scratched his arm.

"Thank goodness," Ingrid exhaled.

Looking up from his injured arm, Viggo met his former fiancée's concerned gaze, but he immediately turned his eyes away.

"It's only a superficial wound," he said. "I'll be fine."

Ingrid tore her eyes away from Viggo as Edmund touched her shoulder.

"There isn't anything we can do here, sweetheart. You need your rest," he said.

The young beauty looked back at the king, who nodded in agreement. Heaving a sigh, Ingrid let her father lead her out of the library and back to her room. As the maiden finished her nightly routine without her earlier levity, a strange kind of hope welled up in her heart. Though she witnessed the beginnings of Viggo's heart change hours before, his merciful response to Anton's assault was further proof of his miraculous repentance.

The man who had his heart set on executing Anton only hours before practically promised the young man his parents' kingdom. Furthermore, he sent the prince back to the luxury of his room instead of a cell in the tower. Of course, this didn't mean the King of Villriket was magically healed of the pain Ansgar caused, but he chose the path of righteousness over retribution.

Viggo was a new man through and through, and she couldn't wait to see what he could do for a kingdom in dire need of the same healing and transformation.

Chapter 6

Upon rousing the next morning, Ingrid dressed for her journey back to Anselm with Edmund and Liesel. The women bid goodbye to Ava and Annette, who wept with joy upon hearing Viggo's decision. The homebound ladies vowed to write to the princesses once they returned to Anselm and to visit them as soon as they could.

When the time came for the Count of Anselm, his daughter, and her friend to leave, the trio departed with Espen and Johan accompanying them for their protection. Though Ingrid thanked God for allowing her to return to the familiarity of her childhood home, she couldn't muster up true joy in her troubled heart.

Just as the three travelers were halfway to the gold and black wrought iron gate surrounding the Schlagefilde royal palace, the carriage bumped and jerked violently before coming to a stop.

"Are you all right?" Edmund asked.

"Yes," Ingrid said while Liesel nodded in agreement.

A moment later, Espen appeared at the window to address his charges.

"One of the wheels broke, my lord. We need you to leave the carriage while a new one is put on. It should take less than an hour to fix."

"Thank you, Espen," Edmund said.

After the three travelers stepped out of the carriage, Ingrid realized they were a stone's throw from the cherubic fountain in the palace garden. Seeing the marble bench only a few yards from the gorgeous spectacle, an idea was conceived in her heart.

"Why don't we have a seat in the garden while we wait?" she suggested.

"Marvelous idea," the count agreed.

When they reached the bench, Ingrid realized only two could comfortably sit on it. Remembering her father's age and Liesel's past hardships, she opted to take in her surroundings while her father and her friend rested and enjoyed the fresh morning air.

As Ingrid wandered through the artfully sculpted hedges and pruned bushes, her eyes soon rested on a bush of scarlet roses much like the ones she and her mother had cultivated in Anselm. The young lady leaned over, but as she inhaled one bloom's sweet scent, she noticed the multitude of thorns adorning each rose's stem. Seeing the prickly scourges reminded Ingrid of something her mother had once said.

"People are like these roses, Ingrid. When they grow wild without anyone pruning their branches, they fail to be as beautiful as they were created to be. However, even with the best pruning, they still can't be embraced without causing pain because of their thorns. Likewise, we imperfect humans are painfully flawed because of our sinful nature."

The late countess had pulled a rose from her basket and removed the thorns one by one until the bloom's stem was perfectly smooth and safe for Ingrid to take in her tiny hands.

"A rose can't take away its own thorns and neither can we take away our sins. Only Christ can do that. He allowed His hands and feet to be pierced and his blood to be shed so we can be sinless just like this rose is now thornless," Carina showed her daughter where a thorn had pricked her index finger, drawing a single bead of crimson blood.

"God only does this work once. Yet, we must still be pruned and shaped so we can grow into the men and women God created us to be and become more like Christ," she explained. *"When you grow into a woman one day, you will be tasked with choosing a husband. I pray the man you marry will be a faithful, loving man, but never make the mistake of thinking you're without your own thorns or he's without his. If you both realize your deep dependence on God in every aspect of life, he can continuously prune you with His capable hands, and you'll bloom together beautifully."*

As the long-forgotten memory faded into the recesses of Ingrid's mind, she pulled the rose from the bush and her heart was suddenly aflame with conviction … and an unexpected, incomparably sweet flurry of emotions. A grin spread across the young maiden's freckled face and she flitted back over to Edmund and Liesel.

"My goodness, child. Are you all right?" the concerned count asked, rising to meet his flustered daughter.

"Yes, I'm perfect, but I can't leave without speaking with the king. Can you please wait here for me?"

"Of course, but perhaps I should go with you."

"No, your presence isn't necessary. If anything, I might lose my nerve if you accompany me."

Seeing the jubilant light in Ingrid's wild, hazel eyes and the flush in her cheeks, Edmund realized what his daughter meant to do. Though he consented to her marriage to Viggo what felt like eons before, the aging count suddenly experienced the sweet pang of loss that stings every father's heart as his first daughter grows into womanhood and leaves his household.

"Liesel and I will be right here waiting for you," he smiled, kissing her forehead.

With her father's approval, Ingrid hurried back to the palace to find the contrite king. Of course, her first destination was the library, where Viggo had spent most of his time since their arrival. Bursting into the room moments later, the maiden's eyes immediately fell upon a sharply dressed nobleman.

The formidable man stood at the window with a canvas before him and a paintbrush in his hand, and her cheeks reddened as she berated herself for barging in and interrupting his private moment. Ingrid jumped with a gasp when the door swung shut with a loud click, but she recovered in time to greet the man with a curtsy as he turned around to see the commotion's source.

"My apologies, my lord. Do you know where His Majesty is?"

Though the blue-eyed, blue-blooded man was strikingly handsome with his high cheekbones, cleft chin, and full lips, she still felt uncomfortable under his silent scrutiny and averted his questioning gaze by fixing her eyes on the floor. The man turned to look outside once more, holding his brush between his teeth as he mixed a new shade for his painting using a palette knife.

"Do you know where the king is?" she inquired. "I must speak with him concerning an urgent matter."

"Is something wrong?"

"Well, I'm supposed to return home with my father, but I can't leave without speaking with him."

"Is something wrong?" the nobleman repeated.

"No. Not exactly."

"Tell me what you need, and I'll relay the message."

"I-I can't tell you."

"Why not?"

"This is a private matter, my lord … something I can't say to anyone but him."

Footsteps filled Ingrid's ears as the man abandoned his brushes and canvas to join her in the center of the room.

"What do you want, Ingrid?"

Identifying the man's voice at last, the young maiden furrowed her brow and lifted her gaze from the rug. With the man standing less than two feet away, Ingrid realized that she knew his icy blue eyes, which were now alive with undisguised emotion. She also recognized the shiny long-healed scar splitting his dark left eyebrow in two. Without thinking, Ingrid reached up and touched his newly cut hair, marveling at his dark waves' unexpected silkiness. Then, her trembling, soft hand caressed his clean shaven cheek, and he leaned into her touch ever so slightly, making her breath catch in her throat.

Good heavens! What am I doing?

Realizing her breach of propriety, Ingrid ripped her hand away. The young lady fixed her eyes on the floor again, embarrassed by her second invasion of the king's personal space. An onslaught of emotions she could scarcely put words to also overwhelmed her thundering heart.

"Why aren't you on the road to Anselm?" Viggo asked.

"A wheel on our carriage broke."

Viggo furrowed his brow and pulled away, walking to the door.

"Well, I'll have another one prepared so you can be on your way."

"I don't need another carriage."

"Don't be ridiculous. You can't ride all the way home on horseback," Viggo chided without a trace of exasperation.

"I don't want to go home at all."

Ingrid heard Viggo turn around to face her again, but she dared not meet his gaze just lest he see how her chest heaved with every anxious breath.

"I'm not going to give in to my rage again. We set Ansgar's and Bettina's trial dates this morning, and their children are safe. You can trust me."

"I know. *You* are the reason I don't want to leave."

Her heart filling with the boldness she'd initially lost in the transformed king's presence, Ingrid turned around and faced Viggo, lifting the rose in trembling hands.

"When the wheel broke, I decided to walk through the garden. There, I came upon a rose bush and remembered something my mother told me a long time ago."

"And what did she tell you?"

"That no one is perfect. We all have our thorns, and we can't be anything but scourges to the people around us left to our own devices. However, we can still love and enjoy one another despite our imperfections as long as we depend on God and turn from our sins in repentance," Ingrid summarized. "I know our engagement hasn't been easy, but I want to honor my promise to marry you."

"Ingrid, you're not obliged to marry me out of duty or pity. You're free to return to your home and marry whomever you choose."

"But I choose you!" she blurted. "And it's not because of obligation or pity. I care about you deeply."

Ingrid took a deep breath and closed her eyes for a moment before looking at the king straight on and speaking once more.

"Your Majesty … Viggo … I want to spend my life with you if you'll have me."

Rather than responding, Viggo left the room, letting the door close behind him. Ingrid's heart sank and her rapidly watering eyes dropped to the bloom in her hands. She chastised herself for not selecting her words more carefully before approaching the king or sending her father to patch up their broken engagement. In her haste, she invaded Viggo's space and foolishly threw her heart his at feet only to have him trample on it by rejecting her in her most vulnerable moment … and she couldn't even blame him after she'd been so harsh with him in recent days.

What kind of man would want such a quarrelsome wife?

But the door opened again.

Ingrid lifted her eyes from the rose to see Viggo stride back into the room with a handkerchief. Taking the rose from her, he pressed the white cloth against her palm, but he didn't withdraw once he finished. Instead, the king gently held her hands, marveling at how soft and delicate hers were compared to his.

"The thorns pricked you," he pointed out. "I couldn't let my bride bleed out right in front of me."

Laughter bubbled from Ingrid's throat as her tears of sorrow transformed into tears of joy. Viggo promptly wiped them away before giving her a grin that made deep dimples appear in his freshly shaven cheeks.

"I'm sorry for concealing my identity. I didn't want to prolong a painful goodbye, but my cowardice doesn't excuse my deception. Will you forgive me?"

"Of course, but I'm not sure if I would've believed you without hearing your voice clearly and looking into your eyes. You look so different. Why did you change?"

"I wanted to look like a new man. My passions ruled me until I was nothing more than an animal driven by instinct and wrath, so I let myself look the part. I even swore never to wear anything but a military uniform until I avenged my parents. Now that I'm resolving not to be a beast, I decided to stop looking like one. I hope you think it's an improvement."

Ingrid looked away for a moment, butterflies fluttering in her stomach as newfound attraction mingled with the affection in her heart.

"You look very handsome."

Ingrid earned a bashful smile from her fiancé, who nervously rubbed the back of his neck and averted his delighted gaze. Viggo hadn't heard a kind word spoken of his appearance in longer than he could remember, and having his future wife's approval meant more to him than the compliments he received from his barber that morning.

"Would you like to tell your father or shall I?" Viggo asked, clearing his throat.

"I'll tell him. I think he knew what I came back to do, but he needs to hear this from me so he can see how elated I am."

"And I will tell my brother. Halvard has been against our marriage from the start, but this won't be the first difficult conversation we've had today."

Ingrid knitted her eyebrows together in concern.

"What happened?"

"I removed him from his position as my general and advisor. I love Halvard, but I cannot trust his counsel when he's as blinded by his grief and animosity as I was. He also lost a great love in his youth, and our engagement being built on affection instead of obligation might add insult to injury."

"I'm sure he'll come around in time."

"I hope he will as well, but you should go share the happy news with your father and Liesel before they freeze to death in the garden."

With one last smile, Ingrid released Viggo's calloused hand, savoring the lingering sensation of his touch as she hurried back to the garden. As she passed through the palace, the young lady remembered the first time she agreed to marry Viggo. She had been afraid for her people, her family, and herself, but determined to do whatever she could to keep everyone safe. Now, as she began their second engagement, her heart soared with unparalleled mirth, affection, and hope.

Chapter 7

A dimpled grin lit up Viggo's face when the chapel's doors opened three days later to reveal his beautiful bride. Ingrid beamed at him from her father's side with equal jubilation. The bride's walk from the doors to the altar seemed unbearably slow as it transpired, but she felt as if she entered the chapel only seconds before once she stood beside the king.

The priest began the ceremony by reminding those in attendance that the marriage they were witnessing was a picture of the union between Christ and His church, and such a covenant was not to be entered into lightly. As he spoke those words, the bride and groom both smiled. God, in his mercy, turned their hasty, imprudent engagement into what would soon be a happy, fruitful marriage.

"Your Majesty, King Viggo Ingvar Lund, will you take this woman to be your wedded wife, to live together in accordance with God's design in the holy estate of matrimony? Will you love, comfort, honor, and keep her, in sickness and in health; forsaking all others, clinging only to her, so long as you both shall live?"

"I will," he swore.

"My lady, Ingrid Carina Kappel, will you take this man to be your wedded husband, to live together in accordance with God's design in the holy estate of matrimony? Will you serve, love, honor, obey, and keep him, in sickness and in health; forsaking all others, clinging only to him, so long as you both shall live?"

"I will," Ingrid grinned.

"Who gives this woman to be married to this man?"

"I do," Edmund responded, taking a step back and leaving Ingrid and Viggo at the altar with the priest.

The old man took Ingrid's right hand and placed it in Viggo's. Her heart fluttered as she remembered the moment the king placed a handkerchief in her hand days before and renewed his pledge to marry her.

"Repeat after me, Your Majesty," the clergyman instructed.

After the priest recited the vows, Viggo repeated the holy oath.

"I, Viggo, take you, Ingrid, to be my wedded wife, to have and to hold from this day forward, for better for worse, for richer for poorer, in sickness and in health, to love and to cherish, until death do us part, according to God's holy design. This I swear with my heart, and soul, and spirit."

Once Viggo finished his vows, they released their hands and grasped them again. As before, the priest spoke Ingrid's vows, which she reiterated with heartfelt, smiling devotion.

"I, Ingrid, take you, Viggo, to be my wedded husband, to have and to hold from this day forward, for better for worse, for richer for poorer, in sickness and in health, to love, to cherish, and to obey until death do us part, according to God's holy design. This I swear with my heart, and soul, and spirit."

Forcing himself to let go of his bride's hand, Viggo took Ingrid's simple, gold wedding ring and set it on the priest's Bible. After a brief prayer, the man of the cloth picked up the ring and handed it back to Viggo. Then, the king slipped the ring on Ingrid's fourth finger until it touched her mother's ruby ring.

"With this ring, I bind myself to you in holy matrimony. All that I am and all that I have is now yours, in the name of the Father, and of the Son, and of the Holy Spirit."

After Ingrid recited the same pledge and gave Viggo his ring, the two knelt before the altar as the priest prayed over the couple's marriage in the sight of their loved ones. Listening to the prayer, which entreated God to help them live in perfect love and perfect peace, Viggo was humbled.

Nothing resembling love or peace resided in his heart when he began invading Schlagefilde. Now, his proficiency as a husband largely depended on his ability to keep those virtues at the center of their relationship. He would need God's help more than ever to live up to his holy standard and to give his beautiful wife the life she deserved.

Ending the prayer with a solemn affirmation, the priest gestured for the two to rise to their feet. Then, he placed their hands together and announced with a joyful finality, "What God has joined together, let no man put asunder. I now pronounce you husband and wife in the name of the Father, and of the Son, and of the Holy Spirit. You may now kiss your bride."

Viggo lifted the lace veil from Ingrid's radiant face, and her heart thumped wildly in her chest as he leaned in to seal their marriage with their first of many sweet kisses. When his lips touched hers for that brief moment, her very soul sang a song of tenderness and joy. She never wanted the moment to end, but the devotion and awe she beheld in Viggo's sparkling blue eyes took her breath away more than his kiss had.

As Ingrid looked away shyly with flushed cheeks and her rosy lips curved into an easy smile, Viggo recognized the love shining on her face. After all, it mirrored the adoration in his softened heart. The king lifted his wife's hand to his lips and kissed it, earning another rident grin.

In that delightful moment, he marveled at how he had miraculously earned not only the respect but also the love of a woman like her. Ingrid was lovely beyond compare in his eyes, but he knew her true beauty came from her heart … A heart which had somehow done the impossible task of seeing the good in a king who had shown himself to be nothing more than a beast.

About the Author

Kristen Reed, a graduate of the University of Texas at Dallas, is an artist, filmmaker and author from Dallas, Texas. As a Christian, her faith influences her writing and is the driving force in her life.

Visit kristenreedauthor.com to learn more.

www.ingramcontent.com/pod-product-compliance
Lightning Source LLC
Chambersburg PA
CBHW072259130726
47910CB00012B/2175